Angel in
Armani

Also by
Melanie Scott

The Devil in Denim

Angel in Armani

Melanie Scott

St. Martin's Paperbacks

This is a work of fiction. All of the characters, organizations, and events portrayed in this novel are either products of the author's imagination or are used fictitiously.

ANGEL IN ARMANI

Copyright © 2015 by Melanie Scott.
Excerpt from *Lawless in Leather* copyright © 2015 by Melanie Scott.

For information address St. Martin's Press, 175 Fifth Avenue, New York, NY 10010.

ISBN: 978-1-250-04040-4

Printed in the United States of America

St. Martin's Paperbacks edition / January 2015

St. Martin's Paperbacks are published by St. Martin's Press, 175 Fifth Avenue, New York, NY 10010.

10 9 8 7 6 5 4 3 2 1

For Hamish.
Best dog ever.

Acknowledgments

The Chinese curse goes something like "May You Live in Interesting Times." This book was written during some very interesting times that included my inner ears deciding that vertigo was the cool new thing for a few months. I'm very glad they've given that particular obsession up. I'm also very grateful to Jennifer Enderlin for being a patient and fabulous editor! I need to thank Miriam Kriss, who continues to be an agent of awesome, and the St. Martin's art department who have given me another cover that I want to hang on the wall and just ~~drool over~~ gaze at. A special shout-out to Richard for answering my dumb baseball questions (any baseball mistakes are mine, all mine). And finally, to all the usual suspects who have provided sounding boards, champagne, chocolate, cheering from the sidelines, hugs, distractions, laughter, inspiration, love, and general Mel support, I couldn't do it without you. Thank you!

Chapter One

It was like having a tiger in the back of the helicopter.

The knowledge of something big and dangerous and ruthless riding behind her. Something that could squish you like a bug and not blink a big golden eye.

Of course, the man behind her had blue eyes, not golden ones. Very blue.

So maybe a tiger wasn't the right metaphor. Maybe—

"Got another chopper coming in about five, Sara. You getting airborne sometime soon?" The crisp tones of Ronnie, running control today, broke her train of thought. *Just as well.* She shook her head. *Because you, Sara Charles, are being an idiot.* There was no room for distraction when she was flying.

"Any second now," she replied. She twisted in her seat to look at her passenger. "We're ready to go, sir." She called all her passengers sir or ma'am, unless instructed otherwise. Most did—or the regulars, at least. Not this one, though. He seemed to accept "sir" as though it were his due. Which was weird because, unless she was way off the mark, he wasn't ex-military. And he wasn't English royalty slumming it in New York. No, his accent was firmly American. Not that he'd spoken more than about six sentences to her in the three trips she'd flown for him so far.

Short sentences. Things like "Good morning." And "Thank you." His voice was deep. Cool. Controlled. His silence should have been annoying but instead it was somehow compelling. Made her want to hear more.

"I'll have us in the air in just a minute," she added, just in case he might break his streak and say something rash like "Great."

He didn't look up. He rarely looked up. He just nodded and kept his eyes on the screen of the slim silver laptop open on his lap. Focused. Intense.

His powers of concentration were clearly excellent. Even with the headsets on, it was loud in the helo, but he didn't let anything distract him. She had to admit that there'd been the odd idle moment when she'd let herself wonder what it might be like to have all his attention focused on her. What it might be like to hold his focus and be the thing he didn't want to be distracted from.

But that was about as likely to happen as her sprouting wings and being able to fly without a helo, so she tried to ignore the thoughts when they arose.

She did wonder where he'd learned to shut the

world out, though. Maybe it came with being a doctor. She knew that much about him. He was a doctor. Dr. Lucas Angelo.

That was the name on the bookings. She didn't know much more than that. She refused to Google a man she barely knew and wasn't likely to. That would just be sad.

Sadder than comparing him to jungle cats?

Suppressing a sigh, she turned back to face the controls. Time to forget about tigers and get this bird in the air.

For the first few minutes, the joy of the flight took her mind away from the puzzle of the man she was flying. The city had turned on a perfect winter day. Fine. Sunny. Just enough breeze to make things interesting. Good light. Good visibility. The helo hummed under her hand, seemingly as pleased as she was to be in the air.

Away from all the problems down there on the ground. Nothing to think about but the sky and her destination for a few hours, at least.

She cut a path around the city, feeling the familiar rush as the gleaming buildings and the swath of the park slipped beneath her. Best view of Manhattan for sure. Best view in the world maybe.

Of course, Dr. Mystery back there was ignoring it as usual.

She frowned and straightened the helo now that she had her heading. She didn't know how he could just sit there and not even look up, let alone out the window. Focus or no focus there was nothing a

laptop could possibly hold that could compete with
the view from up here.

Hell, most of the time the passengers were paying her for exactly that view—sightseeing flights
made up a good chunk of the charter business. She
loved listening to the excited voices of the tourists
as they took in her city. Of course, a few of them
turned green and spent the flight barfing, but those
were the exception.

No barfing from her current passenger, of course.

No, he wouldn't do anything that might risk
ruining his perfectly cut suit.

Three times she'd flown him and every time, no
matter where she was taking him, it had been a suit.

Deep charcoal for the time she'd taken him to the
hospital in New Jersey.

A medium gray for a hop to Staten Island.

Navy with the faintest of pinstripes to JFK.

She'd liked that one. The navy and the deep-blue
tie he'd worn with it had made his eyes even bluer.
She'd decided he should always wear blue.

Until he'd walked into the terminal this afternoon
wearing a tuxedo. Most guys looked better in a tuxedo, of course, but very few of them actually looked
like they were born to wear one. It was unfair. Stark
black and white shouldn't turn a man into a god. But
damn, the man's tailor was genius.

She'd taken one look at him, forced herself to tear
her eyes away, and beaten a path for her A-Star, leaving the checking-in of tuxedo-clad perfection and his
immaculate luggage to the terminal staff. It was one
thing to admit that the man was intriguing, in an an-

noying sort of way, and too handsome for his own good; it was quite another to hyperventilate at the sight of him. Particularly while she was standing there in her pilot's uniform of sensible black pants, sensible black shoes, and sensible blue shirt. With headset hair.

She'd talked sternly to herself as she'd done the preflight checks. One did not get crushes on clients. Because the sort of client who could afford regular chartered helo services had money and power with a capital Money and Power. They did not notice pilots with headset hair. They noticed supermodels. Therefore there would be no inconvenient hormonal responses allowed. Besides, she needed money, not man-candy.

And Dr. Lucas Angelo had hired her three times. Almost a regular. Which she desperately needed. Eyes on the prize, not the scenery.

It had been a good speech. She'd almost convinced herself. Then he'd climbed into the back of the helo and she'd started thinking about tigers.

Though now, as they sped through the air, heading for the Hamptons and whatever no doubt ridiculously expensive event he was attending, she was thinking that tiger wasn't the right metaphor for the sensation. No, the way his silent presence seemed to fill the cabin, impossible to ignore, was more like riding the edge of a storm, feeling the weight of the air and the tingle of electricity. Knowing that if you were foolish and let the storm tumble over you it would sweep you up and control whatever happened from there.

Not going to happen.

She was a damned good pilot. She knew how to avoid a storm.

Even when she wasn't sure she wanted to.

Lucas studied the patient films on the laptop screen in front of him and tried to ignore the steady *thwap thwap thwap* racket of the helicopter around him. Even with headphones he was far too aware of the engine noise. Of the fact he was God only knew how high in the air in a high-tech tin can.

Focus on the problem.

In front of him the X-ray showed the fractured clavicle clearly. It would heal fine once he got to work on it. It was a simple surgery and one he didn't perform that often these days, but this particular clavicle belonged to a promising male figure skater and his parents were willing to pay for the best to ensure that promise could still be fulfilled.

He couldn't blame them.

The surgery wasn't complicated enough to distract him, though, and he keyed up the next file. The helicopter dipped a little, and his fingers clutched the edge of the laptop a little too hard.

Freaking helicopters. Supposedly Leonardo da Vinci had come up with the design for the first one. Crazy bastard. Lucas didn't care how much of a genius the guy was supposed to have been. No one sane would think that a helicopter was a good idea.

He made himself loosen his grip. He wasn't fond

of planes in general, though he ruthlessly suppressed the illogical nerves they brought to life in his stomach because not flying wasn't an option in his life. It was harder in a helicopter, though. Too small. Nowhere to hide from the empty air surrounding him.

He understood flight theory and aerodynamics. He knew how helicopters—and planes—stayed airborne. He'd made it his business to know, but that still didn't ease the fear.

His first time in a helicopter had been an emergency airlift to a hospital, a race to repair his shoulder. He'd been in pain and shock and reeling from the aftermath of the explosion that had put him there, spitting ash and bile as the nurse and doctor in the chopper had tried to sedate him.

All the while feeling like the ground was dropping away from beneath him and he was never going to find his footing again.

Turned out that instinct had been right.

The surgeon had done a brilliant job on his shoulder. It was fully functional. But there'd been no chance that it would stand up to the demands of a career pitching pro ball.

And just like that his dream had been over. All because a bunch of deluded young idiots had decided that they'd had a grudge against the government and that blowing up a college baseball game was a good way to protest. And because he and Alex and Mal hadn't been able to follow their coach's instructions to get the hell off the field and to safety. No, instead they'd stayed and tried to help some of the people trapped in the crumpled wreckage of the stands. He still didn't remember what he'd done that had torn up his shoulder, but he had.

Leaving him with a shattered dream and a new path to find. He'd found it in medicine, but it had taken some time. And it had left him with an unshakable fear of flying.

His brain knew that the explosion and helicopters weren't the same thing, but his body didn't. Every time he stepped into an aircraft, his mouth turned to a desert and his stomach to water.

But in his profession, flying was inevitable. People were hardly going to wait while their crack orthopedic surgeon took the bus across the state or across the country.

So he sucked it up and flew when he needed to. But he didn't like it and he never would.

Focus.

He took a deeper breath, schooling himself to be calm, and tried to send his attention back into the next patient file.

Which would be easier if he were back in his office in Manhattan rather than flying to the Hamptons to attend a party he had no desire to attend.

Socializing was another necessary evil of his career. Hospital fund-raisers, charity golf games, and all the hoopla that came with being a member of the oh-so-wealthy, oh-so-philanthropic, oh-so-full-of-expectations Angelos.

But this party wasn't one his family was roping him into. No, this one was due to the latest piece of insanity to enter his life.

The New York Saints.

He still wasn't sure how his best friend, Alex Winters, had convinced him—and their other friend Malachi Coulter—to join forces to bail out the baseball team they'd all supported since childhood.

There'd been bourbon involved but also a good dose of crazy.

He didn't do crazy.

But he did do baseball. And for once, he hadn't been able to resist a bad idea. Owning a baseball team. He'd imagined it as a kid, as his parents made him attend cotillions and play golf and learn to sail and tried to discourage his love of baseball.

It hadn't worked. It was an incurable disease.

His presence in this helicopter was firm proof of that. As was the fact that he was now officially part owner of a Major League Baseball team. Even if it was the worst team in the MLB.

"We're about twenty minutes out, sir." The voice of his pilot buzzed in his headphones. He liked her voice. It sounded confident and relaxed and had a pleasant female thrum to it that was a small distraction from his discomfort.

He flicked his gaze up from the laptop but saw only the back of her head. The ends of her medium-brown hair curled out in wisps under the cap she wore; the set of her shoulders in the very plain blue shirt was relaxed, but he couldn't see much more than that.

He hadn't seen much more than that in three trips so far. She was always seated in the pilot's seat when he boarded the chopper, already wearing a cap and her headphones or whatever you called the radio-mike thing that let them communicate during the flight.

He did know that she had pretty eyes. Blue. Not bright blue like his. More ocean-y. A hint of gray and green lending depth. Sea-blue eyes and a cute smile, though he'd only seen that once.

The main thing he knew about her—other than the fact her name was Sara Charles, as attested to by the neat name badge on her uniform—was that she seemed to be a very good pilot. She got him where he was going in one piece, with no flashy maneuvers to shatter his hard-won calm, and she didn't bother him with chitchat.

Which was why he'd hired her again after the first time he'd booked her when his regular guy couldn't fit him in. And why he'd booked her again for this trip.

He was glad she'd taken the job. Though any sensible person would, given he was paying quite a nice bonus to have her hang around and wait to fly him home again after the fund-raiser. With Sara Charles, for some reason, even though being in a helicopter still sucked, it wasn't quite as bad as usual. Still, he'd be happy when they were both safely back on Manhattan soil at the end of the night.

He intended that the end of the night would come sooner rather than later. He had surgeries lined up in the morning and roughly four hundred other things to juggle around in his schedule ahead of the Saints decamping to Florida for spring training in a little over two weeks.

Alex and Mal had decided that he, as an orthopedic surgeon, was the one most qualified to keep an eye on things in Florida. Most qualified and also the one with less Saints business already on his plate. Mal was busy trying to bring Deacon Field—the Saints' home stadium—out of the security Stone Age, and Alex was wheeling and dealing with finances and TV deals and the money stuff. Which left Lucas to deal with the team, the potential new players, and getting everyone ready for the coming season. The Saints' first season since they'd taken over.

Of course, that was mostly the job of the coaching team and the trainers and the scouts, but he was going to be boss man on the ground as much as possible. Which meant the weeks between now and the beginning of the season in April were going to be a nightmare as he tried to split his time between New York and Florida. And that was before he even thought about all the air time that was going to involve.

He didn't want to think about that.

So he wouldn't. Instead he'd finish reviewing the files he'd brought with him so that he was ready for tomorrow's procedures, and then they'd arrive at their destination and he'd do his duty at the damned party and get the hell back to New York.

Sara led the way across the airfield to the small building that served as the terminal. Dr. Angelo—she didn't really feel like she could call him Lucas—had thanked her politely when he'd climbed out of the chopper, taken a moment to straighten his impeccable bow tie, slung his black leather laptop bag over his shoulder, and then asked, "Which way?"

That had been the sum total of their conversation. The afternoon light had turned golden, the weather warm for this time of year despite warnings of possible storms later on. He looked not quite real as he walked smoothly across the grass, the gilded light playing on his hair and face.

He moved a bit like a tiger, she thought. Lithe and powerful. Graceful for a tall guy. She was five six and he easily had half a foot on her. She wondered if he'd played a sport of some sort before he'd become a doctor. She'd spent a lot of time around guys who kept themselves in good shape in the army, but even among them it was the ones who'd been great athletes who, in her experience, moved like the man walking besides her. Totally in control of every inch of his well-honed body.

The one she wished didn't make her skin spark with awareness every time she saw him. The one that made her desperately need a little more control over her own body.

Thankfully the walk to the terminal building was a short one. Dr. Angelo held the door for her—of course he was the kind of guy who would hold a door for her—and she walked into the terminal, looking around to see who was on the desk.

She spotted Ellen Jacek, who ran the airfield with her husband, before Ellen spotted them. But not much before. Ellen's dark eyes widened and a smile of appreciation bloomed on her face as she took in Dr. Angelo. Which was gratifying in a way. It meant it wasn't just Sara who was dumb enough to react to the sight of him.

But like her, Ellen was a professional, and her smile smoothed into something more welcoming as she came toward them.

"Sara, honey. How are you? How's your dad?"

Sara returned her brief hard hug. "I'm good. And Dad's doing better. Hoping to get back in the air in a few more months." She remembered why she was there. "Ellen Jacek, this is Dr. Angelo. I think there should be a car waiting for him?"

"Oh sure, Dean delivered it a while back. It's parked out front." Ellen turned her attention to Lucas. "Nice ride. I've got the keys over at the desk." She headed in that direction and Lucas strode after her, leaving Sara to follow behind. She did so, listening to Ellen chatter and Lucas give short answers until Ellen reached the desk, leaned over it, and grabbed a set of keys before passing them to Lucas.

"It's the red one out front," she said.

"Red?" Lucas queried.

"Dean said to say he was sorry but there was an issue with the car you requested. So he gave you this one instead." Ellen grinned at Lucas. "If you don't like it, you're welcome to borrow my truck and I'll take the Mercedes for a spin."

Lucas tilted his head at her. Sara couldn't quite see his expression from where she was standing but Ellen's cheeks flushed slightly and she smiled, so presumably it was amused not angry.

"I'm sure it will be fine," he said, dropping the keys into his jacket pocket. He turned back to Sara.

"I'll call you when I'm leaving the party. It should be around ten."

"That's fine, I'll be here."

He nodded just as his phone started to ring. He fished it out of his jacket pocket and glanced at the screen before taking the call. While he spoke, Sara watched him, getting in a few more seconds of tuxedoed-glory-appreciation time. There was much to appreciate. But sadly appreciation was all there was going to be, so she forced at least part of her attention onto making a plan for the hours ahead. Hopefully Ellen would lend her the truck so she could at least drive to the beach and get in a walk on the sand and pretend she was wealthy enough to own one of the gorgeous houses lining the shore.

After that there was paperwork stuffed in her flight bag that needed her attention. More correspondence with her dad's insurance company in dense legalese that she had to interpret and decide how to respond to. That painful task would earn her a few hours vegging out with her eReader and take-out in the tiny upstairs pilots' lounge while she waited for the good doctor to be done with whatever beautiful-people gathering it was that he was attending.

Not actually that much different from what she'd have been doing on a Friday night after a long week anyway, when she thought about it. Which was just sad. She couldn't, off the top of her head, think of the last time she'd been out. With her dad out of action, there'd just been too much work picking up the slack to want to do more than stay in and catch up on sleep when she got some downtime. Do the good and sensible thing.

Tired pilots made mistakes. And Charles Air really couldn't afford another mistake. She'd flown exhausted and riding on adrenaline in the service but she didn't have to now. She wouldn't. Even when there were a thousand and one things calling for her attention, she tried to make sure she didn't wear herself out. Sleep and rest were more important than bars and restaurants and the dating merry-go-round right now. Even if her therapist had made a few pointed comments about rebuilding her social life in their last session. Her best friend, Viv, had started to nag, too.

Lucas hung up his phone at last and Sara dragged her thoughts back to the present and him. Her client.

Her *paying* client. She was here to make his life easier, not obsess about her own. Was there anything she'd forgotten to tell him about the arrangements for the flight back? Nothing sprang to mind. Which meant it was time to stop admiring him in his tuxedo and let him disappear. But she allowed herself one last quick once-over and her eyes snagged on the laptop bag ruining the line of his jacket as it hung from his very broad shoulder. "You're welcome to leave your laptop bag here with me," she said. "Save you dragging it around."

"We have some secure lockboxes," Ellen added. "It'll be safe."

He nodded. "That would be helpful, thank you." He held out the bag and Sara took it, ignoring the tiny flare of heat that rippled through her when her fingers brushed his. Holding his laptop was as close as she was ever going to get to Lucas Angelo. And as she watched through the glass terminal doors while he climbed into a red convertible and then sped off into the distance, she tried very hard to ignore the part of her that really, really wished she was speeding off with him.

Chapter Two

Intent on working the party, Lucas didn't notice the rain.

The hum of conversation and the music playing through the sound system was loud enough to drown the world outside. Besides, he was focused on doing what he had come to do. Hunting for potential season ticket holders and corporate sponsors. Winning people over. Making them want to throw cash at the Saints.

Cash they needed. He and Alex and Mal had all put their share in, but they couldn't keep throwing their personal funds into the team. Well, Alex probably could, given he was richer than God, and Lucas was not without his own resources. But that didn't matter. The team needed to become self-sustaining. Had to function as a Major League Baseball team. Otherwise they, too, would eventually have to cut their losses. And at that point the chances of the Saints surviving without leaving New York were about a million to one.

Baseball teams were expensive to run. They were even more expensive when you were trying to recruit new talent and replace some of the existing team who'd decided to ply their trade elsewhere after the change in owners. They'd lost their second and third best pitchers and several other players. Pitchers were expensive. All players were expensive.

So they needed supporters. The Saints couldn't compete against the deep, deep pockets of the top teams, but every little bit helped and Lucas would do his best to add to the coffers tonight. So he shook hands and made small talk and smiled at women in expensive dresses and even more expensive jewelry and shut everything else out of his mind for the time he had allocated to this task.

He did, however, notice when the lights flickered and the room went still for a moment. Then laughter broke out as the bulbs steadied and everyone clinked glasses, shrugged, and moved on. Which was the sensible reaction when you were down for the weekend and had no pressing need to be back in the city first thing in the morning.

A storm didn't matter in those circumstances.

It did matter if you were planning to fly back to the city in a helicopter.

He excused himself from the conversation he'd been having with a couple who knew his mother and had spent the last ten minutes grilling him about her various charities. Stepping out of the main room, he pulled out his phone.

The signal was low—another casualty of the weather perhaps—but he had enough to open the weather app and find out what exactly the weather was doing. As he viewed the less-than-good figures on current rainfall and wind speed, the lights flickered again.

He didn't need to read the warnings on the app to know that wasn't good.

Just his freaking luck.

It was only nine o'clock, earlier than he'd planned on leaving, but making it back to Manhattan and his morning surgeries was more important than another half an hour of schmoozing. He just didn't have any room in his schedule right now. If he didn't make it back to the city, then some of his surgeries would be bumped. And for what he did, time was of the essence, particularly when it came to athletes. A delay in surgery could mean the difference between merely a good recovery and being able to compete again.

Delays meant him failing.

He didn't fail.

So. First order of the business was to get back to the airfield, get Sara to fire up that infernal helicopter—his stomach swooped a little at the thought of flying through a storm of all things—and hopefully they could get back to the city.

There, a plan. Everything was just fine.

Mind made up, he went to find his host, say his good-byes, and make a getaway.

* * *

"Not going to happen," Sara said bluntly. She'd been waiting for him at the tiny terminal, had even come out to the car with an umbrella for him when he'd pulled up outside the main doors. She looked cute slightly damp, the moisture making the ends of her hair curl even more, her eyes taking on some of the storm in the odd glow coming from the lights outside the terminal. He'd been taken for a second by the sight of her, braced against the wind that lifted her hair, but that was only until he'd asked her how long it would be before they could get in the air and she'd looked first apologetic and then determined as she delivered the bad news. Cute apparently came packaged with uncompromising.

Lucas blinked. "Excuse me?"

"I'm sorry, Dr. Angelo," Sara said. "And we will, of course, refund you the return flight." Her expression turned vaguely regretful as she said this before it went back to being resolute. "But I can't fly you back tonight."

"The weather isn't that bad, is it?" he asked hopefully. As if in answer, thunder rumbled overhead. A few seconds later the terminal—which was only half lit—brightened considerably as a flash of lightning followed on its heels.

"Trust me, you do not want to be in a helicopter that's struck by lightning," Sara said.

He tried to ignore the mental image *that* conjured up. "Couldn't we get ahead of the storm?"

Thunder rumbled again, and she started a little. Then jerked her head toward the window and the rain pouring from the sky. "The storm's already here," she said. "So no."

"I have to be back in the city in the morning," Lucas said.

Her determined expression didn't alter. "I'm sorry but I can't fly you. Not until the weather clears."

Lucas scowled out at the storm. He had patients who needed surgery. So he needed to get home. "When is that likely to be?"

"Best-case scenario is somewhere close to first light. More likely to be midmorning, though, looking at the size of the storm."

Sunrise. At this time of year, that was about seven thirty. So he wouldn't be at the hospital until nine, depending on the traffic from the heliport. Two hours after his first surgery was scheduled to start. Meaning a screwed-up schedule and guaranteed chaos. And if the storm didn't lift until midmorning, things would be even worse. He didn't do chaos.

Crap. Though, as lightning flared across the sky again, he decided that he couldn't argue with her about the fact that flying through an electrical storm wasn't the smart solution to his problem. Which meant he needed another way.

Like the car waiting outside the terminal.

It was a long drive back to Manhattan, and it would be longer given the weather and the fact it was already getting late. He scrubbed a hand over his face and wished he'd had more coffee at the party.

He needed to be alert.

He turned to Sara, who was staring out at the sky, a mix of irritation and wariness in her frown.

"I need to get back. I'm going to drive."

Her eyebrows lifted.

"My weather app doesn't show the storm being so bad in that direction. So here's my proposition. Keep me company so I stay awake. And keep my return fare, of course."

She stared at him for a moment. "But my helo is here."

"I'll pay for a car to bring you back down here tomorrow morning, and you can fly back. You said it yourself, you can't fly anywhere tonight. So what do you think?"

Thunder boomed suddenly and he thought he saw her flinch, though it was difficult to tell in the darkness. But as the sound rumbled on, her shoulders squared and she nodded. "Okay," she said. "It's a deal."

This might have been the stupidest thing she'd ever done, Sara thought as she climbed into the Mercedes and sank into a leather seat that curved around her invitingly. The car was low and sleek, and Lucas was an uncomfortably large presence beside her. She would have felt better if they were in an SUV or something built for bad weather.

Who was she kidding? She would have felt better anywhere but in such a small space with Lucas Angelo. Because then she would have been able to maintain her denial about just how gorgeous the man was. Gorgeous enough to talk her into driving for hours through a storm.

Of course, the money didn't hurt, either. If there was one thing she needed, it was cold hard cash. And after this evening's debacle, no doubt Dr. Gorgeous would be finding a chopper pilot who was more willing to do his bidding and fly him into a hurricane if need be, so there went the likelihood that he'd become what she'd been hoping was her first new regular client since she'd taken the reins of Charles Air.

It was hard to get new clients when the first thing that came up in any Google search about your company was a chopper crash.

No, it hadn't been her dad's fault—even the NTSB investigation agreed on that point—and he'd had no passengers in the chopper at the time. But it was a crash all the same. It wasn't a great first impression, and she'd fought for every booking since she'd come home to run things. But couple the crash with the fact that she was operating with only one helo and she was barely covering expenses. She needed clients like Lucas. Rich, frequent fliers who needed to get somewhere fast.

Only less pretty.

Because then she could keep her eyes firmly on the prize.

She drew in a breath. Mistake. Because the air inside of the car carried a hint of whatever it was that he wore as cologne or aftershave. It was faintly spicy, a touch smoky, and seemed purposely designed as Sara-bait.

The scent made her stomach warm. Made her want to lean in and breathe deeper. Which she so wasn't going to do.

She was quite close enough already, with only a foot or so separating them.

Lucas was focused on driving as they wound their way back from the airfield to the main road. The car might be small but it was powerful, and he steered it with a skill that spoke of confidence and familiarity. The way pilots handled a helo they'd flown a thousand times before.

Maybe he had the same car?

She tried to remember if she'd ever seen his car, but no. He'd booked his first flight through their website, and he'd never been to the small airfield where they hangared the helicopters. She'd always picked him up from a heliport.

But if she had to guess, she'd put money on the fact that he did drive something like this. Something expensive and built for speed.

He'd want a car that would get him where he wanted to go fast.

He didn't like being delayed, that was clear from his determination to get back to the city.

The rain seemed heavier when they cleared the town and Lucas bumped the windshield wipers to speed them up. Even so, the windshield ran with water, blurring the world outside.

"Are you sure you want to do this?" Sara asked. "It's not too late to turn back. Ellen has a couple of rollaways upstairs at the terminal." *Dumb, Sara.* If

Lucas needed a bed for the night, he'd probably just pick up his phone and have any number of people who owned ridiculously expensive houses here willing to offer him a bed.

No doubt the females among them would be glad to share it with him.

"I mean, you could get some sleep and leave early. The storm might blow over sooner." She had her doubts about that but hey, optimism never hurt anyone. That was what her therapist kept telling her.

Lucas glanced in her direction. "We'll be fine." He flashed a grin that was almost as brilliant as the lightning flickering above them. "Trust me, I'm a doctor."

She laughed, startled. A joke? From silent but gorgeous? He'd already spoken more words to her today than in the entire time she'd known him—and now he was cracking jokes? "You did not just say that."

"Hey, it's a classic line. And it worked."

"Worked?" she echoed.

"It made you laugh," he said with another blinding smile.

He wanted to make her laugh? Why? Was he flirting with her? Dr. Gorgeous?

Surely not. She was headset hair and engine grease. He was designer tuxedos, fancy Hamptons parties, and chartered helicopter flights. It was very clear she was Not His Kind.

Damn it. She squelched the depressing thought and tried to keep herself focused on reality.

"After all," Lucas said, "you're meant to be keeping me awake. You can't do that staring out the windshield."

"I don't want to distract you." There was another flash of lightning as she spoke, and the rain intensified. The sound of it competed with the rumble of the car's engine, the beat making her neck tense.

"You won't distract me."

He sounded confident. At least one of them was. She really didn't like being out in storms.

She tried to think of the plus side of getting back to the city. Sleeping in her own bed. Being able to get home and get Dougal back from her neighbor early. He didn't like storms, either. Which made for interesting times when a ninety-pound dog tried to crawl into her lap at the first rumble of thunder. Lightning flashed again, even brighter, and she ran out of ideas. Maybe Lucas Angelo wasn't going to be distracted, but she was starting to crave a little distraction herself. So. Talking. To the gorgeous doctor. The relatively complete stranger gorgeous doctor.

She flailed for a suitable topic of conversation. Small talk wasn't her thing. "So," she managed eventually. "What kind of doctor are you, Dr. Angelo?"

"It's Lucas," he said. "And I'm an orthopedic surgeon."

A surgeon. Of course he was. And orthopedics. Most of her knowledge of medicine came from TV and her first-aid training. But she knew that one from her dad. A smashed-up leg had meant they'd gotten some quality time with the orthopedics department. "That's bones, right?"

"Bones and muscles," Lucas said, steering the car around a bend in the road. "I specialize in sports medicine, mostly."

Sports. Something else she knew little about. Her dad was a football fan. Her brother had been too. But Sara had never had much time for games involving teams and balls. Her teen obsession had been flying. That hadn't changed. "Sounds, um, glamorous," she managed.

Lucas laughed. "People are all the same on the operating table. But yes, I meet some interesting ones."

"Is that why you have to get back to Manhattan? For a patient?" That would be a semi-reasonable excuse for undertaking this reckless trek through the elements.

"Yes. I have a shoulder to fix."

"That doesn't sound like an emergency."

"The kid's a figure skater. A pairs skater. His shoulder is important to him." His tone sharpened a little.

"I understand," she said. She didn't, not really. Could a few hours really make a difference? Enough to risk driving through this weather for?

Lucas didn't reply. Damn. Had she upset him? Dissed his specialty?

Way to go. She really had no chance of keeping him as a client. She couldn't even manage to talk to the man without insulting him.

After all, it wasn't like she could ask him about the operation or anything. She wasn't fond of blood and guts, and surgery was all about that.

"I'm sure he's in good hands," she managed eventually.

"He is," Lucas agreed.

O-kay. Well, he didn't suffer from a lack of confidence, that was for sure. But she couldn't fault him for that. She figured you needed to be confident in your skills to pick up a piece of razor-sharp metal and slice into someone and believe that you could put them back together again better than when you started. Just like she was confident that she could take someone up into the air in several tons of metal and bring them back down again in one piece. Some things you needed to know you were good at.

Pity that she was all too aware of the things she wasn't good at tonight. Things like major storms and ridiculously hot men and small talk.

She wriggled a little against the leather seat.

"Are you cold?" he asked. He stretched his right hand toward the screen on the dashboard. It looked more complex than the instrument panels in the A-Star. And a lot more high-tech.

But he apparently was more than familiar with it, pressing the touch screen without really looking.

"No," she said. "I'm fine." The seats were heated and the car itself was warm enough, though she could feel the cold air outside from the chill emanating off the window. Far better to be inside the car than out, even factoring in the disconcerting company.

"Good," he said. "But let me know if you are." He nodded toward the dash and the display. "The temperature is dropping out there."

"Odd to get a thunderstorm in winter," Sara said. "Crazy weather."

"According to science, crazy weather is going to be the new normal," Lucas said seriously.

"Don't say things like that to a pilot," she said, only half joking. "I like nice calm weather."

"You should become a pilot somewhere with a more temperate climate then," Lucas said. "Find an island somewhere warm."

"Tempting," she said, trying not to picture Lucas in swim trunks lying on a tropical beach. "But I'm a New York kind of gal. I like the city. Staten is as island as I get."

"Me, too," Lucas said. "Though there are times when a tropical island seems appealing," he added cryptically. He shifted down a gear to take a corner and another bolt of lightning cracked across the sky, giving Sara a better glimpse of the world outside. The trees lining the road were bending furiously in the wind. She shivered.

They drove on a little longer in silence, the road becoming all either of them focused on.

"So how did you become a helicopter pilot?" Lucas asked when they were safely back on a stretch of straight road and the rain had eased up.

"My dad's a pilot. He used to take me up with him from when I was tiny," Sara replied with a shrug. "I can't remember ever not wanting to learn how to fly."

For a moment she thought she saw him shiver but dismissed it. Overly confident gorgeous doctors didn't do human things like shiver, after all.

"You never wanted to fly a plane?"

"Nah. Helicopters are more fun. Planes feel very . . . closed in. In a helo you're closer to the sky."

Another flash of lightning and the drumming on the roof bumped up a notch or two in volume. Right now the sky was a little too close for comfort.

"I guess," Lucas said. He didn't sound excited by the idea, either. "And is the Charles in Charles Air you or your dad?"

"Dad," Sara said. She bit down on the desire to say more. About how it was meant to be her dad and her brother. Here in the dark little bubble of warmth of the car, it would be easy to relax and tell him all her troubles. About the exhaustion of trying to single-handedly run a business that needed at least two more people to function properly. Or dealing with a parent who wasn't taking being out of action very well. Every time she saw her dad, even though he never said anything, Sara was sure he was regretting the fact that she was the one here to pick up the pieces instead of James. After all, sons were meant to be the heirs to the family business, weren't they?

But James was dead and had been for six years now and there was nothing that either Sara or her father could do about that.

And tempting as it was to talk to Lucas as they drove through the darkness, she didn't think crying on his shoulder was going to help keep his business. She bit her lip for a moment, pushing the bad stuff away again. She was aiming for *Born and bred a pilot*, not *Can't cut it*. "Though really, it was my granddad. He flew a Sioux in Korea. That's why Dad wanted to be a pilot."

"Something in the blood, then."

"I guess."

"Have you always worked for your dad?"

She shook her head. "No, I did a tour in the army. I—watch out!"

Lucas swore and braked heavily. The car skidded but he steered into it like a pro and they came to a halt about a foot clear of the massive tree that lay across the road, blocking both lanes. Sara's seat belt snapped her back against the seat.

"Fuck," Lucas said. Sara could only agree with him, but she didn't trust herself to speak just yet. She was too busy convincing herself that she was still in one piece.

He twisted toward her. "Are you okay?"

The sound of her heart beating was roaring in her ears but she wasn't hurt. They hadn't hit the tree. All was good. "Y-yes," she managed.

His eyes narrowed. "Are you sure?" He snapped his own belt free and leaned toward her.

She held him off with a hand. "I'm fine. But you need to move this car before someone else comes up behind us."

"Shit. Yes. You're right." He straightened and pulled his seat belt back into place. He backed the car up and then swung it into a U-turn. "We need a safe place to stop. I can't see what's on the shoulder in all this rain."

Sara couldn't, either. The entire outdoors seemed

to have turned into water sheeting from the sky. "I'm pretty sure I saw a motel sign a couple of miles back."

"A motel?"

She waved back at the tree. "Well, we're not getting past that. And while I'm sure this car has a fancy GPS that could get us onto some side roads, I'm guessing that there are only going to be more trees down. Same thing if we try to get back to Ellen's."

"I—"

"I know, you have to get back to the city. But it's not worth dying for, is it? Let's go to the motel and hope they have some rooms. You can get a few hours' sleep and try again when it's light. The emergency crews might have cleared this by then."

She watched him think about it, his dark brows twisted in a scowl as he gazed out the windshield, and silently kissed her last hope of keeping his business good-bye. The tree was hardly her fault, but this night was turning into the kind of disaster that was guaranteed to make him wish he'd never heard of Charles Air. Or her. If he argued with her, she would politely ask him to take her back to the motel; then he could do whatever the hell he wanted. "I know this sounds like the start of every bad horror movie ever made, but the motel is our best option."

His hands tightened on the wheel—her attempt at humor didn't seem to have lightened the mood—but then he gave a single nod. "You're right. This is too dangerous. We'll try the motel."

Chapter Three

The clerk manning the tiny reception area didn't look like the type to have a dead mother stashed upstairs. He looked about twenty with a red baseball cap pulled down over dark hair and horn-rimmed hipster glasses looming large on his face. He was reading a photography magazine and listening to a static-interrupted weather station on the radio.

That seemed fairly sane.

More sane than her anyway. Lucas had put his hand on her arm to steady her as they climbed the front steps after dashing through the rain and her body had responded with a good old-fashioned flash of lust-delight-more-please that had left her half dizzy.

"Two rooms," Lucas said.

The clerk pushed his glasses up his nose a little but didn't lift his head. "Sorry, only one left."

Damn it. Apparently they weren't the only two

riding out the storm. Only one room. Which meant sharing with Dr. Gorgeous.

Her body did that flash-of-lust thing again while her mind went a little crazy with images of her and Lucas together in the dark.

Not going to happen. Sara somehow managed to wrestle control of her brain back, telling herself that she was only reacting to him like this because of the adrenaline rush from their near miss with the tree. So time to stop giving in to inconvenient bodily chemical responses and actually think about the situation.

And whether it was a good one. After all, she didn't exactly know Dr. Gorgeous very well, and they were in the middle of nowhere. She was able to take care of herself if she had to, but no point being dumb. The only problem was how to ask Lucas to prove himself the good guy that her gut insisted he was.

Just in case her gut was being deceived by her apparently easily-swayed-by-a-gorgeous-face hormones.

"Do you have a business card?" she asked Lucas as he pulled out his wallet to hand over a credit card.

He nodded. "Why?"

She looked at him a moment. "Because I don't know you very well and we're about to share a room for the night." This made the clerk lift his head from the card details he was taking down and waggle his eyebrows at her. She shot him a look, and he ducked his head down again—but she could still see the grin on his face.

Lucas frowned, then his face cleared. "Oh. Right." He pulled a couple of cards from his wallet then passed one to the clerk. "These are my details." He hesitated a moment then handed over his driver's license as well. "Take a copy of that, too, if you have a copier." The clerk nodded and disappeared through a door behind the desk.

He handed the other business card to Sara. "Okay, text all that to someone you trust." He nodded in the direction of the door. "That guy knows all my information, too, now. Can pick me out of a lineup if he has to."

"Won't help if you're a crazed serial killer, you could just murder us both," Sara said with a half smile, but she took the card and snapped a picture of it with her phone. Then she sent a hurried text to Viv, with the pic and a short explanation of where she was and why, and told her she'd check in by six a.m. If Lucas wanted to get back to the city in the morning, they'd surely be up by then. Viv was ex-army, too. She'd raise all sorts of hell if Sara didn't call her on time.

"I'm not a serial killer," Lucas said. "And I promise, I'm not a creep, either. You're perfectly safe." He sounded serious, which was good.

She nodded then tucked the business card into her purse as the clerk came back with Lucas's license. He passed it over, along with the key, and pointed them toward the room at the very end of the long, low building.

And, because there could be no other possibility, there was only one bed in the room. One bed that looked narrower than the queen size the information sheet on the bedside table proclaimed it to be.

It was the only piece of furniture in the room other than a single wooden chair that looked like it might collapse if anyone sat on it. There was a TV bolted to the wall on a kind of shelf thing, but that hardly counted as furniture. Neither did the two low square shelves on either side of the bed that she guessed were meant to serve as nightstands.

Lucas put his laptop bag on the floor. Sara put her bag on the chair and then opened it. Her uniform pants were half soaked from the dash from the car, and she kept spare clothes in there in case she ever got stranded.

"I'm going to change," she said and slipped into the tiny bathroom, locking the door. When she emerged, Lucas was still standing by the door, studying the bed.

"I'll sleep on the floor," he said.

Sara shook her head, regarding the carpet. It was a dull mottled beige shade and more than a little sticky underfoot. God only knew what might be lurking in those fibers. She wouldn't have asked Dougal to sleep on that floor, let alone Lucas Angelo. She'd slept on hard dirt plenty of times but she didn't think he was the kind who roughed it. Besides which, the motel carpet wasn't covered in good clean dirt; it was kind of disgusting.

"We can share." That woke up her hormones again, making her stomach tighten. She mentally smacked them back down.

Lucas looked at the bed. "Are you sure?"

Yes, said the hormones with enthusiasm. Stupid hormones. Even if they did share a bed, sleeping would be all that they would be doing.

She looked at Lucas, trying to see past the face to the man underneath. She'd done the smart thing back in the reception, and he'd taken no offense. He'd never treated her with anything but courtesy, he hadn't thrown a tantrum when she'd told him she couldn't fly him through the storm as some clients would have, and he was a surgeon who fixed teen-age figure skaters, for Pete's sake.

He didn't set off her Spidey-sense in any way that wasn't 100 percent good. And what with the army and working in the very male world of helicopters and life in general, she'd been around enough jerks to learn to trust her Spidey-sense when it came to detecting creeps.

True, her Spidey-sense hadn't always gotten it right when it came to jerks, but that wasn't an issue. She wasn't planning to date Lucas Angelo.

Still, the fact that he did set off her Spidey-sense in the 100 percent good way made her question whether it was a good idea to climb onto a bed with him for a whole other set of reasons.

But there wasn't a lot she could do about it. She was just going to have to be a big girl and ignore how hot the man was.

Having him in the back of her helo had been bad. But she was discovering that it was nothing compared with being stuck in a very small motel room with him on a bed that was also very small but looming very large in her consciousness.

Which was ridiculous. The man hadn't done anything other than smile at her a little and hand over his details to strangers when she'd wanted proof he could be trusted. It didn't matter if she was drowning in lust, because he quite clearly wasn't.

Outside the world was still drowning in plain old rain. The rumbles of thunder made her shiver a little.

"Beer?" Lucas held out a bottle with another polite yet gorgeous smile. They'd found a six-pack in the trunk of the Mercedes when they'd been retrieving their bags. It had been chilled from the weather but was warming now in the overheated room.

"Okay." Sara took it and twisted the top free. One beer. Which she would sip slowly. It would at least give her something to distract her from the fact that she was alone with Lucas Angelo.

She perched on one side of the bed and watched as Lucas removed his jacket, undid his bow tie, unbuttoned his collar, and took off his shoes and socks. Which left him in tuxedo pants and a glorious white shirt, tanned feet bare, looking like every female fantasy picture of a male movie star she'd ever seen.

She looked away as he took a seat on the far—not far enough, really—side of the bed. He sat propped against the wall and some pillows—the bed at least had a good supply of those—as he cracked open his beer.

Warm beer, the weird fan whistle of the motel's heating, and the weight of a man lying on the bed beside her.

The first two she could cope with. The third was driving her a little crazy.

Which was ridiculous. *Just a man*, she told herself firmly. *Just a man, just a man, just a man*. And a client besides.

But try as her brain might, her body insisted on fighting back. Not just a man. A bona fide gorgeous man. A bona fide only-in-the-movies gorgeous man who smiled at her when he passed her a beer and who smelled like nothing on earth—warm and clean and male with that damned perfect cologne doing wicked things to her insides.

Who was just a few tiny short inches away from her, lying on the bed as he sipped his own warm beer.

Her heart was beating so fast, she was sure he must be able to hear it.

She was pretty sure that the sight of her, in the old black pants and KEEP CALM AND FLY ON T-shirt that she'd found stashed in her flight bag, wasn't having the same effect on him.

Life really was a bitch sometimes. And lately it was a bitch who seemed to have it in for Sara.

Couldn't just one little thing go her way? Just one tiny miracle like the male Adonis going for the normal girl for once?

Not that she should be even thinking that sort of thing about a customer.

He's going to be an ex-customer. So what does it matter?

That was the evil part of her brain. The part that apparently had her confused with somebody entirely different who could make a move on a man like Lucas.

She was hardly a virgin and she'd coaxed a man or two into her bed in her time. But never one who looked like Lucas. And to be honest, most of the time she'd let the guys do the coaxing.

But damn, he smelled good. And looked even better.

She stared at the ugly brown floral curtains covering the window, fingers clenched around the beer bottle so she wouldn't do anything stupid like roll over and reach for him.

The edges of the window lit up suddenly. Lightning. Thunder boomed close on its heels, and she winced and turned away from the window.

Toward Lucas.

"You don't like thunder, do you?" Lucas was regarding her over his beer. She hadn't picked him for the beer type but he seemed to be enjoying it. Even now, he tilted the bottle back again and took a swallow. Then he tossed the bottle toward the trash can near the door. It landed neatly, dead center. Of course it did.

"It's fine." She managed an everything's-normal-here, don't-worry smile as she picked at a loose corner of the label on her beer. Lucas Angelo didn't need to know why storms could make her squirrelly. Everything was fine. She wasn't out in the storm and neither was anyone else she cared about. She tilted the beer, swallowed quickly. "Don't worry, I'm not going to have hysterics and try to hide under the bed or anything."

He tilted his head, and the light from the lamp on the bedside table did something that made his eyes seem even bluer. "I didn't think you were."

"I never liked storms, actually," she said, desperate for something to talk about. Something that would distract her from him. From the fact that it wasn't just the storm making her shiver. "Even as a kid. There's something about the thunder that . . . I don't know. I just don't like it. At home, I'd just put on the TV and my headphones and be fine." Plus at home, she'd have Dougal to hug and make her feel better. He smelled like dog rather than delicious man, but that was a small price to pay for sanity.

"My gran said I must have been hurt in a storm in a past life." She offered a smile meant to prove that she didn't believe that. "Gran was Irish. Superstitious. I think I just don't like storms." Which was true, she didn't. But she was leaving out the part where Jamie, her brother, had died in one and her dad had crashed his helicopter in another.

Another swallow of beer while she forced her thoughts away from that particular reality. And another. The bottle emptied. The slight buzz—luckily it wasn't anything stronger or she'd be heading toward drunk after downing it so fast—began to push away her nerves. Lucas sat beside her apparently content with silence for a time.

The trouble with that was that as her nerves about the storm faded, her exquisite awareness of Lucas flooded in again to take their place. All her senses zeroed in on him, taking in each tiny detail. The scent of him. The tingle in her nerves, which were far too attuned to his presence so very close by. The dip in the mattress from his body that meant her side of the bed was angled ever so slightly toward him. Just inviting her to slide over and . . . Another clap of thunder boomed above them and she jumped.

"If the storm's going to bother you that much, I think we need a distraction," Lucas said.

They both stared across at the tiny TV bolted on the wall. The screen was dark. The clerk had informed them that the cable was out due to the storm after he'd handed them the keys. Sara tried not to think about the other most obvious form of distraction for a man and a woman alone on a bed.

Maybe she should get her eReader out of her bag. Pretend to read something . . . though that would be kind of rude.

"TV's out," Lucas said. "The best option I can offer is more beer." He rolled a little and reached across her for the beer.

Before she knew what she was doing, she rolled toward him, too, and her leg, apparently having a mind all of its own, hooked itself over his hip.

Lucas froze.

So did she.

"Sara?"

"Um, yes, that's me," she said.

He laughed then. A soft low rumble of a laugh.

Move your leg. Move your leg. Move your leg. Her body was having none of it, though. Her leg stayed right where it was. Stupid body. It had heard that laugh. It wanted more of the man who'd made such an enticing sound. Damn it.

She almost fainted when Lucas's hand settled on her waist. "I know it's you," he said. "What I'm trying to figure out is what exactly is going on here."

Which wasn't exactly, *What the hell is your leg doing hooked over me, you floozy?* Her throat went dry as her mind went into overdrive. Did that mean he was happy about the leg? Or was he just too polite to push her the hell away?

She swallowed, trying to make her brain work. His hand was warm and heavy and she was fairly certain that every inch of her that it was touching was about to burst into flames.

What the *hell* was she doing?

"Um, I'm not sure," she said. He'd said *distraction*, and apparently her hormones had used that moment to seize control of her body and stage a coup.

"Can I tell you what I think is happening?"

Oh God. He was going to let her down gently or something. Make some chivalrous speech. But then his hand moved a little on her waist. A small stroking flex of his fingers that sent her skin even closer to the point of spontaneous combustion. She bit the inside of her lip so she wouldn't moan at the sensation.

"I think you're making a pass at me," he said.

"I—" She stopped and swallowed again. He didn't sound angry or horrified. A little amused, maybe, but maybe the prospect of sex made him happy. She wasn't sure it made her happy despite the fact her skin was melting under his touch.

In fact, the way that she was reacting to him

meant she wasn't sure that the idea of sex with Lucas Angelo wasn't downright terrifying. And there she was, thinking about sex with a client again. So she had a decision to make. Pull away and blame it on storm nerves or woman up and go after what her body was strongly suggesting she wanted, to hell with professionalism and common sense.

She really wanted door number two. Really, *really* wanted it. The way she hadn't wanted anything since she'd gotten back from the army and been sucked into the maelstrom of dealing with her dad and insurance companies and the business and . . . good God, his hand was moving again. Doing that little coaxing stroking thing.

She looked up at him. His eyes were very blue. Very very blue. And he was watching her very intently. With the sort of look that, unless she really had lost touch with every female instinct she possessed, was telling her he wasn't unhappy with the situation.

Oh hell, it was door number two. "Would that be a bad thing?"

"Not bad," he said. He smiled and she felt her brain fog a little. "But—"

"It's all right," she said. "I'm clear on the situation. I'm not going to turn into a crazed stalker in the morning and tell the friend I sent your details to that you attacked me. This is about sex. For one night only. Deal?"

His eyebrows flicked upward. "Deal. And just to be clear, if you change your mind, just tell me." His hand moved to her back, pulled her in a little closer.

"So, lady's choice, Sara Charles. Where do you want to start?"

"I think—" She didn't really. No, she was far too distracted by the hardness of his body against hers. And by the look in his eyes, which was suddenly hot and focused all on her. And by the curve of his mouth while he waited for her answer. That mouth. "Isn't kissing traditional?"

"Excellent choice," he said and put his mouth to hers.

He took his kissing seriously, this man. That became apparent in the first few seconds. Any thoughts of *How do I get out of this if he's a terrible kisser?* flew out of her head with the last shreds of her sanity when he settled his mouth on hers and began to light every nerve ending in her body on fire with a series of soft gentle exploratory kisses that were the work of a master.

She made a humming sound of pleasure and moved closer against him, curling her hand behind his neck as his lips teased and nipped and played.

When she began to grow impatient and arched a little more into him, opening her mouth, he didn't need a second invitation. The kiss turned deeper. Hotter. His tongue was just as skilled as his lips.

He tasted as good as he smelled. A little like the beer they'd been drinking and a lot like . . . well, Lucas, she guessed. Delicious. Male.

And all hers for just one night. She was suddenly eager not to waste any time.

She reached for the first button on his shirt and popped it open. Lucas stopped kissing her for a moment. Then started again when she moved her hands to the next button and the next. It didn't take very long to free them all. She pulled her mouth back from his kisses and pushed his shirt open, eager to see if the body beneath was all she'd imagined.

The power chose that very moment to go out.

Chapter Four

"Are you kidding me?" she muttered, frustrated.

Lucas laughed, the sound somehow even sexier in the dark. "Like to look, do you?"

"Depends on the scenery," she said, still annoyed. "Yours had potential."

He laughed again. "You know, in medical school they taught us that when one sense is deprived the others become heightened."

"Not sure super-hearing is what I need right now."

"I was thinking more of touch." One of his hands took hers, lifted it, and placed it on his chest. Her palm tingled at the feel of warm solid muscle. "Touch is much more fun."

He had a point. And at this moment, following doctor's orders seemed like a pretty damned good idea.

He recommended touch. So touch it was going to be. Greedy now, she pushed at him and he rolled obediently and lay on his back. She swung a leg over him and settled astride him, pushing the shirt open with the impatience of a child tearing open a Christmas present.

If he was to be hers for one night only then she was going to make the most of it. Enjoy every inch of him.

She laid her hands on his chest and felt the bump of his heart under one of them, rushing fast like her own. So maybe he was human after all.

Flesh and blood.

She wriggled a little and felt the flesh part all too clearly. Nice. Very nice. But that would come later. No point rushing the touching. Start with the chest and work her way down. A smile bloomed on her face.

Her palms warmed from the heat of his skin, tingling as his chest rose and fell beneath her. He didn't talk, just lay quietly. The room was still very dark, though her eyes were starting to adjust a little, but somehow she knew that his eyes were focused on her face.

There was something intimate in the weight of his unseen gaze. Too close, almost. More intimate than the fact that he was nearly half naked and she was straddling him, only thin cotton and wool separating them from being flesh to flesh.

They stayed that way, breathing together until she began to be able to see him, a little. Even half hidden by the lack of light, he was beautiful.

She bent down and kissed him again, wanting to be lost again, to not have to look at him a moment while she caught her breath.

His hands came up around her upper arms and she sighed into him as their tongues met and the pleasure of his kiss cut off the thinking part of her brain with ruthless efficiency.

So good.

So very very good.

Maybe they could just kiss until sunrise. Kiss like teenagers, lost in discovery.

But that would mean wasting the rest of him. And that, no matter how glorious his kisses, would be something she'd regret until she was old and gray. And probably beyond.

Lucas Angelo was a once-in-a-lifetime opportunity.

She'd seen enough in her life to know that you shouldn't waste those.

So she had to seize the day—or the night—and make the sort of memory that would make her eighty-year-old self very happy when she looked back on it.

She began to kiss her way down his neck, taking a moment to press her face into the place where the muscle of it started to curve in his chest and breathe him in. She still didn't know what it was he smelled like, but up close it was intoxicating.

Intoxicating was good. She moved lower, mouth drifting downward, kissing his skin and sucking. Her right hand found his nipple and pinched it. He made a suitably pleased noise.

Good. Something he liked.

She did it again and he groaned this time, and the sound sent a shiver down her spine to light every nerve between her legs. She wanted to hear him make that sound again. She wanted to know that it was her who'd made him make it.

Plain old Sara Charles.

And suddenly she wasn't so sure she had the patience to explore him slowly.

She sat up and ran her hand down his chest, following the trail of dark hair that led the way, and made herself stop when she reached the waistband of his trousers. Curling her fingers around it and just slightly under it, feeling his stomach muscles tighten and tremble as she touched warm skin.

"God," he muttered, but he still stayed still, letting her do what she wanted.

What she wanted, she knew, was to see him naked. She reached for the button of his fly and dealt with it and the zip.

He lifted his hips and she tugged his trousers down and away. He kicked free of them. Sara tossed them off the bed where they landed in a heap on the grimy carpet—which would no doubt have horrified whoever had made them, but she didn't care.

His boxer briefs were dark. Black or dark gray, she couldn't tell which, but they hugged every inch of him. There were plenty of inches to display, too, and even in the dim light, she saw the outline of his cock straining against the fabric.

She sucked in a breath, lost in the sight of him for a moment, and then tugged at the briefs, too, eager to see what lay beneath.

His skin was hot to the touch, and the muscles of

his stomach tensed and tightened as she brushed over them. As the briefs slid free, he muttered something under his breath that she couldn't make out but the humming frustration in the sound made her stomach tighten and her breath catch.

His cock was free and she hated the lack of light that meant she couldn't see it clearly.

But the weather gods weren't cooperating and there was no sudden flash of lightning to show her the way; nor was there a sudden return of the electric lights. So touch it would have to be. Touch and . . . wait, yes. There was a whole other sense to be indulged.

Taste.

The thought settled into her head. Of setting her mouth to his skin and finding out what he tasted like. It made her throat dry and she froze for a moment, the mental image blanking out her senses.

"Sara?"

The question was just loud enough to jolt her back to action. She shifted herself backward on his legs so she could get a better angle to explore him.

"Everything okay?" Lucas asked.

She nodded, then realized that he might not be able to see that response. "Everything's just fine," she said and wondered who it was exactly who was talking with that husky edge to her voice. "Just admiring the view."

"Do helicopter pilots get superpowers then? Can you see in the dark after all?"

"No, but I do have excellent night vision," she

said. "And I've been told that I have very good hands." She let her fingers drift then, one hand making an arc up his hip and across his stomach before trailing down to trace a circle around the very tip of him, which earned her another of those very pleasing noises. Really, sound was an underrated sense. She laid the flat of her hand over him then curled her fingers around him.

His skin here was even hotter, and the warmth combined with the smooth-over-hard texture of him made a little gasp escape her throat.

He felt extraordinary.

Even in the darkness where she could only dimly see the gorgeous face, her body was reacting to him like he was 100 percent whatever the Sara equivalent of catnip was.

She touched him gently, exploring, and then— unable to resist any longer—she bent her head and let her tongue follow the path of her fingers.

This time the noise he made was deep and urgent. His hands came down, fingers twining in her hair. And his hips flexed up.

Liked that, did he?

Well, so did she. She licked again and slipped her hand around him before taking him into her mouth fully.

Heat and salt and darkness. Lucas groaned again and his hands came down onto her head. She didn't need any more encouragement to keep doing what she was doing.

Slide. Taste. Tease.

His skin hot against her tongue, his muscles flexing against her legs, tightening with every glide of her mouth. She let her world narrow to the taste and feel of him, the sound of his breath getting harsher, the noises he made.

Everything else blurred and disappeared. There was just Lucas and just the answering heat blooming over her own skin knowing that he was reacting this way to her.

Just her.

His breath came faster and his hips flexed up again and then she heard him say, "Wait."

She stopped, lifted her head. "Something wrong?"

"Very far from wrong," he said, and she could hear the kind of dazed pleasure she was feeling in the depth of his voice. "But I want a turn."

That made her shiver. Touching him was one thing. But the thought of those hands and that mouth and . . . "What happened to lady's choice?" she said.

"You woke up my inner caveman," he said.

She laughed. The thought of the always immaculate Lucas Angelo having an inner caveman was kind of hilarious. Until she pictured him wearing not much more than a strategically placed loincloth. Her hand ran along the length of his torso, feeling the muscles there. Maybe there was some caveman after all.

"And what happens if your inner caveman doesn't get his way?" she asked.

"If not getting his way means you keep doing what you were just doing, then I think I can reconcile him to it," Lucas said. "He'll lie back and take it. But he'd prefer if you let him do his thing for a while." He lifted himself up and shifted them effortlessly so he was sitting up while she was still sitting across his lap. And then he kissed her.

Fiercely enough to make her forget what she was doing at all.

"If it helps," he said, pulling his head back. "Just remember that my inner caveman comes attached to an outer doctor." He grinned at her, the expression a flash of white teeth and a just visible rapid change of the planes of his face. "An outer doctor who has spent a lot of time studying anatomy."

He slipped a hand between them and flicked open the button of her waistband—damn it, why was she still wearing her trousers—then slid his fingers between the fabric and her skin, and down between her legs. He found her clit with no trouble at all. Heat spiked through her.

"So I see," she managed.

Another stroke. "Is that a yes?" His lips pressed against the curve where her neck joined her shoulder, and she shuddered.

"Hell, yes."

"I like your enthusiasm," he said.

"I like your hands," she gasped as he pressed again.

"This will be easier if we're both naked," he said and suddenly she found herself lying on her back with him above her. Her trousers and underwear vanished like magic.

"Do they teach you that in med school as well?" she asked. "Or are you just naturally talented?"

He laughed but then bent and pressed his lips to her torso, where the arches of her rib cage met. His tongue flicked against her skin and she shivered as a nerve she didn't know she had went live with a force she felt deep in her stomach.

"I'm going with naturally talented."

He lifted his head. "I also take direction well."

"I find that hard to believe."

He pressed another kiss, this one a little lower, then stopped again. "Feel free to try it out." He slipped a hand under her thigh, coaxed her to drape a leg across his back as his mouth moved a few inches lower.

Good Lord, the man was trying to kill her. "Right now, you're doing okay."

"Really? No—" Kiss. Lick. "—needs you want to—" Kiss. Lick. Nibble.

Oh Lord. Who knew that teeth pressing oh so carefully into her hip bone could feel so good?

"—tell me about?" he continued. He wriggled a little lower and pressed a kiss to her thigh. Her stomach clenched as her body throbbed. She wanted to feel his mouth right where it was hottest. And apparently all she had to do was ask.

Her head fell back as her face heated. Thank God for darkness. In the darkness, maybe she could be the sort of woman that asked a man to go down on her. After all, her body had thrown her brain under a bus way back when she'd first touched him. So maybe she just had to let it take over completely.

She licked her lips, felt his lips drag across her inner thigh again. Swallowed hard. "I want your mouth on me," she said. It was half a whisper, which thankfully sounded much more man-eating sexy than she was.

"Hell, yes," he whispered back, and then his head moved and his hands coaxed her legs wider and then his tongue slipped across her clit. And set to work.

God.

She really was going to catch on fire.

He hadn't been boasting, and he knew what the hell he was doing. Each stroke drove her deeper into the swirl of heat and sensation and oh-so-damn-good-she-couldn't-think. She might have moaned. Someone moaned, anyway.

She couldn't keep track of who. Couldn't think, couldn't do anything but lie there and let him set every last inch of her on fire with his clever tongue and talented fingers. Until she had her fingers buried in his dark hair and was calling out his name as she came.

Lucas stayed where he was a moment or two then pressed a final kiss and rolled away. She heard a crinkle of foil but was still too floaty and buzzed to think much more than *Oh good, condom*.

When she finally managed to catch her breath and a thread of sanity, he was poised above her, his cock pressed hard against her, sending off a second mini shock wave.

The fuzziness receded as hunger for him took

over. "Star pupil," she said, twining her arms around his neck. "What's your next trick?"

"This," he said and buried himself inside her with one long slow thrust.

Lucas Angelo is inside me, she thought for one wild minute, and then he bent to kiss her and started to move and once again all rational thought fled. Her legs wrapped around him, hooking above those slow driving hips, pulling him closer. Closer still.

She wanted to crawl inside him. Or have him crawl deeper still inside her, she wasn't sure which.

Just knew that she wanted to stay here a very long time, riding the dark with Lucas and maybe never, ever leaving this bed again.

"Lucas," she said and he kissed her again. Deep sure kisses that matched the rhythm they'd settled on. Kisses that felt both new and familiar, like she'd spent a long time kissing him in her dreams, or a prior life, or something that meant that she knew the taste and feel of him and felt like he knew her, too.

Each thrust stole her breath and each kiss gave it back to her. And the pressure started to build again and she started to move more fiercely beneath him, arching and retreating, closer and . . . "More," she whispered. "More . . ."

It grew faster then. And deeper. Wilder. She wanted to tell him something but try as she might she couldn't gather her thoughts to figure out exactly what. "More," she managed again until more was suddenly too much and she dissolved again and spiraled away into pleasure.

* * *

It took her a moment to figure out exactly where she was. And what had woken her. Then she heard it again. The buzzing. Her phone doing a little vibrating tango under her pillow.

She rolled over and realized she was naked. And that there was a naked man beside her. Lucas Angelo.

It all flooded back. All that sex. They hadn't been able to stop touching each other. Which resulted in all that very good sex, which, as she remembered, made her body buzz as happily as her phone.

The phone.

Damn. Who was calling her at whatever ridiculous hour this was? Surely it was too early for Viv to be checking on her? She reached out and grabbed the phone off the bedside table and peered at the time. Five a.m.

Too early.

But Ellen—and it was apparently Ellen unless her caller ID was lying to her—wouldn't be calling her if it wasn't important.

She slipped out of bed, holding her breath, hoping that Lucas wouldn't wake because really, how to deal with the very hot guy who'd given her several memorable orgasms during the night when they'd agreed this was just for one night was not something she was ready to figure out.

So she would deal with the more immediate problem and then come back to that one.

She reached the tiny bathroom with a few cautious, silent steps and, closing the door carefully behind her, tapped the screen to answer the call as she pulled one of the skimpy towels off the rail to wrap herself in.

"Ellen?" she asked quietly.

"Sara? Is that you? I can't hear you very well." Ellen's voice sounded rough. Tired.

Worry gripped Sara's stomach but she wasn't going to shout and wake up Lucas. "The line is bad," she said. "Is everything okay?"

"No," Ellen said bluntly. "It's not. Sweetie, you have to come back. The storm—well, your helo got damaged."

"Damaged?" Sara's voice rose. "What do you mean?"

"Just come back," Ellen said. "Where are you anyway? Manhattan? That's what your note said."

"No, we didn't make it all the way back. There was a tree down. Blocking the road. I'm in some motel about an hour away from you."

"Then turn around and come back," Ellen said. "You need to deal with this." She hung up and Sara sat down on the cold tiled floor, legs suddenly weak with panic.

Her helo.

What had happened to it? She couldn't run Charles Air without a helo. Her dad had put their other helicopter out of commission in his accident, and his medical bills were doing a good job of eating up the payout from the insurance company, so they hadn't been able to replace his helo.

She'd told herself that she would get ahead of

things by the time he was back in the air and they needed two helicopters again, but so far she was only going backward.

Shattered legs, it turned out, cost a lot of money to fix. Even more when you got infections in the pins and other complications. Her dad, apparently, didn't believe in doing things the easy way. Even now, when he had been out of hospital for months, the physical therapy bills were killer. Especially when he seemed to have stopped making progress.

If the A-Star was out of action, too, they were toast. Because she doubted the insurance company would be keen to pay out again to them. The deductible alone would be massive. And the way their cash flow was currently dwindling, renting a replacement wasn't going to be an option, either. She needed a healthy customer base to cover rent on a helo—assuming she could find somebody willing to rent her one—and her operating costs. Right now, the only way to describe her customer base was "in need of intensive care." Possibly about to flatline.

And she had just slept with one of her few customers. She put her head down and pressed her hand over her mouth so she wouldn't swear out loud.

Lucas.

Out there in the bed, sleeping the sleep of the well-satisfied male. Or of a doctor who'd learned to sleep hard when he got a chance. She'd learned that skill herself in the army.

Oh God. Lucas.

Lucas who had a *car*.

She stared down at the phone. Just after five. She couldn't hear rain anymore—so she assumed the weather had settled down—but who knew if the road was clear?

So there was no guarantee that he would be able to make it back to Manhattan on the road. He must already be cutting it fine.

It was a rationalization and she knew it. It wasn't even a very good rationalization. But she had to get back to Ellen and see what had happened to the A-Star. The sooner she could start the processes of getting whatever needed fixing fixed and lodging any insurance claim, the sooner she could get back in the air. And every minute counted because without it, Charles Air was going to be history.

Which might just kill her dad.

So that meant she needed the car. Lucas was rich. He would find another way back to the city. That's what rich people did. Used their money to get what they wanted. She'd dealt with enough rich customers to know that.

She pushed to her feet, feeling sick to her stomach. Damn it.

Last night, apart from the storm and the near death by tree, had been one of the best nights of her life and now she was going to ruin it.

They'd agreed it would be one night only and she had steeled herself to honor that even though the thought made her body protest loudly. Not to mention that she'd enjoyed Lucas himself. The funny playful guy he'd been in bed was very different from the serious doctor in the suits.

Which one was the real him?

It didn't matter, she realized. She wasn't likely to see either version of him ever again. Not after she did what she was about to do. Not unless he decided to have her arrested or something.

She crept back into the main room, tiptoed around picking up her clothes and donning them as fast and silently as she could. When Lucas turned over, muttering something under his breath, she nearly had a heart attack. But then he stilled again, his breathing slow and steady.

The whole room smelled like him, which made her feel even worse.

Well, she could do one thing to make it right. Her checkbook was in her flight bag. So she carefully wrote out a refund for his charter—though the thought of what that would do to their already shaky bank balance made her cringe—and the amount she guessed he'd paid for the car rental.

And, because it seemed like the honorable thing to do, even when she was abandoning him like this, she wrote, "I'm sorry. I had to go," on a page from her notebook and left that and the check weighted down by the heavy watch on his bedside table.

She stared down at him, sleeping there, the lines of his face—as much as she could see in the darkened room—still one of the most beautiful things she'd ever seen.

Life really was a bitch.

Couldn't even let her have this one thing without turning it into a disaster, too.

But that was the reality, and she was good at dealing with reality.

So she shoved away the guilt and regret, scooped the car keys up from beside his watch, and let herself out of the room.

Chapter Five

Ellen met Sara at the door to the terminal. She looked pale and wet and exhausted, her hair scraped back in a rough bun and her mascara smudged.

"Sara, honey," she said. "I'm so sorry."

Sara braced herself. All through the ninety-minute drive—she'd had to take a couple of detours around downed trees and power poles to get back—she'd been holding out hope that it wasn't going to be too bad. That whatever had happened to the A-Star could be fixed. A few days' downtime and she'd be back in the air. No problem.

But looking at Ellen's face, she wasn't so sure. "Show me."

She followed Ellen through the terminal and out to the airfield. The wind cut through her jacket like it wasn't there but wasn't howling as badly as it had last night. The ground squelched under her feet, muddy and slippery, rain still falling steadily. She concentrated on staying on her feet until they reached the place where her helo should have been, sitting patiently and waiting for her, the bright blue-and-silver paintwork shining. She'd tied it down properly. It should have been fine.

But it wasn't.

Instead, it was on its side. She could see from here that at least one rotor blade had snapped off. About ten feet past it, a small plane was flipped on its back, looking far more mangled than the helo, but still. She looked back at the rotor and had to swallow hard as her throat went hot and tight.

No helo. She had no helo.

No helo. No work. No work. No money. "Oh *God.*"

"Sara—" Ellen put her hand on her arm.

"What happened?"

"Near as we can tell, it was the wind. The Piper came untied and flipped and got blown into the helo. That wind was nearly hurricane-force last night."

Sara stared at the A-Star, blinking back the sting in her eyes as the rain hit her face. Did her insurance even cover freak wind gusts . . . what did they call them, acts of God? That was it. Though what she thought about whatever deity had decided to mess with her was firmly unprintable.

As to whether she was covered . . . she had no idea. Hopefully whoever owned the Piper was.

Regardless of insurance, she did know she was looking at a helicopter that was kind of screwed.

Much like she was.

* * *

I'm sorry. I had to go.

Lucas stared down at the note, still not believing what he was reading though he'd read it at least ten times now. The handwriting was neat and perfectly legible. It was just that it made no goddamned sense.

She'd left. And, he'd deduced from the lack of car keys on his bedside table, she'd taken the car.

When he'd first noticed the lack of keys, he'd stomped over to the window and confirmed it by flicking the blinds up. The Mercedes was gone. And so was Sara Charles.

She of the innocent face and the seaside eyes and the mouth that had made him think he'd gone to heaven. She'd spent the night with him—hell, that was too tame a term for what they'd done, because sex with Sara had been very good and very hot and damn he was getting hard just thinking about it.

Which meant his cock was stupid. Because the woman who had done all those things with him— kissed him, whispered sweet nothings, laughed and teased and let him inside her—had run off with his car and left him stranded.

Fuck.

She had refunded his money but that was hardly the point. She'd run away and left.

I'm sorry. I had to go was not a suitable good-bye. And it was an even worse explanation.

He had no idea why she might have left. Last night had been good. More than good. They'd both enjoyed it. So why would she just get up and leave? Had she gotten embarrassed about the one-night thing? Decided the walk—or drive—of shame back to Manhattan was going to be too awkward or something?

Double fuck.

He allowed himself a small moment of regret and then locked it down and focused on the bit where he was, quite rightly, pissed off about the whole situation.

First things first. It was past six and he needed to get back to the city. So he would shower, get dressed, and then go see if the powers of cash or unlimited credit could find someone in this motel willing to either give him a ride or let him hire a damned car.

He was doing it again. Lucas stared down at his fingers. Which held a slightly ragged piece of folded notepaper.

The note Sara had left him two weeks ago.

The one that he'd shoved roughly into his wallet when he'd left the motel and had meant to throw out. Only he hadn't.

And, every now and then, he kept finding it in his fingers. Fingers that remembered the feel of Sara Charles's skin precisely.

He was famous for his hands—surgeons had to have good hands—but right now that seemed like a curse, not a blessing.

He didn't want to remember the exact texture of her skin or the taste of her mouth or the sound of her voice laughing with delight in the darkness.

The woman had snuck out and left him abandoned in the wake of a near hurricane.

He didn't want to think about her. Normally if he dismissed something from his mind, it stayed dismissed. But Sara Charles was bucking that trend.

Which meant he had to decide what to do about her.

His first trip to the Saints' spring training camp in Florida was in two days. Which meant the travel schedule from hell started, too. Every second he could save on travel was time he had for his patients. And that meant using choppers to get around where he could.

So he needed to find another pilot he trusted. Sara's check refunding his fare seemed to be a fairly clear message that she didn't expect him to patronize her business again. Combined with the hire car boosting and the near-dawn abandonment, that was.

Christ. Near-dawn abandonment? He needed to get a grip. They'd agreed to a one-night thing and she'd taken that to its logical conclusion and left first.

He'd done his share of leaving women's bedrooms at the end of one-night stands. A few had left his, too. True, he usually tried to be gentlemanly about things and offer breakfast, but that didn't always work out.

He always made his position clear. Short-term only. One night usually.

He just didn't have time for anything more complicated. Not now. Relationships were always complicated, in his experience.

His mother had started trying to throw eligible girls in his path when he'd been in college. He'd avoided those—the girls his mother approved of were generally the kind who wanted to have the same sort of life she had, and he'd been doggedly working to avoid the life his parents expected him to have for as long as he could remember.

In medical school and during his internship he'd barely had time for women. But he'd had a few longer-term relationships. With beautiful intelligent women who should have been perfect for him. But either they hadn't liked playing second fiddle to his crazy schedule—which he couldn't blame them for—or they revealed themselves to be more interested in the Angelo money than in Lucas himself. Or things just hadn't worked out.

And then there'd been Elena.

Elena whom he had met at one of his mother's fund raisers. Elena who was beyond beautiful and smart and busy with her own career. Elena the biochemist.

He'd thought she was perfect. Until she, too, started talking marriage after only a few months and he'd realized that once again his name was more interesting to her than anything else he might have to offer.

Since then he'd decided that, until his life was more under control, and God knew when that would be, casual was the better option.

He'd broken up with Elena well over a year ago now, and he'd stuck to that plan since then. Which was just as well, given that becoming part owner of the New York Saints hadn't exactly freed up his schedule.

So sue him, he hadn't said no to Sara Charles when she'd made a move.

He hadn't been expecting it—hadn't pegged her for the type—but he'd been more than happy to oblige.

And now he was wondering exactly why he couldn't consign her to memory where she belonged.

What was it about her exactly? He had no idea. She wasn't the most beautiful woman he'd dated. But there'd been something about her.

His hands flexed . . . remembering. Her skin. Her mouth. The way she'd felt wrapped around him and calling his name.

Maybe he'd lost his mind due to the storm or something.

Maybe there was a scientific explanation for it. Wasn't a near-death experience meant to draw people together? It was certainly a theory espoused by almost every Hollywood action movie he'd even seen. He didn't know the science, though. He'd never been terribly interested in psychology. Too much theory. Not enough scalpels.

The close encounter that he and Sara had had with the tree counted, he supposed.

So was that it? The fact that their systems had been flooded with adrenaline, heightening the experience? Maybe that explained her unexpected pass as well.

He swore suddenly and shoved the paper back into the wallet.

What did it matter why he couldn't forget her?

She obviously hadn't wanted to see him again or she wouldn't have snuck out. And if she'd regretted it since, she'd made no attempt to contact him. She knew who he was, and he wasn't exactly hard to find on the Internet these days. A few seconds with Google and she would have had contact details for him at the hospitals he worked at, at his office, and at Deacon Field.

So no, it was clear enough that he was the only one having inconvenient flashbacks.

Which meant that he was going to have to do what needed to be done. He was going to accept the situation and really put her out of his mind. And the first step in that was finding another helicopter firm.

Four days later Lucas stood in Alex's office at Deacon Field, having caught a red-eye back from Orlando to perform emergency surgery on a world-class golfer who'd managed, of all things, to roll his golf cart and smash up his knee pretty good.

He'd endured five hours of flying and twice that in getting through all the airport security bullshit that came with flying these days. All for just over twenty-four hours in Florida. Barely time to be introduced to all the potential players they were trying out or speak to Dan Ellis about the training program.

He was tired and hungry and he very much did not want to turn around and drive back to Manhattan and catch a plane to get back to Vero Beach in the morning. But he definitely didn't want to get back in a helicopter with the cowboy who'd flown him back from JFK. The guy had decided to show off a little, and it had been only a very iron force of will that had kept Lucas from reacting to the swooping maneuvers he'd put the chopper through or from punching him when they landed. He was the third pilot Lucas had hired so far. And the third who'd come up short in the fly-the-chopper-in-a-manner-that-didn't-make-him-think-of-imminent-death stakes.

Sara didn't swoop.

The thought of Sara Charles and the fact that so far, he hadn't found another chopper pilot who managed to fly the way she did, didn't improve his mood.

He scowled down at the field, currently empty with the team in Florida.

"What's eating him? Girl trouble?" Mal said from behind him. Lucas didn't turn around. He wasn't in the mood for Mal's idea of wit.

"Lucas doesn't do girl trouble," Alex replied, his voice somewhat amused.

Lucas gritted his teeth.

"Remember, he has his new tap-'em-and-toss-'em policy," Alex continued. "No trouble to be had."

Lucas turned at that one. "I do not," he said, trying not to give in to the urge to toss Alex somewhere, "toss women. We come to mutually agreeable terms"—he held up a hand before either of his so-called best friends could come up with some stupid joke about that—"and we part ways amicably."

"That's what he thinks," Alex said to Mal. "How much do you want to bet there's a trail of women a mile wide across Manhattan pining for ol' blue eyes?"

"I don't have to bet on that," Mal said. "There've been women pining after ol' blue eyes for the last twenty years. Ever since Texas."

Lucas rolled his eyes at Mal. "I never noticed you lacking for female company at college, either. Nor," he pointed out in a steely tone, "do I see any sign of you having a regular girlfriend. And yet, I don't think you've taken a vow of celibacy. Those who live in glass houses . . ."

"I'm not throwing stones," Mal said. "But if it isn't girl trouble, then what's put the bug up your butt? Because Alex was just talking to you about TV licensing and you nearly took his head off."

Had he? Fuck. He was more tired than he thought. He parked himself back in one of the chairs facing Alex's desk. "I'm sorry. I need sleep." He didn't sleep on planes, and he'd gone straight into surgery and then come right on out to Staten Island for this meeting.

Alex regarded him, head cocked to one side. "Are you sure that's it?"

"What else would it be?"

"I don't know, but you've been in a mood ever since you got back from that party at Margot's a couple of weeks ago."

"Like I said. I'm tired. In case you hadn't noticed, the schedule is kind of crazy around here."

"I noticed," Alex said. "And I'm sorry you got the short end of the stick with the travel. I'm trying to get everything else set up as fast as possible so I can get to Florida more often myself. But these things take time."

Lucas nodded and dug his fingers into the muscles at the back of his neck. "I know." Owning a baseball team was a lot more complicated than it sounded. And he'd been thorough about weighing the pros and cons before he'd agreed to sign up to this insanity. He'd gone in with his eyes open.

This was just the hard part. Getting things established. They'd known the Saints were in trouble when they'd bought them, known there was work to do. So he just had to plow through and get it done.

"You really need to learn to nap on planes," Mal said.

Lucas gave him a death glare. Mal, thanks to his years of being the globe-trotting soldier, slept anywhere at the drop of the hat. Lucas, who had also learned to catch any sleep he could as an intern, could usually sleep like a log in almost any situation, too.

But he didn't sleep in the air. Never had since that airlift to the hospital twenty years ago. It was irrational and he knew it, but he hadn't managed to convince his body that if he fell asleep in a plane or a chopper, he wouldn't wake up in a hospital again. Or maybe just not wake up at all.

"You worry about your wheeling and dealing," Lucas said. "Let me worry about me."

Alex and Mal both frowned at him. "You're no good to us if you keel over," Alex said.

"I can do twelve-hour surgeries, I'm not going to keel over from a little travel."

They both kept frowning at him. It was their way of expressing concern, he guessed. They both knew he didn't sleep in planes, but he'd never let them know why exactly.

"Fair enough," Alex said. "But don't be stupid about it. If there are things that will make this easier, then do them. Whatever you need."

What he needed was Sara Charles.

Wait. What? No.

He stomped down on the thought but it sprang back up with annoying persistence. Sara Charles piloting for him. Sara Charles doing—

He stomped harder. *Not* going to happen.

"What was that?" Mal asked.

"What was what?"

Mal cocked his head, dark eyes narrowing. "Your face went kind of weird."

"My face is not weird."

"Have you looked in the mirror lately?"

"No, because it broke last time you looked in it," Lucas retorted.

Alex held up a hand. "Much as I love this little double act you've got going on, I have to agree with Mal on this one. You were thinking about something."

"Is thinking a crime?"

"No, but that wasn't your usual analyze-the-situation-six-ways-from-Sunday look."

"I do not have an analyzing look."

"Yeah, you do," Alex said. "But that wasn't it. What's up?"

He started to say *Nothing* but then his mouth seemed to detach itself from his brain and said, "I think we need a helicopter."

Alex's eyebrows shot skyward. Lucas couldn't blame him for that. He was pretty surprised by what he'd just said himself.

"You want us to hire a helicopter?" Alex said.

No, Lucas thought. Then "Yes," he said. "If I'm going to have the commute from hell then this will make life easier."

"Helicopters aren't exactly cheap," Mal pointed out. "And there are many other things we need."

"Leasing the chopper will work out cheaper than me chartering one several times a week, surely?"

"It's a helo, not a chopper," Mal corrected.

"I'm not in the army," Lucas said. "Normal people call them choppers."

"Normal people don't rent helicopters all that often," Alex said. He was wearing his usual combination of blazer, business shirt with no tie, and jeans, and he shoved his hands into his pockets while watching Lucas, looking vaguely amused.

"Yeah, well, normal people don't buy baseball teams, either. And they don't try and run a baseball team and a surgical practice at the same time. So I'm not putting myself in the category of normal just now. I'm putting myself in the category of guy whose friends are making him spend insane amounts of time traveling and whose life would be made much easier if he had a *helo*"—he grinned at Mal as he stressed the word—"on standby."

Mal folded his arms. He wore jeans, too, and Lucas suddenly wished he had a job where he could wear jeans. But nope, his wardrobe was suits for patient consultations and business stuff and scrubs the rest of the time. Mal's jeans were paired with a faded black Metallica T-shirt rather than Alex's shirt-and-blazer combo and only looked even more appealing because of it. Why hadn't he gone into security?

Because he didn't want to spend the decade in the army being shot at in exotic locations prior to that? Right.

"And exactly who is going to be flying this on-standby chopper?" Mal asked.

"Well, obviously we'll need to hire a pilot as well," Lucas said. "Or come to an arrangement with one to be on standby. Though hiring one would be better. They could travel with me, fly me in Florida as well." Okay, he was seriously losing his mind. Mal and Alex were going to have him committed.

"If the pilot travels with you, then the rest of us wouldn't be able to use the chopper," Alex said. "If we're going to spend that much money, I think the rest of us should benefit, too. You're not the only one commuting."

"I'm the only one commuting to Florida. And it would save me the drive to and from Vero Beach," Lucas said. "You're welcome to use the chopper when I'm in New York."

"So really you want to us to hire two choppers, one here and one in Florida?"

"We can probably make a deal with a charter firm in Florida to use a chopper," Lucas said.

"You could do the same thing here in New York," Alex said. "And use their pilots."

"I want a pilot I can trust," Lucas said. "I swear the guy who flew me today had a death wish."

Mal looked unsympathetic. "Did you have someone in mind?"

"Perhaps," Lucas said.

"Ah," Alex said. "The plot thickens. Who is she?"

"Why do you think it's a she?"

"Because you're suddenly on fire to have a helicopter at your beck and call, which makes me think that maybe something else is on fire, too," Alex said. "Who is she, Angelo?"

Lucas looked at Mal, who only shrugged and grinned at him, as if to say, *I'm with Alex on this one, buddy*.

"Well, as it happens, there is someone I used a few times who was reliable. Her name is Sara Charles."

"Know any guys named Sara?" Alex said to Mal.

"Not that I can think of," Mal said. "Sounds pretty female to me."

Damn right she was female. But that was beside the point. He wanted her for her piloting skills, nothing more. Part of his mind snorted at that. Apparently he wasn't fooling himself very well. Hopefully he was doing a better job with Mal and Alex. "Yes, she's a woman," he said. "She's also an excellent pilot and that's all I care about."

"Looks like Lucas has found a way to distract

himself from his fear of flying," Mal said. "Improve the scenery."

Alex laughed.

Lucas began to wonder why he was friends with them. "I am not afraid of flying. People who are afraid of flying don't fly multiple times a week."

"You don't enjoy it, though."

"There are many things I do I don't enjoy," Lucas retorted. "It's called being an adult."

"So this Sara Charles . . . what is it? Do you like her or something?"

"I told you, she's a good pilot. I trust her. Isn't that enough? You said whatever I need."

Alex raised one eyebrow. "I just want to be clear on what need she's fulfilling. Because things are complicated enough around here."

Lucas blew out a breath. "Look, she was the one who flew me down to Sag Harbor when there was that big storm. You know, Margot's fund-raiser thing."

"I remember," Alex said.

"So she was good in a crisis." He left out the part where she'd left him stranded. Up until that point she had been good in a crisis. Very good.

Very very good, the unhelpful part of him piped up.

He stomped again. "And we need someone who can cope with a bit of chaos."

"It's a lot of money for us to spend," Alex said, still looking somewhat skeptical. "Plus it'll take some time to organize."

"Surely one of your companies already has a chopper somewhere that's not being used? You could lease it to us. Or sublease it or however the hell helicopter financing works."

Alex shrugged. "Maybe. I'd have to check what's in the fleet at the moment. And how it's being used." He opened his sleek silver laptop and typed something quickly.

Sometimes Lucas forgot just how much money Alex had. His own family was wealthy, but they didn't keep a fleet of aircraft. "If you do, we can use it, and if it turns out we don't use it as much as we think or that it's not working out, we can give it back."

"You've got this all planned out." Alex flipped the laptop closed. "Have you asked her already?"

"No. I'm not an idiot. It would be cruel to make an offer I couldn't follow through on."

Mal nodded. "Yes, it would. As would giving her a job because you like having her around. So you need to be clear why you're doing this. If you like this girl, then hiring her is not the smartest thing in the world. Just ask Alex."

"I hired Maggie before I liked her," Alex said. "And it's worked out pretty well. But Mal's right. It's not an easy situation. If you are interested in her. So are you?"

"That's nobody's business but mine right now," Lucas said.

"That means yes," Mal said. "Which means it is our business. Literally."

Lucas threw up his hands. "All right. Fine. I found her . . . interesting. Is that a crime?"

"No," Mal said. "Just a potential complication."

"That's my problem."

"Lucas Angelo dating a helicopter pilot," Alex said. "Must be true that opposites attract." He grinned then. "Have you introduced her to your mother?"

"No. And we're not dating yet." Lucas said shortly. "And even if we were, I would have no intention of subjecting her to that particular can of worms until I have to." He knew his mother. Knew what her opinion of him being involved with a woman who flew helicopters and had no money was likely to be. He wasn't going to put Sara through that just yet. Not until he was sure this was more than one of those odd high-intensity sexual things that burned themselves out.

He flashed on Sara again, asleep beside him in the motel. It didn't feel like that. Hot sex. Mind-blowing sex. Yes. But he was interested in more than that. Wanted to know what made her tick. Wanted to know why he felt safe with her. "So you'll look into the chopper thing?" he said to Alex.

"You really think you need it? That you'd be asking if the girl wasn't . . . holding your attention?" Alex said.

She'd held more than his attention. But that didn't change the fact that the helicopter was a good idea. "You must be getting tired of driving back and forth as well. With the chopper you can be back at Ice headquarters or your apartment in, what, fifteen minutes or so?"

"There's the small question of where exactly this helo would land," Mal pointed out. "We don't have a helipad. And I think the grounds staff would revolt if we land a helicopter on the field."

"There's always the parking lot," Lucas said. He had no idea if Sara could land a helicopter in a parking lot. He assumed so. Wasn't that the point of helicopters, after all, that they could land in tight places? "Besides, the airfield where her company is based is only five minutes away. That's how I found her in the first place." On a drive back to Manhattan he'd passed the sign outside the airfield advertising charter flights. "Local business and all. Can't hurt with that improving-relations-with-the-community thing you have going on."

It hadn't been all smooth sailing since the other MLB team owners had approved their purchase of the Saints. Along with players walking, there were a lot of nervous supporters eyeing the new boys in town and wondering if they were going to screw up their team completely.

Alex nodded. "I guess not," he said. "All right, I'll get Gardner to look into it and do some costing. If you're okay, with that, Mal?"

Mal shrugged. "Far from me to get between Lucas and a girl. If it's workable on the money side, let's give it a try. I could do with some reduced commuting time now and then."

"Okay," Alex said. "We're agreed. And now,

speaking of community spirit, I want to get back to the subject of cheerleaders."

"No cheerleaders in baseball," Mal and Lucas said in unison and Lucas watched as his friend squared his shoulders and prepared to argue his cause once more.

Chapter Six

Lucas should have known Alex wouldn't mess around once he'd decided on doing something, but he hadn't expected a message waiting for him when he stepped off the plane in Orlando, telling him that yes, Ice did have some helicopters in their fleet and that one could be made available if necessary.

It seemed too simple. Of course, the less simple part was still to come. The part where he convinced Sara Charles to be his personal pilot.

He still hadn't figured out exactly what had possessed him to raise the idea back at Deacon yesterday, but despite several hours arguing with himself afterward, he hadn't been able to bring himself to call Alex back and tell him to forget the whole thing. Not when he couldn't stop thinking about Sara. Damn it.

Lucas handed the driver his overnight bag and climbed into the back of the car waiting to take him to Vero Beach. Then he pulled out his phone and found the number for Charles Air.

Where a polite female voice that wasn't Sara's informed him that the office was currently closed until further notice.

He frowned at the phone as he left a message for Sara, asking her to call him. Then, trying to ignore his rising frustration, he banished her from his mind and turned his attention to the trip ahead, hauling out his laptop to review the files on the players who were trying out.

They needed a pitcher. They still had Brett Tuckerson, their starter, but their second- and third-string guys had both accepted offers from other teams. So pitchers were a priority. Plus another couple of gun hitters couldn't hurt things.

Pity that true gun hitters cost more than they could afford. So they needed to buy smart. That was what Dan Ellis and his staff kept telling him as they spouted statistics and theories ad nauseam.

It wasn't until later in the evening, when he was back in his hotel room, that he had time to think about Sara again. And the fact that she hadn't yet returned his call.

He pulled up the Charles Air website. But instead of the familiar image of a blue-and-silver chopper he was used to—okay, so he liked that their helicopters were kind of the Saints' colors—there was a neat white page with only the company logo and a blue-bordered announcement that the company was not currently taking customers and providing a neat list of links to other charter firms.

That brought the frown back to Lucas's face.

Not taking customers?

And for long enough that they were referring them to other companies. That wasn't good business sense. If it was a short closure, then surely they'd have a date when they'd be reopened for business. And if it was for a longer period of time, then what the hell had happened?

His gut went cold.

Shit.

Had Sara been in an accident?

He'd never opened Google so fast in his life. But a few minutes of searching revealed no Sara Charles in a helicopter accident. No chopper accidents at all for a good few months. There was, however, a raft of stories about a Sean Charles in a crash. Almost twelve months ago.

Sara's dad, he assumed. The stories all named Charles Air as the company involved.

It looked like bad luck to him. The chopper had been struck by lightning—and that explained Sara's flat-out refusal to consider flying him in the storm—and according to the coverage of the story the electrical system hadn't recovered the way it was supposed to.

But Sean Charles had survived. Looking at the images of the half-mangled chopper, Lucas couldn't see how exactly. But that had been a year ago. Obviously Charles Air had survived, too. Because Sara had been flying him around perfectly happily just a few weeks earlier.

But not now.

Where had she vanished to?

It was too late to ring again but he found himself dialing the office number anyway.

Same polite voice. Same cool message about being closed.

"This is Dr. Lucas Angelo calling for Sara Charles," he said. "Sara, please call me back." He recited his cell and office numbers and hung up again.

He couldn't do much more right now. So he would sleep on it. See if she called him back.

She didn't call. And by the time Lucas got back to Manhattan, he was moving from frustrated to outright irritated. She was the one who'd slept with him then left him stranded, after all. Couldn't she at least do him the courtesy of returning his calls?

There was no Sara Charles in the Staten Island phone directory. Not in Manhattan, either.

She apparently liked her privacy.

He should take the hint perhaps and give up. Hire another pilot.

And he would. As soon as he could stop thinking about her.

Finally, he called the airfield outside Sag Harbor that Sara had used and asked to speak to Ellen Jacek.

"Sara?" she said, sounding wary. "What do you want with Sara?"

She obviously didn't remember him.

"Actually I'm looking to hire her. She flew me down to the Hamptons a few weeks ago, we landed at your terminal. I hired the Mercedes. It was the night of the big storm."

"Ah." Her voiced turned regretful.

"Is there a problem?"

"Charles Air is closed at the moment."

"I know. I've been trying to contact them but no one is returning my calls. What I'd like to know is why."

"You didn't hear?"

He went cold again, fingers gripping the phone too tightly. "Hear what?"

"The night of the storm. Sara's helo got damaged."

"Damaged?"

"Yes."

"Is Sara okay?"

Ellen sighed down the phone. "If she's not returning your calls, then I have to assume she doesn't want you knowing her business."

Lucas gripped the phone harder, trying not to give in to frustration. Ellen was being sensible. Cautious. In her place, he wouldn't give out information about a friend to a man she'd met for about five minutes, either. He could be a crazed stalker.

He was starting to feel a bit like one. "Okay," he said, keeping his voice calm. "If you speak to her, could you please let her know I'd like to talk to her?" He once again recited all his details and heard Ellen typing, which gave him some hope she might actually be taking them down. And maybe, just maybe, she might even pass them on to Sara.

Though if he hadn't heard from Sara by tomorrow, he was just going to go to Charles Air and see what was what. Someone at the airfield where they were based might know something.

"Wankers!" Sara pushed the phone across the desk, tempted to hurl it across the room. Damn insurance company. She'd just wasted another two hours on various levels of hold and being shunted around from person to person passing the buck and she still had nothing more than "Yes, we are pursuing the claim with the other party's insurance company, and yes, we are hopeful of a timely resolution."

Which meant, as far as she could tell, *You'll get a check, maybe, but only when we're good and ready*.

No check equaled no repairs to the A-Star.

No helo.

No helo equaled no customers.

No money coming in. Still quite a bit going out. Rapidly sinking bank balance.

And she was pretty much fresh out of ideas as to how to fix that other than her looking for work elsewhere.

Telling her dad she thought she should do that—that closing down Charles Air wasn't going to be as short-term as she hoped—might just give him a coronary.

She kicked the trash can by her foot, which raised a *whuff* of protest from Dougal who was lying next to her chair.

She looked down and he pushed himself up,

shoving his broad black head forward under her hand with a happy wriggle.

She rubbed his ears. But not even Dougal could make this better. Besides, he was happiest when he had Sara to himself. And Charles Air being closed meant no mechanics and other random men around. Which meant Sara could bring Dougal to the airfield with her instead of having to leave him with her parents.

Douglas was ninety pounds of big black softy, except when it came to men. Put him in the path of a guy and he turned into ninety pounds of over-protective barking, growling idiot dog. So far Sara's dad was the only exception to the rule, and even that had taken years of Dougal staying with her parents before Dougal had stopped slinking around and barking at him as though Sean was a dog-eating monster.

God only knew what his issue was. She'd gotten Dougal when he'd been only three months old, right after Jamie had died. He was purebred and raised by a good breeder but at some point a man had obviously done something to scare him. That experience had lodged deep inside his doggy brain and wasn't going anywhere, no matter how much training and conditioning they tried.

She sighed and rubbed his ears again. Right now, she had bigger problems than her anti-male dog.

She'd tried everything she could think of to move the insurance company along, but no dice. She couldn't get them to commit to any sort of time frame.

So, decisions needed to be made.

If she shut everything down, then they could probably cover the hangar fees for a few more months and keep the A-Star from getting any worse than it already was. But shutting down for any extended period of time could be a death knell. Without new cash flow, once the money was gone, it was gone.

Her mom was already back working part-time but couldn't do more than that with her dad out of action. He needed help with his therapy and other things, so he couldn't be alone five days a week. Getting his leg functioning was as important as getting the A-Star repaired. He couldn't work until his leg was better. Couldn't fly a chopper if you couldn't use the pedals.

And getting his leg better was racking up an ever-growing pile of physical therapy and doctors' bills.

That was without thinking about the hospital bills or the rehab facility. He'd had health insurance, but it didn't cover everything. And the company was arguing about some of the costs it was supposed to cover, which meant they might have even higher bills to pay.

She was beginning to hate even the word *insurance*.

But that still didn't solve her problems. Nor would trying to stick her head in the sand and ignore the fact they couldn't keep going the way they were. Nope. Time to woman up and talk to her dad about the whole freaking mess.

She copied the latest file from their accounting software to a flash drive and tucked it into her bag.

Then she locked up and headed for her parents' house.

Her mom's car wasn't in the drive. Maybe that was better. It would be easier to tell her dad alone. Give him some time to come to terms before they had to tell her mom as well.

She sat in the drive, hands gripped around the steering wheel, hot lead weighing her stomach down.

Failed him.

She'd failed him.

She'd left the army to come home to keep Charles Air alive and she couldn't do it.

Couldn't even manage that much.

And even though she knew it wasn't true . . . knew that it was her dad's accident that had started this particular run of bad luck, it felt true. Deep in her gut, where she couldn't shake it.

Her dad would look at her and he'd bow his head and he'd look that little bit older and grayer. More tired. Since the accident he looked tired a lot.

Hadn't seen him laugh much, either.

Now she was letting him down. And he had to be thinking that it would have been better if Jamie were still here to run things instead of her.

She rested her head on the steering wheel for a minute, taken by the sudden sharp stab of pain thinking about Jamie. It had been six years and mostly she remembered him with joy but every so often the grief caught her by surprise, stealing her breath and turning the world gray and cold.

From behind her, Dougal whined softly, eager to be out of his harness now that she'd stopped the car in a place he knew. Eager to get inside and cadge some dog biscuits and claim his place by the heating vent in the kitchen.

The thought made her smile and she lifted her head and took a breath before turning around. "Just a minute, buddy."

Dougal yelped and grinned at her in his doggy way. He liked coming here, liked the extra attention. He'd lived with her parents while Sara had been deployed and he had been thoroughly spoiled.

Just as well, because she was probably going to have to give up her tiny apartment in the city and move back to the island. She wouldn't be able to afford Manhattan rent anymore. Not even rent-stabilized rent.

She'd taken the apartment on a whim, wanting to have a stake in the city and not just come back home to Staten Island when she'd left the army and Viv had found out one of the studios in her building was coming up for lease. It meant earlier starts and later nights but she loved the city. Loved the energy. Loved feeling like she was in the middle of something big and alive.

Maybe she could find a sublet . . . something short-term until she found work.

Someone, somewhere needed a pilot. Surely. There were helos all over the place in New York. Someone would hire her. She tried to quell the cold feeling in her stomach.

Think of something good.

The only thing that came to mind, the last thing that had made her feel safe, was the feeling of Lucas's arms around her as she fell asleep back in that damned motel room.

Which only proved she was crazy.

Because that was never going to happen again.

She'd heard the messages he'd left but hadn't been able to make herself return his calls. Because if he wanted to hire her again, well, she didn't have a helo. And if he wanted anything else then it was more likely to be to yell at her than because he'd decided he couldn't live one more day without sleeping with her again.

It wasn't going to happen. It didn't matter how many times the memory of his hands on her stopped her thought processes, it wasn't going to happen again. It had been one night.

One night that had ended badly.

Seeing him again would just bring another bit of crappy reality into her life.

Which made her a wimp for not dealing with him, but at least a pragmatic wimp. Life was not a fairy tale, and Lucas Angelo wasn't Prince Charming. He just resembled him on paper.

She'd given in and Googled him in a weak moment. So now she knew all about Lucas Angelo and the Angelo family and their many businesses and their charity work and their accomplishments. Or at least what could be gleaned from the Internet, which seemed to be a large *about*.

And she knew that Lucas had just bought a share of the New York Saints, which spelled out the fact that his net worth had to be pretty damn healthy in no uncertain terms. She'd been vaguely aware that the Saints had been sold. It was hard to completely avoid baseball on Staten Island, but she hadn't paid much attention to exactly who had bought the team.

Finding out that Prince Charming was one of them had been a surprise. She hadn't pegged him as a sports nut. So maybe he wasn't quite so perfect after all.

She'd never been the least bit interested in sports.

But sports nut or not, there was no denying that Dr. Gorgeous had a pretty good life.

For a moment she wished fervently that she could be Lucas Angelo. She didn't want Prince Charming to rescue her, she wanted to have Prince Charming's resources so she could rescue herself. Have so much money that she didn't have to worry about anything.

What would life be like?

Glorious. Easy.

She sighed and cut off the fantasy. Because money would solve her problems yes, but that didn't mean her life would magically be trouble-free. So she had to keep putting one foot in front of the other. Starting with getting out of the damned car and going to talk to her dad.

Her dad had insisted on making her lunch and she'd given in, happy for a few more minutes' reprieve before she had to talk to him. She'd almost finished her sandwich when she noticed that her dad had barely touched his.

Uh-oh.

Almost every day of her life that she'd eaten lunch with him, her dad had eaten a tuna melt on whole wheat with a dill pickle on the side. Demolished it with about five rapid bites of each half. He believed in food as fuel, and didn't like to waste time on things like choosing a different sandwich or making small talk while he ate.

He liked things simple and practical and uncomplicated.

Not that any of those things applied to their current situation. He'd been very quiet for the few weeks since the A-Star had been damaged. Which made her feel even worse about it all.

"Is your leg bothering you?" Sara asked. Pain was one thing that could kill his appetite, but she'd thought it had been well controlled lately. Maybe he'd tried to wean himself down a dose on the meds again.

Her dad shook his head. "No more than usual." He looked up at her then back down at his plate then back up at her.

The expression on his face made her nervous. "Then what's up?"

Sean gripped the edge of the table. "Ron came to see me yesterday."

"Ron?" Her mind was blank for a moment. "You mean Ron Harris?" Ron Harris who was one of her dad's flying buddies and business rivals not to mention the father of one of her exes, Evan. Evan who was a perfectly nice guy except for that small inability to be faithful to his girlfriend. Or to her, at least.

She'd heard he was engaged now—her mother had included the clipping of the announcement in one of her care packets, God knew why—so maybe he'd learned to keep it zipped in the time since they'd parted.

"Yup."

"That's nice." She didn't know if Ron had been to see her dad since the accident.

Though she didn't think it likely that Ron dropping by was the news that her dad wanted to share with her.

"He heard about what happened," Dad said.

Hope bloomed in the pit of her stomach. Ron Harris also had a helicopter charter business. One that was about five times bigger than Charles Air. He had helicopters aplenty. "Can he loan us a helo?" If Ron could help them out there might be some hope.

"No."

Well, shit.

"He came to offer you a job," Sean continued. He looked down again and Sara's stomach clenched again, not in a good way.

"He needs a pilot?"

"He needs someone to work in reception."

"Reception?" Her throat tightened.

"Taking bookings, handling customers, you know the drill."

She did. Because she'd done all of that and more for Charles Air, but she was a goddamned pilot. "I want to fly, Dad."

Sean held up his hands. "I know you do. I told him that."

She could just imagine Ron's smug expression when he had. He wasn't exactly the poster boy for equality. Come to think of it, that should have been a warning about his son.

"Pretty cocky of him to offer a job when I have one," she said.

Sean stabbed at his cooling tuna melt with his fork. "Darlin', he can do the math." He looked up, nailed her with his steel-blue eyes. "And so can I. How much money is there?"

It was the first time he'd asked her about the business in ages. And she was going to have nothing but bad news for him. Her stomach twisted. "Some . . ."

"Do we need to shut down properly?"

The twist tightened. "Maybe for a little while. Just until the insurance coughs up to fix the rotor."

"That could take a while."

"I'm working on it," she said defensively.

Her dad nodded. "I know you are. But darlin', if we need to close, then this would be money in the meantime."

Money. Money they needed.

And it wasn't like pilot jobs were a dime a dozen. There were plenty of pilots—more than ever thanks to the war—and she knew all too well that given a choice between a guy and a woman, 95 percent of the charter companies would pick the guy. It was a boys' club in all too many ways and her trump card—her dad, who formerly could've opened those doors for her—was persona non grata. A jinx. Pilots could be a superstitious bunch, and none of them would want to catch a dose of the current Charles bad luck.

Which left her with the option of going out and doing something completely mind numbing like temping—she at least could claim some office skills on her résumé—or setting her sights a bit lower and taking any job with a charter company that she could with the hope that luck would swing her way and at some point they'd need a fill-in pilot and she'd be right there on the spot.

Or maybe the insurance gods would suddenly smile on her and decide to cough up the money to fix the A-Star.

Both options seemed equally remote. But here was Ron Harris with his offer and her dad looking wretched about it. Blaming himself for their current predicament, probably. Or blaming her.

She stared down at her plate a moment, willing the urge to scream a protest at the sky away before she either gave in to it or burst into tears.

Working reception for Ron and Evan. It was a job, no matter how much it might stick in her craw to watch Evan swan past her and jump into a helo— she could fly the pants off him any day. A job. Money. Survival.

But she couldn't quite say yes. Not yet. "Let me think about it, Dad, okay? Just for a couple of days."

Chapter Seven

"Die, you little bastard," Sara muttered as she shoved down on the hole punch and pierced the last of the day's bills with a satisfying *chomp*.

She tugged the paper free, wriggled it into place in the binder, clipped the rings closed, and shoved the whole thing back into place on the shelf next to her in-tray. Another day conquered, and there was still some money in the bank.

Some. Not that much. And there was that job offer staring her in the face. A job. Cash. Something to keep them going. The offer she'd been avoiding giving an answer on for nearly two days now.

A job with no flying.

She pushed away the nasty little thought, her gaze straying to where the A-Star sat in its hangar, rotor still broken. Sadly no magic helicopter repair fairies had appeared to get her out of this jam. She looked away, setting her jaw. Getting the helo trucked up from the Hamptons had been another expense she couldn't afford, but she couldn't leave it sitting out in the open at the Jaceks' airfield. Where anything else could happen. She rubbed her temples, trying to think. Just a few more days. Surely the insurance company would get things in motion by then?

If she just kept on them. Kept nagging. Or begging.

Hell, she'd get down on her knees if it meant not having to work with Evan Harris. She really didn't know what she'd seen in him, except she'd been young and foolish and Evan had been one of the few guys her age who hung around the airfields as much as she did.

She really didn't want to be reminded of her past every day of the week. See him smirking past her as he got to fly and she sat in reception taking bookings. He would love that.

He'd never been slow to gloat, Evan.

If only the flow of bills could slow down until she could pry the money out of the insurance company.

They had to slow down.

She pushed her chair back, finger poised over the OFF button of the computer, and then the bell over the office door chimed.

"We're closed," she sang out as she swiveled in her chair. "I'm sorry—"

The words died on her lips as she saw who was standing there.

Lucas freaking Angelo.

The suit was black this time and the shirt a pristine icy white. The tie was black, too, with only a few small dark-red diamonds breaking up the silken darkness. Against all that black and white, his eyes were very blue.

Lucas freaking goddamned Angelo.

Her chest suddenly felt like it had been stomped on, her mind a blur of kiss-night-hands-touch images that ended in oh-God-I-kind-of-stole-his-car, which was almost enough to cool the rush of heat warming her skin. Almost.

Why was he here? Had he finally gotten around to calling the cops on her? She leaned sideways a little, trying to see if there was anyone with him.

"Don't worry," he said drily. "I didn't bring the police."

She straightened hastily, pasting her best I-have-no-idea-what-you're-talking-about expression in place and trying to ignore the memories of their night together that were whirling through her brain again now she knew he wasn't going to have her arrested. "Why would you bring the police?" she asked, going for innocent.

Brilliant-blue eyes studied her a moment. Then, slowly, one very dark eyebrow lifted at her. "Well, there was that time where you stole my car."

Her eyes narrowed. "I did not steal your car." Denial, that was the ticket.

"I woke up, you were gone, and so was the car."

She folded her arms across her chest, calling his bluff. "I returned a rental car for you. I even paid the bill. That's not stealing by any definition. I don't care how much your lawyer charges by the hour, if you try to get that through a court, you'll get bounced." Now she was the one bluffing. Hopefully he didn't know that.

"You left me stranded in the middle of nowhere." His tone was very flat.

"It looks like you made it back to the city in one piece to me, Dr. Angelo."

"No thanks to you," he muttered, mouth thinning.

Even thinned his lips looked pretty good. Nope. She straightened further. She was not going to think about his lips. Or any other part of him.

Yeah, good luck with that.

"I refunded your fare," she said. "Was there a problem with the check?" Her mind went horribly blank for a moment as she tried to remember if that payment had gone through already. Because her dwindling bank balance would dwindle a lot more if she'd miscalculated by five grand.

"No problem with the check."

If he thought she was going to ask him if he had another problem, then he was crazy. "As I said, we're not open right now—"

"I need a pilot." His voice, if anything, had gone even flatter. A muscle ticced on the side of his jaw. Her pulse bumped in response.

Oh dear. Dr. Gorgeous was annoyed about something. About what, exactly, other than the car, she had no idea. And the car had been nearly three weeks ago, so surely—if he wasn't upset enough to involve the police—he should have cooled down about that by now?

Then what he had said finally registered with her brain. He wanted a pilot. Hope flared like a rocket then died just as fast when she remembered she had no helo.

"Well, New York has plenty of those," she said, trying not to let the disappointment creep through to her voice.

"I want a pilot I know," he said.

"Is that doctor-speak for you're offering me a job?" she asked. She was going to have to say no, so might as well just get it over with fast.

"Yes."

She could have cried. Here was Lucas Angelo on her doorstep. Exactly what she needed.

Exactly what she *wanted*, the evil part of her brain piped up. She stomped on the thought. Hard. She needed his money, not his body. Yet once again the universe was conspiring to make it so that she couldn't have it. "I'm sorry, but no."

"Is that no because you don't want the job or no because your helicopter is damaged?"

She started. "How do you know my helicopter is damaged?"

"You didn't return my calls. I called Ellen Jacek while I was trying to track you down. She mentioned it. And I made a not-so-gigantic leap of logic to conclude that it hasn't been fixed yet because you aren't taking customers."

"There could be other reasons."

"Are there other reasons?"

Sara sighed. "No."

"Why isn't it fixed?"

"Because the insurance company is dicking me around," she snapped. "And I don't have the money to hire a team of lawyers or whatever it takes to speed up insurance companies these days."

"I see. Okay. We'll deal with that in a moment. But you haven't answered my first question. Do you want the job?"

"You haven't told me what the job is."

"Helicopter pilot for the New York Saints," he said. "You know I own one-third of the Saints, yes?"

She nodded as her brain tilted and spun a little. Piloting for the Saints—baseball team or not— sounded a lot better than working a reception desk for Ron Harris.

"I believe someone might have mentioned that," she said. No way was she confessing to Internet-stalk—er—*researching* him.

"Good. Anyway. We need to someone to ferry people around. Here in New York and in Florida."

Florida? She hadn't expected that. "What's in Florida?"

"Spring training," he said. "February to April, the teams go to states where it's warm and not snowing and we try out players and start getting ready for the season. Play games, shuffle things around, get every-one fit again. Half the teams go to Arizona and half to Florida."

Florida. Sunshine. Warmth. Oranges. Disney World. Alligators. That was about all she knew about the state. She'd never been there. She looked past Lucas at the gray sky outside. It had rained ear-lier and snowed last night so there was nothing but freezing gray slush on the ground. That made sunshine and warmth seem pretty tempting. As did the man standing before her. "And the Saints go to Florida."

"Yes."

"And why do you have to go?"

"Like I said, we're trying out new players. The guys I bought the team with—well, Alex is good with money and Mal is more the security guy. Because I'm the doctor, I get to deal with the players."

"You pick the players?"

He half shrugged and shook his head. "That's mostly up to the coaching team. But if they're not sure they'll ask me my opinion. And it's good for me to know what the players can do and work with the coaches on how they're being trained. After all, I'd rather that none of them end up in my operating room."

"Baseball players get injured?" She asked the question and then realized what a dumb thing it was to ask. Her mental image of baseball involved a lot of guys standing around a field not doing much that was dangerous, but that wasn't the reality. "Sorry, stupid question."

"Lots of minor scrapes and bruises and sprains," Lucas said. "Playing so many games in a season is hard on their bodies. But in terms of serious injuries, well, shoulders and arms mostly. Pitchers get those. And batters. And then of course people fall when they're running bases or fielding, et cetera, and screw up knees and legs."

"Well, your team will be lucky, you can fix them."

"That's the plan. But it doesn't always work. An injury can end a career." He hitched his shoulder again—the right one—and grimaced.

Thinking about athletes he hadn't been able to fix or something else? "So you're down there supervising. How does that work with you being a surgeon up here?"

"It means I don't get a lot of sleep and I'm going to clock up a lot of frequent flier miles over the next few months. All year, really. I want to see as many games as I can, though my partners can share that load during the actual season. Florida isn't so bad. It's only a two-and-a-half-hour flight to Orlando. And it's the same time zone as New York. So no jet lag. But I'm currently commuting between New York and Florida at least twice a week."

"That's a lot of travel."

"Yes, and I'm looking to cut down on the time it eats up. And Alex and Mal—those are my partners—need some transportation, too."

"So you want a full-time pilot?" It was nearly the perfect solution to her problems. Of course, it was only nearly perfect because she'd had sex with Lucas. And just looking at him had certain parts of her voting to do that again. Which absolutely could not happen. Because he was offering her a job.

"Yes."

She gestured at the office around her. "I kind of have this."

Lucas nodded. "Yes, but your helicopter is out of commission, so I imagine this"—he echoed her gesture—"is just costing you money at this point."

"That's none of your business."

"Yes it is. I'm offering you work." He looked around the office, and Sara suddenly saw it through his eyes. She did her best to keep things tidy, neatness having been drilled into her by first her mother and then her army training, but there was no hiding the fact that it had been a while since they'd painted the walls or gotten new carpet.

Her dad's desk, where she currently sat, had been a flea market find of her grandfather's. It had sentimental value but had been ugly to start with, and forty years of use hadn't improved things.

Lucas finished his inspection and then his gaze returned to Sara. All that blue, focused on her. Just like it had been back in that damned motel room.

And even though he was only here to offer a job, even though she knew that she was not the sort of woman that men like Lucas sought out for other reasons, there was something deep in that blue gaze and the way he watched her that made her want to do something very stupid.

Like ask him to kiss her again.

Which would be crazy because he was only here to offer her a job. But the fact she was imagining something more meant she really should say no. Saying yes because she couldn't think straight when he was around would be an invitation to disaster. After Evan, she'd decided she'd wanted her next relationship to be based on off-the-charts chemistry.

Which was how she'd ended up dating Kane in the army. And that hadn't exactly worked out well, either. So now she really needed to keep her hormones in check and make the smart decision. "I'm not—"

"Look, the busiest time for me is the next few months." He came a little closer, near the edge of her desk. His scent drifted across the desk, and she fought the urge to close her eyes and breathe deeper. Instead she rolled her chair back a little.

Lucas smiled.

One quick smile. One quick knowing bloody smile that meant he knew she was unnerved by him. That he liked it.

And what did that mean?

"A few months?" she managed.

"Just until the season starts in April. It's not that long and it will give you a chance to get your chopper fixed. Then we can reevaluate."

It sounded too good to be true. In her experience, too good to be true usually was. Which was another indication that she needed to be very careful about the decision she made. Because he would become not just a client but her only client. Her boss, really. "My insurance could come through any day now. So you're asking me to potentially give up several months' profit."

He shrugged. "Yes. We'll compensate you for that once your chopper is fixed. Alex came up with an offer."

"Oh really?" She wondered exactly how much he thought Charles Air made. "Does Alex know much about running a helicopter charter?"

"No, but he knows about running a multibillion-dollar corporation that has a company fleet. Ice Incorporated? Perhaps you've heard of them."

"Wait, your business partner is Alex Winters?" Sara said. Maybe she should have read all of the articles she'd found about Lucas and the Saints, not just the bits about him. Ice was one of those gigantic companies that did a bit of everything. Including some aeronautical research she'd read about. Alternative fuel sources for planes and helos as well as design.

"Yes. And he said to offer you this." Lucas pulled an envelope out of his jacket pocket and passed it to her.

Sara took it gingerly. What if the offer was terrible? Then she'd have to say no and go work for Ron Harris. On the other hand, if it was good, then she'd be working for Lucas. Lucas who'd seen her naked.

Lucas whose naked body had made her wake from dreams of it hot and wanting too many times since that night in the Hamptons.

She wasn't entirely sure which was the more terrifying option.

"Are you going to open that?"

No point putting it off. She flipped open the envelope and pulled out the paper inside then unfolded it. When she read the figure typed there, she had to sit down for a moment.

"Sara?"

"I always wondered what an offer you couldn't refuse looked like," she said faintly. She read the letter again. The figure didn't change. And it was more than she was likely to clear in three months of running with one helo.

She didn't know whether to be gleeful or horrified. She scanned the letter a third time. Then actually took in what the words surrounding the salary figure said. "What's this part about Florida?"

Lucas leaned back. "I don't want to bother with two pilots. So when I go to Florida, you'll come with me and ferry me between Orlando and Vero Beach. That's where our spring training facility is."

"I'm assuming you don't do day trips?"

"Not usually, why?"

"I have a dog." She glanced down to where Dougal would normally be lying near the desk. She'd left him at her parents' house earlier, wanting to focus on her pile of paperwork. Just as well. He'd be going ballistic with Lucas here.

"Do you have someone who can mind him?"

"Yes?" Her parents wouldn't mind having him a few nights a week. If it was only for a few months. But she didn't have someone who would mind her. Overnight trips with Lucas Angelo. Hotel rooms that were near hotel rooms that Lucas Angelo might be occupying. Her heart started pounding again. She and Lucas and hotel rooms were a dangerous combination.

"So the dog isn't a problem then. So what do you say? I have to be in Orlando tomorrow night, so I need a pilot."

Were his eyes suddenly a more vivid blue? She wondered if he was thinking about hotel rooms as well. Then told herself not to be stupid. After all, the last time they'd shared a room, she'd snuck out before dawn and stranded him.

Yet here he is, another part of her brain pointed out. *Come back to find you. To hire you again.*

He wants you. He said so.

As a pilot.

But looking into those very blue eyes, she wasn't at all sure that was all it was.

She really should say no. It was the sane option. Not financially but from a Sara-doesn't-get-her-heart-stomped-on-by-the-rich-guy perspective, it was definitely the sane option.

"Do you care if I don't know anything about baseball?"

Lucas tugged at his tie, looking amused. "Define *don't know anything*?"

She could lie to him or she could tell the truth. The truth seemed easier. If any of them was going to be offended that she didn't find hitting a ball around a field fascinating then there was really no point taking the job. "Never been to a professional game. Avoided as many high school games as I could. Couldn't tell a Yankee from a Met."

"Really?"

"Yup. Sorry. Never paid much attention to it."

"You grew up on Staten Island and you're not a Saints fan?"

"My dad likes football. And baseball season is more a summer thing. I spent my summers flying."

He shook his head. "Weird. But no, that doesn't matter. I'm hiring a pilot, not a fan."

Well, there went another potential reason to say

no. She looked back down at the paper. Looked at the figure one last time. Thought about her dad and bills and what it might do to him if Charles Air went under.

"If I need help with the insurance company, will the Saints do that?"

"Sure."

The response was so fast she knew he meant it. Damn. She folded the paper up and slipped it back into the envelope. Then she looked back at Lucas and knew that she was about to throw sanity to the wind. "Yes," she said. "I'll take the job."

Chapter Eight

It was just the unfamiliar helo. That was the reason for her nerves, Sara told herself as she went over her preflight while she waited for Lucas to arrive the next afternoon. She'd spent an hour or so flying the helicopter with the pilot who'd delivered it to the airfield earlier and then she'd flown it the short hop to Deacon Field—home of the Saints—without him. It had felt good.

It wasn't an A-Star but she'd gotten the hang of it easily enough. What she hadn't gotten the hang of was the fact that she was now working for the Saints. Working for Lucas. And his partners, though she hadn't yet met Alex or Mal. She'd met Gardner Rothman, apparently Alex Winters's right-hand man, first thing in the morning at Deacon, and he'd walked her through the contract.

And then informed her that the helicopter would be arriving that afternoon and Lucas was going back to Florida that evening. Aka, she was going to Florida that evening. Where another helicopter would be waiting for them so she could fly him to Vero Beach.

She'd spent a frantic half hour at her apartment packing and then spent the rest of the time cramming a flight plan for the Florida leg and familiarizing herself with the new helo.

So it was perfectly normal that she had more than the usual level of pre-takeoff anticipation zinging through her veins.

Nothing to do with Lucas Angelo at all. No sirree. Not one little bit.

It sounded good in theory. Pity she didn't believe it in the slightest.

Lucas was going to be in her helicopter. Close to her. Sitting there all big and gorgeous and—no, she had to shut down that thinking. There was no room for big and gorgeous. She'd screwed things up enough already getting tangled up in Lucas Angelo; now it was time to woman up and treat him like the customer—no, *employer*—he was.

Hands off. Eyes off. Mind off. Nothing to do—or think about—but take off, fly, then repeat in Florida to deposit him safely at their destination.

Easy. Nothing she hadn't done hundreds or thousands of times before. She wasn't going to screw this up. If she did, Charles Air would probably be dead in the water.

She wasn't going to let that happen. So. Hormones were to be reined in, Lucas Angelo was to be ignored as far as possible without being actively rude, and everything would be fine.

She wasn't going to think about the fact that her

luck had turned in her life into something pretty far from fine lately.

But as she stared up at the stadium—they'd wanted to see if the parking lot was a good temporary helipad—she wasn't so sure.

So much space. The stadium, with its tower and the field, suddenly felt enormous. What would it be like to own something like this?

Hell, she'd settle for owning something a fraction of the size. Like a working helo.

But before she could disappear down that particular rabbit hole again, she saw Lucas emerge from one of the gates in the side of the vast concrete structure. He wore a suit as usual and carried a garment bag and a carry-on.

Nerves buzzed. "Just a job," she said and climbed out of the helo so she could wait for him.

As soon as her foot hit the tarmac she almost turned around and climbed back in. After all, she'd never waited for him like this before; always let him be shown to the chopper by the reception staff. He knew the drill of how to buckle himself in and stow his luggage.

But that was in the A-Star, and this was a whole new helicopter. She'd need to show him where everything went. She bit her lip, hand on the edge of the door. She hadn't thought about how she'd have to stand here and watch him walk that goddamned master-of-the-universe stupidly sexy walk toward her.

But she did. And the gloomy day meant hiding behind sunglasses was out. So she steeled her spine and her face and pretended that she didn't care in the slightest that Lucas Angelo was striding toward her dressed in yet another perfectly cut suit.

She couldn't tell from this distance if it was very dark gray or maybe very dark blue, but his tie was mostly silver with blue and yellow stripes.

Which were the colors of the New York Saints. Another thing she'd spent several hours studying last night after she'd accepted Lucas's offer. Given herself a crash course in the history of what seemed to be the worst team in Major League Baseball and the three men who'd just bought the franchise.

It was intriguing, really. Lucas was—other than in bed—a study in control. A surgeon. She was fairly sure that only people who were very fond of being able to order the world around them became surgeons. And yet here he was, taking on what had to be a terrible bet. A team that hadn't won a World Series in so long that it was ridiculous. A team with serious financial woes.

Why? It didn't seem to fit with the rest of him. Which made her stupid heart give the tiniest of hopeful bumps as she watched him close the distance between them.

For one long moment their eyes locked. Then her nerve broke and she turned back to the helo for a moment, fussing with the handle on the door for no reason before she got brave enough to turn back.

And there he was. Just a foot or so away. Close enough to touch. Definitely close enough that a hint of that spicy Lucas scent hit her even through the smell of fuel and machine that surrounded her.

"Sara," he said. "Sorry I'm a little late." He smiled down at her, blue eyes warm.

Too warm. Too close. She felt her face go hot. His smile widened.

She tried to remember what he'd said. Something about being late? He was maybe two minutes past when he'd said he'd arrive. They had plenty of time to get to JFK.

"It's no problem, Dr. Angelo," she said.

"It's Lucas," he said. "I think we left Dr. Angelo back in the Hamptons."

Crap. He'd brought it up. Why oh why had he brought that up? Her face went from hot to supernova, and she looked down at her shoes for a moment.

"So how do you like my ballpark?" Lucas asked.

Change of subject. Thank God. She risked looking up again. His expression had eased to something less intense. Still gorgeous but manageable. "Well, I haven't really seen a lot of it yet. But it seems nice."

Lucas grinned. "That was diplomatic of you."

She smiled ruefully. Deacon Field might be a Staten Island icon but it wasn't going to win any awards for architectural splendor.

"Is that supposed to be a halo?" she asked, pointing at the strange silver glass structure that was built into the angled roof of the office tower spiking above the stadium.

Lucas shook his head. "Apparently so. Butt-ugly, isn't it?"

"Not exactly the most beautiful building I've ever seen," she admitted.

"If I had my way, we'd tear it down and rebuild," Lucas said. "But that's not in the budget just yet. Besides which, the fans would probably picket us."

"People like it?"

"People like history," he said. "That halo is older than either of us."

She looked up at it. Squinted sideways.

Tried to see the big silver ring as something more than a blight on the landscape. It didn't magically become more attractive. She shrugged. "To each their own."

"Baseball fans are sentimental. And superstitious. The Saints need all the good luck they can get, so we can't go messing with our good-luck symbols."

"That's a good-luck symbol?" she asked. "Maybe that's your problem. Anyway, aren't the Saints like the worst team in the league?"

"I thought you didn't know anything about baseball." He slapped a hand against his chest, looking mock-wounded "But the one thing you do know is that my team is terrible?"

"I did grow up on the island," she said. "I might not pay attention to that, but it's pretty hard to miss the mass depression of the entire male population at the end of the season."

Lucas looked skyward, muttering something. Suddenly he looked very Italian.

"Are you telling me they aren't the worst team in the league?" she asked, half teasing. If he couldn't joke about his team and take a bit of ribbing, it was best to know now. For one thing it would make it easier to forget about him. She liked her men to have a healthy sense of the ridiculous to go along with a healthy ego.

And for another, it was going to stop her shoving her foot in her mouth if he was touchy about it. Not that being touchy about the Saints seemed sensible. He was going to give himself a nervous breakdown owning the Saints, if their reputation was true and he was too set on being a winner or something. Evan had been big on winning. Even mini golf and supposedly friendly Frisbee in the park turned into a contest with Evan. And Kane had been another competitive flyboy, with an extra dose of high-octane army testosterone. She was over men who needed to win at all costs.

She held her breath as Lucas studied her a moment, blue eyes unreadable.

"We finished seventh in the American League last year," he said eventually.

"Is that good?"

He groaned theatrically. "You really don't know anything about baseball, do you? Seventh means we didn't make the play-offs, but it's also not dead last."

"Well, that's something." She reached out and held out her hand for his bag. "Not last is good."

"Of course," Lucas said with a grin, "if you look at our average performance over the history of the team, we are definitely the worst team in baseball."

"Which begs the question of why you'd want to buy this team?" Sara said. She waved a hand at the stadium. "I mean, this is kind of sweet and all. But don't you want to win?"

His smile turned rueful. "To tell the truth, I'm still

not entirely sure how Alex talked us into it. I think he put something in the bourbon that night. But no, it's not about winning. It's about being part of something that I've always loved. I've been a Saints fan my whole life."

"But you grew up in Manhattan," Sara said. Manhattan and the Hamptons and all the other playgrounds of the rich and privileged. "Why pick the Saints?"

He shrugged a shoulder and said, "Trying to explain that is like trying to explain why you fell in love with someone. My dad kind of followed the Yankees. But the first proper game of baseball I ever went to was the Saints versus the Red Sox and I just kind of . . . fell. I liked their spirit." Another shrug. "Or maybe it was the fact that their mascot is an angel."

"Why Dr. Angelo. That's very sentimental of you," she said.

"I know," he said. "Not logical. It horrified my dad. Still horrifies my whole family really." He nodded toward the helo. "Shall we?"

Apparently they were done with chatting for now. Which was good. The more she talked to the man, the more she remembered what she'd liked about him back in that hotel room.

"I'll show you where to put your bags," she said. There. Pretend he was just another customer.

Thankfully he didn't call her on it but listened attentively as she showed him where to put his stuff and how to use the headset and adjust the seat. Then she left him to settle himself and climbed up into the pilot's seat to ready for takeoff, running through her mental list of checks and tasks while trying not to notice the very familiar scent of Lucas Angelo that had spread through the helo way too quickly.

Ignore it.

Focus on the flight. She started the helo and wasted no time getting them into the air and pointing the helo toward JFK.

As her ears filled with the steady familiar noises of flight, she couldn't help the happiness that swept through her. In the air again. At last.

For this, she would put up with Lucas Angelo and whatever else the universe decided to throw at her. She allowed herself to revel in it for a minute or two, and happily Lucas stayed silent. She assumed he had his nose buried in his laptop as usual. Which meant it should be safe to sneak a look.

Just one.

After all, it was her responsibility to ensure her passenger was comfortable. And she was determined to be hands-off with Lucas from here on in—but that didn't mean she had to completely deprive herself, did it?

But when she twisted her head to check on him, she found herself caught in the spotlight of those brilliant blue eyes. He lifted one eyebrow at her. She turned back, cheeks heating.

"Did you want to ask me something?" Lucas's voice came over the headset.

She shook her head.

"My mother always says it's not polite not to look at someone when you're talking to them."

"Your mom isn't flying a helicopter," Sara said. "Besides, I wasn't talking to you."

"Oh, just admiring the scenery, then?" Amusement was clear in his voice.

"I was making sure my passenger was all right."

"I see." He paused. "You know, I could come up and sit beside you."

Panic flared. She might have thrown sanity to the wind by taking this job but she had retained enough common sense to know that she needed to keep some space between them if she was going to keep her distance from Lucas. She glanced at the empty second pilot's chair beside her. "Nope. It's not safe for you to move around while we're in the air." She worked the controls a little, just to make the helo bobble a bit. "And see, it's a bit bumpy. You stay where you are."

"Okay. As long as you tell me something."

She gritted her teeth. "What?"

"Why didn't you wake me up?"

Wake him up . . . ? It took her a moment to figure out what he was talking about. Then her cheeks got hotter. Her stomach tightened and something lower down throbbed as suddenly the helo felt full of tiger all over again. She swallowed. *Play dumb, Sara*. "Wake you up?"

"Back in the Hamptons." His voice sounded lower. "Why didn't you wake me up and ask for some help?"

"Because I didn't think you'd let me take the car," she said. "Why would you? You had to get back to the city and let's face it, I'm just the girl you slept with because you were stuck in a dodgy motel during a storm."

"As I recall, I slept with you because you made a pass." His voice was definitely lower.

She didn't know if that was a bad or good thing. *Do not turn around and look at him.* It was bad enough that she could feel him sitting there behind her. Feel him as clearly as though he were pressed against her. "Blame the beer."

"Do you often make passes at men after one and a half warm beers?" He sounded curious.

Only when they look like you. She swallowed again, tried to ignore the tingle on the back of her neck. He was watching her. She knew it. But she wasn't going to turn around. "No."

"Then let's be honest and chalk it up to mutual attraction."

Mutual? Her mouth dried. "I—"

"Which brings me back to my question. Why didn't you wake me up? I had a damned good time." His voice roughened, and she had to suck in a breath as it sent a shiver fluttering down her spine. "I'm pretty sure you did, too. So why wouldn't you ask me to help you?"

Because if I woke you up, I wouldn't have been able to leave? Nope. Wasn't going to say that. "I like to solve my own problems."

"Car theft was easier than asking someone to help out? Isn't that taking independence a little bit too far?"

"I wasn't thinking straight. I was worried about the helo."

"Helo trumps guy?"

"Helo trumps one-night stand that was a bad idea."

"A bad idea? It felt pretty good to me." There was that low hot tone in his voice again.

There were so many reasons. "You were a customer. I don't get involved with customers." There, that was the simplest explanation.

"I don't usually sleep with my chopper pilots, so we're even on that score."

"It's not the same thing."

"Why not?"

"Because you're the one who can afford to charter helicopters and I'm not."

"I'm a bad idea because I have money?"

"No. You're a bad idea because—" She waved a hand in the air, frustrated, trying to work out the diplomatic way to get him to end this conversation. "Because we're different." She looked down at her instruments, calculating the flight time left. Too long to just stay silent the whole time.

And then there was the flight to Florida and another helicopter flight before she'd be able to get away from him. Maybe she wouldn't be sitting with him on the plane, though. That would be something. But it didn't really matter. She was going to be spending enough time with Lucas over the next few months that they might as well get this sorted out now.

He needed to understand that there would be no more sex. No matter how much heat might spark between them.

"Different seemed to work okay in that motel room," Lucas said, breaking the silence.

"That motel room wasn't reality."

"It felt real to me."

Her stomach twisted, warming as she remembered just how it had felt. And tasted and sounded. *God*. Was she ever going to be able to forget? "It was just for one night. That's all it was ever going to be. So please, can't you just let it go?"

"No."

"Why not?"

"Because I haven't been able to forget what it felt like when I was inside you," he growled.

Her hand jerked on the controls and the helo tilted. Much like her world just had. She righted the helo easily enough but she couldn't do the same to her pulse.

"Well, try harder." She was amazed she could still speak with an ocean of lust flooding through her.

"Why?"

"Because I don't sleep with clients and I definitely don't sleep with men who are, for all practical purposes, my boss."

"Why?"

"Do I really need to explain that to you? Workplace relationships are bad news. I prefer nonfraternization." And not just with employers. Lucas Angelo was out of her league. All the great sex in the world wasn't enough to bridge the gap between them. And she'd learned the hard way what happened when people from her world tangled with the very rich when Jamie had died.

"Nonfraternization?" He sounded amused.

"That's what we called it in the army. Keeps things simple."

"Do I get a say in this?"

"You hired me as a pilot. That's all your money buys."

He coughed. "If you think that I expect you to sleep with me because I'm paying you then you really don't know me." Now he sounded indignant. Which was better than sexy.

She resisted turning around to see if she was reading him right. "Exactly. We don't know each other. And that's best for both of us. You need a pilot, I need a job. Which means our relationship is business. This money is important to me, Lucas."

"I understand that."

"Do you?" she said. "Have you ever actually had a problem in your life that you couldn't fix by doing your rich-guy thing and fixing it all with cold hard cash?" She tried to keep the bitterness out of her voice and didn't entirely succeed.

"My rich-guy thing?"

Her hands tightened on the controls. "Wave your black Amex, watch everyone jump to do whatever it is you want and solve all your problems."

"I think you've been hanging around with the wrong rich guys," Lucas said. He sounded annoyed now.

She still didn't look. "I don't generally hang out with rich guys."

"Oh, so you just stalk them to observe their obnoxious Amex-waving behavior?"

"I fly them places. That presents plenty of observational opportunities."

"And plenty of opportunities to make sweeping generalizations. I've never waved a black Amex at anyone in my life."

"No, but I'm sure you've had plenty of people leaping to do whatever you want." *And quite possibly most of them were women.* And ouch, that sounded bitchy even in her head. Why was she being hard on him, anyway? If she didn't care what Lucas Angelo did, she shouldn't care who he did it with.

"Less than you might think."

She snorted. "You're a surgeon. Doesn't that mean you have whole teams of people doing what you tell them to every day?"

"No, it means I work with a team to get the outcome we want."

The outcome he wanted, that was. "Isn't the outcome where you get to be just a teeny bit godlike and put someone back together again? That sounds like snapping your fingers and getting what you want."

"I don't think ten hours of painstaking surgery counts as snapping my fingers."

Ah. No. "You're right," she said. "I'm sorry, I'm being rude." But she wasn't really sorry. For one thing, her irritation seemed to have burned away some of the fog of heat he'd ignited. She could think again. Control it again. Tame the tiger, so to speak.

"Bad day?"

Bad year. But she wasn't going to tell him that.

"Long day," she said. "But I get to fly again and that means it isn't bad."

"You haven't flown since your chopper got damaged?"

Was that an olive branch? Regardless, she would go with it. "No."

"Kind of risky to have only one helicopter, isn't it?" he said.

"Yes. But we don't have one. We have two. The other one is wrecked. My dad had a crash about a year ago."

"I read about that. Why isn't that chopper fixed?"

He'd read about it? Had he been doing a little Internet research of his own? Best not to go there. "Because insurance companies suck. The official investigation cleared my dad but they kept stalling. With the A-Star, another aircraft damaged it so things should be sorted out faster." She didn't want to mention the part where they had spent most of the payout for her dad's helo—once they'd finally gotten it—on his medical bills.

"And is your dad okay?"

"His leg was pretty badly smashed up but he's getting there."

"Is that why you're not in the army anymore? You came home to help your dad out?"

"Yes. Look, I don't want to talk about it, okay?" The story of how she'd joined the army in a fit of grief-fueled insanity after Jamie's death was just too complicated. As was the part where she'd been happy enough to have an excuse to leave it.

There was a long pause. Then, "Why not?"

"Because talking about it doesn't change anything. It is what it is."

"Sounds like you've had a pretty crappy year then."

Damn it. The last thing she needed was him being thoughtful and sympathetic. She made a noncommittal noise.

"You know, what you need is some fun."

"Fun?"

"Yes. When was the last time you did something just because you wanted to?"

Back in that motel room. She pressed her lips together so she wouldn't say it out loud. "I have lots of fun."

He made a disbelieving noise, and this time she did turn her head to glare at him. He was grinning at her.

"You don't know me," she said. "Or what I do."

His head tilted, the shade of his eyes in the odd cabin lighting suddenly a deep deep blue that spoke of night and bed and wicked delicious things. "I know some things you do very well."

"Shut up." She turned back, focused on the horizon, trying to figure out exactly how much longer this flight was going to last. How much longer he could drive her crazy.

"Spoken like someone who knows she's losing the argument."

"Not being interested in having this discussion with you is not the same thing as losing the argument."

He laughed. "Depends on why you don't want to have the discussion. If you were a patient of mine and told me that in the last year your dad had been in a serious crash and you'd had to change jobs and you were obviously working yourself way too hard, then I'd tell you to let go a little. Be selfish, take some time for yourself. Be a little bad for once instead of the good girl."

She felt her fingers tighten on the controls again. Be bad. Do what she wanted. Be free. That sounded . . . dangerous. It also sounded divine. Which only proved that it was dangerous. And that she needed to ignore Lucas Angelo.

"What do you know about being bad?" she said. "You've got *good boy* written all over you."

"Is that so?"

"You're a surgeon. You're successful. You're so well put together it makes my teeth hurt. Textbook good boy. Your family must love you."

"Actually, I'm kind of the black sheep in my family."

"What? What family doesn't want their kid to grow up to be a doctor?"

"Mine. I should have done a good sensible business course and law school or an MBA. Right now I should be running one of the family businesses and having many children. And I definitely shouldn't be buying baseball teams. Like I said, they're still pretty horrified about that."

She squelched the thought of how pretty Lucas's children would be. "So why did you?"

"Because I love baseball. And I'd be miserable

running a business. So I know all about rebelling and being bad. And I recommend it. So, want to give it a go? You could start by having dinner with me tonight."

Yes! Her mind practically shrieked the word. But just then, she heard the chatter of the JFK tower. Thank God for air traffic control. Reminding her of reality. She needed to fly. She needed to work. So she couldn't want or need Lucas. "No," she said firmly and started to concentrate on getting back down safely on solid ground.

Chapter Nine

He was here to think about baseball, not women. But that was proving difficult.

Sleep deprivation, that was it. He just needed caffeine. Which was why he was pouring his third coffee of the morning.

They'd arrived at Vero Beach at o'dark thirty, thanks to a delay in the flight from New York. Sara had slept on the plane. He, of course, had not. Having her curled up under a blanket in the seat next to his hadn't made it easy for him to concentrate on the work he'd brought with him. Not when what he wanted to do was wake her up and see if she was interested in joining the mile-high club. Or even in just talking to him to take his mind off the flight.

His alarm had sounded far too soon after he'd fallen asleep. Which hadn't been for an hour or so after he'd crawled into bed. His body had been far too aware of the fact that Sara was just a few rooms away from him. It didn't seem to care that she'd shut him down pretty firmly on the flight to JFK.

His body was a hopeless, hormone-infested optimist.

He, however, had to be a realist. Do what he was here to do. Ignore the sexy pilot girl.

Ignore the sea-blue eyes and the mouth that curved so nicely when she was putting him in his place. Ignore the quick wit and the determination that made him want to keep her talking so he could work out what made her tick.

She wasn't interested.

Correction. She said she wasn't interested.

Her mouth said it. But he'd seen the way she stole glances at him and the pink stealing over her skin when he looked at her. He'd heard her voice go loose and turned on when he talked about that night in the hotel room. And he knew damn well the way that mouth tasted.

So he didn't entirely believe her, no. Only question was: How he was supposed to get inside the wall of responsibility and whatever the hell it was that she'd erected around herself and get back to the woman who'd seduced him in the Hamptons?

Without making an idiot of himself or behaving like a complete and utter jerk in the process.

There might not be enough caffeine in the world for that.

He frowned, thinking about it. He couldn't quite figure her out. And he couldn't quite figure out what about her made him want to figure her out.

"Lucas, are you coming?"

He jerked back to reality, and coffee—thankfully cooling by now—slopped down his hand. He scowled at it anyway.

"Whoa. Looks like you've had too many of those already." Dan Ellis grinned down at him. He looked annoyingly wide awake in a white Saints polo shirt and jeans with a well-worn blue Saints cap pulled low over his eyes.

"I didn't get much sleep," Lucas said. He squinted at the watch on the un-coffee-splashed wrist. Nine thirty. He felt like he'd been awake for a day already but apparently not.

The coffee provided at the stadium where the team had their temporary digs was nowhere near good enough to kick-start his brain the way it needed to be kick-started. Each sip had left him wishing desperately that he was home with his very expensive, very good espresso machine waiting for him on his kitchen counter.

But no, he was here in Florida, where the day was far too sunny for his current mood.

He'd hidden away from the sunshine in one of the offices, trying to get some surgery-related calls and emails out of the way first thing before he had to switch to baseball. But apparently he hadn't hidden well enough. Dan had found him.

"We're about to start the pitching drills if you want to come and watch," Dan said. "There's one kid in this batch who's looking good. Sam Basara."

Lucas nodded and shut down his laptop. "He's the one you've been telling me about." Dan had had his eye on Sam for a while, apparently. The kid was only in his first year of college ball. Getting called up to the majors at this stage would be a dream come true. Lucas knew that dream.

And also knew how that dream could chew people up and spit them up. MLB was unforgiving.

But the cold hard fact was that they'd lost their best pitchers—other than Brett—and needed to build that capability back up ASAP. Combine that with pockets that were far shallower than most of the other teams and their only option was to go for the underrated players that Dan and his team were picking out. Including kids still in college.

"Yup," Dan said. "Kid's got an arm on him." He took a file folder from the pile he held and passed it to Lucas. "So let's go."

Lucas yawned. "Do I have time for another cup of coffee?"

"If you're quick. But get used to it. None of us sleeps much in spring training."

"Yeah, but you're not sleeping in just one place for the most part. I'm doing it in two," Lucas said.

"Cry me a river," Dan said. "We've got a team to build."

Couldn't argue with that. He grabbed another cup of average coffee and followed Dan out to the field. It was, at least, warmer here in Vero Beach than in New York. He pulled out his sunglasses and put them on as he gazed out over the small park. Small but newer and in better condition than Deacon Field. But a ballpark was a ballpark, and the familiar white diamond and bleachers and scoreboard made him smile despite his bad mood.

Down on the field, a bunch of players in the silver and blue and yellow Saints colors were gathered around the lanky form of Stuart Kelso, the Saints pitching coach, watching intently as he gestured with a bat and made wild arm motions.

Hopefully it was a rousing pep talk and the players would be inspired to do what they did best so Lucas and the coaching team could make some decisions and he could get the hell back to New York.

More likely, half of them were standing down there wishing they could find a discreet place to puke their guts up through sheer nerves.

He'd never actually tried out for an MLB team, but he remembered what it had felt like being scouted at his high school games. The sheer terror that he wouldn't get chosen. Wouldn't be offered the money that would mean he could do what his parents didn't want him to do and go to the school of his choice and play baseball.

"Poor bastards," he muttered.

Beside him, Dan grunted. "Not if they're any good. This is a good shot for them."

Lucas nodded. If any of the players down on the field did turn out to be great players, then it was unlikely they'd stay with the Saints too long. With their finances the owners were going to be playing buy low, trade high with their players for a few years yet, but he intended to make sure that the team served as a good training ground and didn't treat the players like interchangeable bits of meat to be moved around any more than necessary. While they were part of the team, they would be treated well. And eventually, if he and Alex and Mal got this right, the Saints would be in the position not to have to shuffle players around so often.

But they wouldn't get to that point without taking these first steps. So he had to do what he'd been sent here to do. Which meant forgetting about crappy coffee and seeing exactly what the guys down on the field could do.

Dan moved farther down toward the barrier between the stadium seats and the field, and Lucas followed him. As they walked he noticed Sara sitting in the seats a few rows back. She had a cap—not a Saints cap—pulled over her hair and sunglasses hiding her face, but it was her. She wore a short-sleeved blue shirt and black pants and was holding an eReader or tablet or something. But at the moment she was ignoring the device and gazing down at the field, apparently fascinated.

"I'll be there in a minute," he said to Dan and detoured across to where she sat.

"Good morning," he said.

She jumped a little, then recovered and looked up at him, the sunglasses hiding her eyes. "Hello."

"Didn't expect to see you here."

"I went to make sure the helo was squared away this morning," she said. "But I didn't want to just hang around the hotel all day. So I came down here to see if there was anything I could do."

For a second she bit her lip and Lucas had to stop himself from staring at her mouth. She had beautiful lips. And she knew how to use them.

In ways he needed to stop thinking about.

Though, as he stood there, the pause in their conversation while they watched each other growing just that little bit too long, he saw color start to steal across her cheeks and felt a little growl of satisfaction low in his stomach.

She might be denying it but she wasn't as indifferent to him as she wanted to be.

"Lucas!" Dan yelled from down at the fence line.

"Look, I've got to go do this," he said. "But I'm sure we can come up with something to keep you busy if you insist. Until then why don't you come down closer and watch and I'll introduce you to the coaching team."

"Just as long as you don't expect me to say anything helpful," she said.

"You never know, you might be a baseball savant."

"I doubt that," she said as she shoved her tablet back in the big black shoulder bag sitting on the seat beside her. "What I don't know about baseball could fill a book."

That stopped him. "Tell me again how you grew up on Staten Island and didn't learn anything about baseball?"

She shrugged. "Just not that interested." Her expression turned apologetic. "Sorry. Like I said, I was more into helicopters than sports."

"What about high school? You didn't have to go to games, show some school spirit?"

"I was the one hiding under the bleachers with her nose stuck in a flight manual," Sara said with a grin. "Or playing hooky altogether."

"A rebel, huh?" So she didn't like sports. He could hardly hold that against her. After all, he didn't like flying. And she liked plenty of other things he liked. Beer. Beds. Really really good sex.

"Just kind of one-track-minded back then."

"And now? Are there other things that hold your interest now?" He couldn't help the question.

Sea-blue eyes narrowed at him; then she smiled with bared teeth. "Yes. My dog."

His mouth curved up before he could stop it. But he took the hint to back off with the flirting for now. And he could feel Dan glaring at him. Time to focus on the job at hand. "Well, maybe you'll like baseball now, too. Come and see."

Sara followed Lucas down closer to the field but took a seat a couple of rows back from the front of the stands. Lucas stood at the fence with a guy who was a few inches shorter than him and a few years older, if the glimpse she'd gotten of him when he'd yelled for Lucas to join him was anything to go on.

If she had to guess, she'd say he was Dan Ellis, the team's manager—which was the coach as far as her baseball for dummies research could determine.

Lucas was definitely paying attention to whatever the guy had to say, anyway.

But Sara wasn't likely to understand anything they had to say, so she didn't bother trying to make out what they were talking about.

Instead she turned her attention to the group of

men standing on the field, listening to what another man in a Saints jersey was telling them.

They all wore Saints uniforms that were blindingly white and new looking, so they were probably the ones trying out.

From what she'd read and what Lucas had told her, that was what spring training seemed to be about. Trying out new players, getting the team gelled before the season proper started in April.

The guys in the new uniforms varied in age, a couple of them looking painfully young still—all legs and arms and potential.

About eighteen or nineteen, she thought. She'd seen enough fresh-from-basic-training young recruits in her army days to know a lanky not quite a man when she saw one.

It seemed pretty young to her to be trying out for something as big as professional ball.

Then again, she'd started working toward her commercial license at sixteen, so who was she to judge?

Two of the younger guys were bouncing on their toes, swinging their arms, while listening to whatever they were being told. The third, the one with the very short dark hair and broad shoulders he hadn't quite grown into, hung back. She saw him swallow a few times, and her stomach tightened in sympathy.

Poor kid.

She watched him a little while longer, saw him adjust his cap a few times then swallow again. Was he going to barf?

For his sake, she hoped not. If a baseball team was anything like an army platoon, then he'd never hear the last of it if he did.

She turned her attention to the others in the group as the guy who was talking to them finished and they all peeled off and headed in different directions across the field. The nervous guy and his two youngest buddies stayed near the fence.

The guy in the jersey walked over to Dan and Lucas. The three of them conferred.

"You're new," a voice beside her said.

She looked up. A tall guy with dark curly hair and a killer smile was standing at the end of her row. He wore a Saints uniform but it wasn't as painfully new as the ones on the guys trying out. He had a cap and a baseball glove in one hand and a smartphone in the other. His eyes were hidden behind mirrored sunglasses. The expensive weirdly shaped kind.

His smile widened when their eyes met and he moved down the row toward her. "Ollie Shields," he said, dropping down beside her. "And you are?"

"Sara Charles."

"Definitely new. I haven't heard of you. Remind me to chastise the grapevine." He frowned down at his smartphone as though blaming it for his lack of information.

"What makes you think the grapevine should have heard of me?" she said. She studied him warily. He seemed to think she should have heard of him, but she hadn't gotten as far as studying the actual Saints players in her research. She'd wanted the basics, not the details.

But whoever Ollie Shields was, he was not hard on the eyes. Tall, olive-skinned, in great shape. About her age. Maybe a little older.

"This place is one big barrel of testosterone," Ollie said. "Trust me, when a new female walks through the gates, we hear about it."

That was something she was familiar with, too. Being a female in a sea of men. "Well, I got here kind of late last night. Maybe your grapevine was asleep."

"Like I said, chastisement will be delivered. So, what brings you to Florida, Sara Charles, and can I convince you to stay awhile?"

His cheerful assuredness made her smile "Confident thing, aren't you?"

He grinned. She had to admit it was a pretty cute grin. Not as good as Lucas's, though.

"Just getting in early before the masses."

She relaxed a little. He was flirting but it wasn't serious. It was just cocky guy banter. Another thing she'd learned about in the army. The key to cocky guy banter was to banter right back. "And here I thought you'd been struck by lightning at the sight of me."

"Who says I haven't?"

She wrinkled her nose at him. "Somehow I get the feeling you're not the struck-by-lightning type."

He pouted. "I'm wounded."

"You'll survive." She studied him for a moment. "I take it you're on the team." She waved a hand at his uniform.

"You don't know who I am?" He sounded genuinely surprised.

That made her smile. "Sorry, not a big baseball fan."

"Then what brings you to spring training, Sara Charles?" He pulled his glasses off, as though he wanted a better look at her. Well, non-baseball fans were probably a rarity in his world. His eyes were a very dark brown and smiley. Which didn't make him any less attractive. "You didn't tell me why you're here."

"No, I didn't," she said. "You'll just have to live in suspense for a while."

"Ah, that means you're going to be around for a bit," Ollie said. "There's hope for me yet."

"You don't want me," she said. "I'm sure dating a girl who doesn't like baseball would be terrible for your ego. After all, I wouldn't swoon appropriately when you murmured your stats in my ear."

"It's true," he said, "I do like a good swoon."

She smiled again. She had to give Ollie points for being entertaining, no matter what else he might or might not be. And maybe he could teach her a bit more about baseball so she didn't sound like a complete idiot in front of Lucas. "So who are the guys out there?"

Ollie shrugged and pushed his glasses back into place before assuming a bored expression she thought was at least partly for show. "Rookies, mostly."

She lifted her eyebrow. "Eloquent, aren't you?"

"You want chapter and verse?"

"How about just a couple of verses. In non-baseball-speak?"

He shrugged. "Okay. I'll keep it simple. The guys out there are trying out for the team. When we got sold—you know the team changed owners, right?"

She made sure not to look at Lucas. "That much I know."

"Well, when the terrible trio took over, some of the guys got traded and some wanted out. That's why we're down at spring training earlier than usual. We have more gaps to fill than we normally would." He jerked his chin toward the field. "Those guys are pitchers. Couple of guys from the Preachers—that's our minor-league team—couple of kids from colleges, and a couple of guys from other teams who've been dropped."

"Why do you want them if they've been dropped?"

"Means they're cheap," Ollie said. "We at the Saints have a proud history of not having a lot of cash to spend."

"Aren't the guys who bought you gazillionaires?"

That got her another shrug. "Alex Winters is definitely a gazillionaire." For a moment his mouth tightened, and she got the distinct impression that he might not be a fan of Alex Winters. "Lucas Angelo—" Another chin jerk, toward Lucas. "—well, he's got family money and he's a hotshot surgeon so he's not hurting for cash. Neither is Mal Coulter, the other guy. But I don't think they're quite as rich as Alex."

"But rich enough to buy good players."

"It's a business," Ollie said. "I guess they're playing things carefully. They could spend a lot of money upfront but it's not going to guarantee a good solid team. They say they're in it for the long haul, so I guess they're being smart. Seeing if they can find some undervalued talent. Build from there."

He seemed to think it made sense. She didn't know anything about baseball strategy so she'd take his word for it.

"Are you a pitcher, too? Is that why you're here today?"

"Nah, I'm first baseman. Reasonable batter. Can't pitch for shit, though. I'm here to run around a bit and pick up balls once they start trying out. Start getting my hand in, so to speak." He leaned forward as he spoke. Toward the field and the action. Like a puppy eager to be let off the leash so it could go join in the fun.

"Am I keeping you?" she asked.

"No, the coach is still putting the fear of God into them," Ollie said, relaxing a little. "They won't start getting into it for a bit longer."

Sara looked down at the field at the three young guys again. They were all looking seriously tense now.

"Surely that makes it harder for them to do well? Getting them wound up, I mean."

"If they can't perform with just the coaching staff yelling at them, how are they going to do with thousands of fans screaming at them?" He sounded unsympathetic. "Better to know now if they're going to crack at under pressure. This is the big league. Literally."

"I guess."

"If you want something, you've gotta go after it,

no matter how nervous you might be. Feel the fear and do it anyway or whatever that shit is."

"Deep."

He laughed. "Baseball philosopher, that's me." Then he straightened as the coach turned in their direction and jerked a thumb toward the field. "That's my cue," he said, standing. "Don't go falling in love with anybody else while I'm down there." He grinned one last time, hitting her with full-out ridiculous charm, and waggled dark brows at her.

"I'll do my best," Sara said, but even as she spoke the words she felt her gaze drift toward Lucas. It wasn't Ollie Shields's ridiculous charms she had to worry about.

Chapter Ten

After Ollie left, Sara turned her attention back to what was happening on the field. If she didn't have anything else useful to do—and that was a pretty weird feeling, not having something urgent to do— she might as well watch and see if she could make any sense of what was going on.

The players broke off into groups and, once again, the three younger guys stayed closest to where she was sitting. Lucas and Dan Ellis stayed right by the fence, too. Ollie and another player—a tall black guy who'd walked past her swinging a gleaming silver bat idly in one hand—stood beside them.

Sara shifted a few seats over so she could see past the group of men, feeling herself tense in sympathy as the young guys headed over to a batting cage and started stretching and jogging in place, nerves written all over them.

Once again, her gaze was caught by the one with

the short dark hair. He was lanky but he still moved fluidly, hints of grace peeking from beneath the lingering adolescent gangliness. Once he filled out he would be no one to mess with.

The guy with the bat and Ollie strolled over to the three young pitchers with the other coach. Ollie jogged on past and took up position out on the field a fair way from the cage. When he was in position, the batter walked into the cage.

The first of the young guys picked up a ball from the pile of them sitting outside the cage and walked out to the pitcher's mound.

Sara could feel every step he took, her heart pounding in sympathy.

She held her breath as he took his first pitch. And winced when the batter connected solidly and the ball went flying past to where Ollie stood.

Ollie scooped it up easily and sent it back to the pitcher, yelling something that Sara thought was, "C'mon, rook. Get it together."

Not helpful.

The second pitcher was better, she thought, the kid not looking so nervous. He had curly dishwater-brown hair and a solid build and even managed a flash of a nervous amazed grin before he took his shot. But he, too, got his pitches smashed solidly by the batter.

And then the third—the short-haired guy—managed to get in a ball that the batter didn't connect with. He smiled as he straightened, teeth flashing white against his olive skin, but then his face turned serious again as his second attempt suffered the same fate as his friends'. This time, the coach beckoned and the kid came back to where the others stood.

Out of the corner of her eye she saw Lucas start to walk out on the field. She realized, as he walked, that this was the first time she'd seen him wearing something other than a suit. The something being very dark jeans and very expensive-looking sneakers with a navy polo shirt that had a white Saints logo on the back.

The jeans showed off his butt very nicely as he walked and she made herself turn her gaze onto the three baby pitchers instead, who all looked even more nervous as they watched Lucas—their potential boss—coming toward them.

That, she really could sympathize with.

To her surprise, when Lucas reached the three of them, he bent and picked up one of the balls, tossing it idly in his hand as he said something to the rookies.

He spoke to them for a minute or two then demonstrated a pitch, his body moving through the motion as easily as any of the players she'd seen today. He didn't let go of the ball at the end of the movement, though, keeping it in his hand before he did the move again, the actions so strong and sure that she knew he must have done it hundreds of times.

Had he played baseball? And if so, how seriously?

Interesting. Obviously she needed to do a bit more research on the man.

Or just ask him.

No. That was too personal. There was going to be no personal between her and Lucas. All business, all the time, and nothing more. Awesome butt or not, he was not for her.

Except he didn't seem to realize that. As he returned to the fence line, he stopped to say something to Dan and then came and sat next to Sara.

"What do you think?" he asked.

"They're nervous," she said. "You need to loosen them up a bit."

"They need to be able to perform under pressure."

"I get that, but if you want to see what they can really do, you need to get them to relax. Have a little fun with it. You seem to be big on people having fun."

He ignored her dig. "This is major league. It's serious."

"Yeah, well, I had to teach nervous eighteen-year-olds how to fly helos in the army. Trust me, it was always easier if you could get them to forget how terrified they were for a while."

He turned to her, a curious expression in his eyes. "What do you suggest, then?"

"They're guys, make it a contest."

"I think they already know they're competing."

"Yes, but right now the goal is too big. Their whole life's dream dangling over their heads. No one can relax in those circumstances. You need to make it something smaller. A more immediate reward."

"You want me to take them to Disney World or something?" Lucas sounded amused.

"If they like Disney, that might work," she said.

"But they're young guys trying to look tough in front of the pros, so I'm guessing that they wouldn't admit anything so uncool. Make it a cooler prize, though, and you're on the right track."

"Something cool, huh?" Lucas said. He smiled then, and the expression held more than a hint of wickedness. "Like a helicopter ride with the hot pilot?"

She frowned. "I'm hardly the hot pilot."

"I think I'm the better judge of that," he said, his voice dropping low and intent. "And trust me, they'll see it my way." He leaned a little closer. Just a little. They were, after all, in public. But it was enough to make her mind fog a little as she breathed him in.

No. No. No. "Whatever you're thinking, it's not going to happen," she said.

A smile spread across his face. "I was thinking that you could take the guy who does the best for a bit of a scenic flight later on." He cocked his head at her, a clear invitation for her to contradict him.

As clear as the fact that he wasn't thinking about his rookie pitchers at all. No, he was thinking about the two of them. About her.

She didn't know why he wouldn't just quit it. There were plenty of way prettier women than her who'd be more than happy to sleep with Lucas. But here he was. Looking at her.

Thinking at her.

Daring her to ask him what he was thinking about.

So not going to happen.

She was glad of the sunglasses hiding her a little from his gaze. It meant she didn't have to look away. "Well, you are the boss. So sure."

His mouth quirked. "If only you were so amenable to all my suggestions. Have you given any more thought to the whole concept of having fun?"

She held up her eReader. "I have a good book. I have all these nice-looking men to watch, and I'm sitting in the sunshine in Florida rather than freezing my butt off in New York. I'm having plenty of fun."

"Your idea of fun needs work," he said. "I have much better ideas than that."

"Well then, figure out something fun for your baby pitchers to do," she said. "And go bother them."

"Why, Sara Charles, do I bother you?" he said in a voice that was almost a purr, satisfaction underscoring his words.

Her cheeks went hot. "Not in the slightest," she lied.

Lucas lifted his eyebrows, smile widening. But then, to her relief, he moved back and got to his feet.

She kept her eyes firmly on her eReader as he walked away.

Lucas watched the helicopter descend toward the ground and tried not to hold his breath. He couldn't see Sara from this distance—the helo was a dark blur against the late-afternoon sunshine—but he knew she was up there. And he wouldn't feel relaxed until she was firmly back on the ground.

Which was dumb.

"Man, that looks awesome."

He turned his attention to the two rookies standing with him. In the end, Sam had been Dan's pick for having the done the best that day, finally loosening up enough to unleash a series of fastballs that had nearly set the batter's hair on fire. So he was the one up in the air with Sara but Lucas had let the other two—Tico and Walsh—come with Sam to the airfield. A little envy wouldn't hurt their performance, and Sam would be even more pumped if he got to show off in front of his friends.

He remembered that feeling all too well. He'd been about the age of these three when he'd first met Mal and Alex. The three of them had delighted in beating one another in any stupid contest they could come up with.

Teenage boys.

Idiots.

Not that he seemed to have learned that much in the intervening years. At least not when it came to women. He was feeling pretty teenage himself as he watched the chopper bring Sara closer and closer.

He needed to figure out how to convince her to give him another chance. Because the more time he spent near her, the more he knew that there was no way he was getting her out of his system anytime soon.

Every time she looked at him, the blood in his body rushed south and he struggled to think straight.

He really needed to figure out how to win her over.

The chopper was close enough now that he could see the concentration on her face as she brought it in to land, her brows drawing together, eyes fixed on whatever point she was aiming for.

Christ, even that was sexy.

There was something wrong with him.

Yeah, and her name was Sara Charles.

"Will we get another shot at a ride in that?" Walsh shouted as the wind from the rotors started to buffet them.

Lucas shrugged and made himself look at Walsh. "That depends how well you do."

He saw determination light in the kid's eyes. He wanted the ride. Or wanted to win. Either way worked. Sara had been right about getting them to focus on something smaller. She might not know baseball but she'd apparently been right when she said she understood guys.

Which was kind of unsettling, really. Did she see through him as easily as she'd seen through the rookies' bravado?

If so, he was in serious trouble.

The noise and wind from the chopper finally died. The doors opened and Sam climbed out, grinning widely. He jogged across the field and Walsh gave him a high five. "Dude, how cool was that?"

Sam hitched a shoulder. "Pretty cool."

"More than pretty cool," Tico said. "That pilot chick is hot."

Lucas stiffened. "Hey," he said. "Around here, we treat women with respect. Ms. Charles is the team pilot and you will be polite." He heard the snap of anger in his tone. Maybe a little more anger than the dumb comment warranted. There was a thread of possessiveness in it, not just his annoyance at a teenager mouthing off at a woman.

Tico winced then held up his hands. "Sorry, I didn't mean anything by it."

Lucas nodded, once. "Think before you talk then. There are plenty of women involved with the Saints, and they're all more important than you three at this point." He jerked his head back toward the stadium. "The three of you should head back. I'm sure the coach has something for you all to be doing."

Looking suitably subdued, they turned and jogged off immediately. Lucas saw Sam turn back, though, and steal a last glance at the helicopter before he gave up and sprinted a little to catch up with his friends.

Lucas turned back and saw Sara walking around the helo, her expression one of concentration.

He walked over to where she was. "Problem?"

"No, just checking things out. I'll take the helo back to the airfield in a minute." She stopped for a moment. "Unless there's somewhere you need to go?" Her tone was polite. Damn. She was back behind her wall again.

He shook his head. "No. I'm good. Thanks for doing this. You were right about it relaxing them."

"Yeah, Sam had fun." She peered up at him. "What were you saying to them at the end there? You got them looking all nervous again."

"I was explaining to them certain things about the

way we expect women to be treated in the Saints," he said.

"One of them called me hot or something?" she asked. She shook her head at him. "I can cope with a teenager, Lucas. You don't have to defend my honor."

"Yes, I do," he said. "I don't want that attitude on my team. The other players would take their heads off if they caught them talking like that about Maggie Jameson or any of the other female employees, for one thing. For another, it's just wrong."

"So you can hit on me, but no one else can? Wow, you don't like other people playing with your toys, do you?"

He scowled. "You're not a toy. And frankly, that's insulting. I've made my position clear, yes, but it's up to you. Tell me you never want me to mention it again, and I'll never mention it again."

He paused and watched her. Her cheeks, which had a faint hint of pink from the sun, went pinker and she glared at him but, tellingly, she said nothing. Something primal flared in his gut. Desire. Need.

She hadn't said no.

He'd given her a clean shot to tell him to take a hike and she hadn't said it.

She wanted him. So now he had to figure out how to get her to say that part. Because he was going to crawl out of his skin if he didn't get to touch her again soon.

But it was probably wiser not to push his luck just at the moment.

"And sure, if guys want to hit on you, they can. I'm sure you can handle them. But making a genuine pass is different from talking trash. I don't let it happen at the hospital and I'm not going to let it happen here."

"Okay," she said. Then she nodded toward the helicopter. "I really should get this back to the airfield."

He wanted to tell her to stay but it was clearly not the right time. He was going to find the right time. Very soon. But now he just nodded. "I have to be back in New York tomorrow, so we'll be leaving about midday."

"Do you need me before then?"

"No," he said. "But I'm sure Sam and his friends would like it if you came by to watch them again in the morning." They weren't the only ones.

"All right," she said. "I will. See you tomorrow."

She should be home by eight at the latest. That was her plan. Deliver Lucas to Staten Island then deliver herself to her parents to pick up Dougal and head home. She smiled at the thought. She'd promised herself a night off, a tiny reward. Her, Thai takeout, Dougal, and a few hours to catch up on the shows her aging TiVo had hopefully recorded for her while she'd been in Florida. British detectives and melodramatic billionaire vigilantes and reruns of half a dozen other shows she'd missed while deployed.

A night off without having to worry about Charles Air. Her salary with the Saints would take care of the bills for now, and she would start chasing up the insurance company again in the morning. Tonight she was going to just relax.

Something she hadn't been doing enough of lately. Something that she definitely hadn't been doing in Florida. Being around Lucas close enough to twenty-four seven wasn't remotely relaxing.

The fact that it wasn't relaxing, that she was still far too aware of every move he made and the sound of his voice, was even more not relaxing.

She had a knot between her shoulders the size of the Grand Canyon from pretending not to notice him. But a bath, some red wine, and mindless TV should take care of that.

Heaven.

But first she had to get through the final, less heavenly part of the evening. One last flight from JFK back to Staten Island with Lucas.

She should be grateful, she supposed. She was flying again. And she'd been hungry to fly. Starving for it, in fact. Now she would have all the flying she could want. With someone else picking up all the bills.

All thanks to Lucas.

But it was hard to be grateful to the man.

Not when she knew, somewhere deep down and barely acknowledged, that it wasn't the chance to fly again that had made her heart bounce when she climbed into the pilot's seat. No, it was seeing Lucas himself.

Which meant she was all kinds of stupid. He made her all kinds of stupid.

And he was late. He'd stopped to check his messages when they'd gotten off the plane at JFK, and she'd taken the opportunity to put some distance between them for a while and gone on ahead to get the helo ready. But they'd agreed on a time for takeoff, and she knew exactly how long it should take him to get from the terminal to her—and he was now fifteen minutes late. What was taking him so long?

Just as she reached for her cell phone to call him, it buzzed to life. The man himself.

"Sara speaking," she said, trying not to let irritation overtake her.

"Sara, change of plans."

"You're not coming?" A girl could hope. She could leave as fast as she could and be home even sooner than she'd planned.

"I'm on my way. But I have to stop in the city. Can you take me to downtown Manhattan?"

"You're staying the night in Manhattan?" She tried to keep the hope out of her voice. If she just had to do the hop to Manhattan and then fly on to Staten herself, it would hardly put a dent in her plans.

And surely any sensible person would want to stay in town and sleep in their own bed after commuting from several states away. She assumed Lucas lived in Manhattan rather than on Staten Island. No doubt he could afford a place on the island as well, but she didn't picture him as the type to live anywhere but the glittering heights of the Big Bad Apple. Upper East Side, probably. In one of those condos that cost more than most people made in a lifetime. All marble and steel and glass.

A million miles from aging TiVos and linoleum banged up by big black dog paws.

"No, I still have to be in Staten Island later tonight. Can you wait for me and bring me over? I'll only be an hour or two."

Crap. She felt her teeth clench, and the knot in her back twinged in sympathy. But Lucas was paying her the big bucks, so she could hardly tell him that she wouldn't wait for him and, you know, do her job.

"Service with a smile, that's me," she said and hung up before she could say what was really on her mind. So much for a quiet night with her dog. She might still get the Thai takeaway, but hanging around the city for a few hours while Lucas did whatever the hell it was he had to do that was so important was definitely not what she was in the mood for.

She missed Manhattan but tonight, she didn't have the energy to even think of something fun to do. She knew that Viv was out for the night, she'd Skyped her from Orlando the night before, so she couldn't even try and meet up with her for a long-overdue girl talk.

At least she had her eReader in her flight bag. She'd have to make do with a new book instead of TV. And then there was Dougal. Who would be waiting patiently for her to get home.

She made a quick call to her mom, who was happy enough to keep Dougal a little longer. That was all she had time for before she got the message from the terminal that her passenger had arrived.

Chapter Eleven

Sara Charles was not happy with him, Lucas thought as he followed her through the chilly night back out to her chopper. Her greeting had been almost as cool as the wind whipping through his bones. Apparently two days in Florida was enough to make him forget that it was still winter in New York. Other than reconfirming which heliport he wanted to go to, she hadn't said a word to him.

Which made him wonder if his plan was going to work after all. It had made sense at midnight the previous night when he'd come up with it, but maybe that had been some sort of horniness crossed with tropical madness descending upon him.

Tropical madness in the form of the sight of Ollie Shields talking to Sara every time he turned around. He knew Ollie had been hung up on Maggie, but with Maggie now pretty firmly glued to Alex's side, Shields had to be on the hunt for a distraction.

Ollie wasn't going to distract himself with Sara. Nor were any of the other Saints players.

Sara was going to be busy distracting Lucas.

She hadn't been talkative on the flight back from Florida. In fact she'd spent the time either sleeping or reading with her headphones firmly clamped over her ears. The carefully neutral expression on her face now suggested she wasn't feeling any more talkative now.

But damn it, he was going to try anyway. She'd opened the chopper door for him, clearly expecting him to take up his usual spot in the passenger seats behind hers.

Screw that. He climbed into the seat next to Sara's before she could say anything. Hard to ask a girl out when you were sitting behind her after all.

She shot him a look but kept her mouth shut. Better give her some time to cool down a little. He waited while Sara got the chopper in the air and headed toward the sparkling lights of the city before he spoke.

"Sorry about the change of plans," he said. There, that was a nice and gentle, if somewhat boring, opening.

"It's fine," she said.

Fine was never a good sign.

"Did you have plans tonight?" he tried. He fervently hoped the answer was no. In retrospect, he should have tried to get that information out of her. She really was distracting him if he couldn't even think of the basics.

"Nothing important. Like I said, it's fine," she said.

Two fines. Which meant she was annoyed, if not outright pissed, if his female-interpreting skills weren't failing him. "If you did have plans, you could tell me," he said. "We're paying you to be a pilot, not a slave."

This time he saw the muscle on her jaw tighten. "You're paying me to be on call. That means ask and you shall receive."

Oh, how he wished that were true. There were many things he wanted to ask her for. But no. She was stubborn. She'd decided to ignore whatever this was sparking between them. Even if it killed them both.

"It's okay to let me know if you have a problem," he said. "I'm not going to fire you if you disagree with me."

She slanted him a look, eyes a mysterious shade in the odd light shed by the chopper's instruments. "I'll try to remember that."

He shook his head and sat back, watching for a few minutes as Sara flew them through the darkness, working out what he should say next.

Sitting up here in the front of the helicopter didn't make flying any more pleasant other than putting him within reaching distance of Sara. Watching her was a pleasure. Not just because she was gorgeous but also because of the way she flew.

She seemed part of the helicopter, moving with ease as she steered—was that the word?—and checked instruments and kept them moving forward through the air. Almost a dance. The way a good surgical team worked together. Every movement certain. Every movement purposeful.

It was clearly her world.

Despite the fact she wasn't happy with him, he could see that she was happy in the helicopter. Relaxed in a subtle way, some of the tension she always carried with her gone while she was up here in the air.

His own tension at being up here retreated a little just watching her.

He wanted to be able to watch her more often. And not just when they were in helicopters.

The question was, how did he convince Sara to give them a chance? He watched the lights of the city growing closer and brighter as they sped through the darkness and the small half smile on Sara's face as she flew.

At least, she was smiling until she noticed that he was watching her. Then the smile became pursed lips and brows drawing down. "What?" she asked.

"Nothing," he said. "Just admiring the view."

Her eyes narrowed and he grinned at her. "What, you don't like the sight of Manhattan by night? Or did you think I was talking about something else?"

"Don't try and charm me."

"Why not? You seem eminently worth charming. Actually, no, scrap that. I know you're eminently worth charming, remember?"

Her mouth flattened, and he knew that she was going to tell him off. But he'd also seen the tiny flare of her pupils. Which told him that she remembered, too.

And that she liked that memory, even if she was trying not to.

He settled back in the seat. "You do remember, don't you?"

"There's nothing wrong with my memory," she said in a cool tone.

"Then—"

"There's also nothing wrong with my common sense," she said. "So stop trying to charm me."

"Can't help it."

"Try harder."

"Oh, I've been trying. But I'm not a slow learner. I know that banging your head against the wall doesn't help anything. So when trying not to think about you didn't work, I decided to change tactics."

She sucked in a breath, and he wondered what she was going to say about that. But then the radio crackled to life.

"Land the helicopter," he said as she glared at it then back at him. "We can talk about this on the ground."

Lucas waited for Sara while she completed her postflight and got organized. Of course he did. He was annoying that way.

She wanted to tell him to go, go have his fancy dinner or whatever it was his detour to the city entailed, and leave her in peace. No flirting and charming and making her forget her resolve.

She would find out how long he was going to be and then she would walk to her favorite little deli near the heliport and get some dinner, and then she'd wait for him and deliver him back to Staten Island. And out of her hair.

It was an excellent plan.

A simple plan.

Somehow, though, as she came around the helo to where he stood, looking into his very blue eyes, she didn't think Lucas was going to let things be quite that simple.

"Don't you have somewhere to be?" She gestured him toward the walkway that led to the terminal building.

"Do you?"

"Well, if I did, that would've been ruined by your little side trip, wouldn't it?" she muttered.

"That depends," he said. "You said you didn't have plans. Have you been holding out on me, Sara Charles? Did you have a hot date tonight?"

She almost laughed. Her and a hot date? Apart from the moment of idiocy with Lucas back in Sag Harbor, there had been very little heat in her life lately, and what there was 100 percent self-service. There'd been no time for dating since her dad's accident. Not that any of that was any of Lucas's business. "Are you always this nosy about your pilots?" she said, hoisting her flight bag up on her shoulder and turning toward the terminal.

"Only the pretty ones," he said. "And there's only been one pretty one."

"Oh yes, and who was she?" she said, only half joking.

"Don't do that," he said.

"Do what?"

"Put yourself down."

"I'm the pretty one, am I?"

"Yes."

He reached a hand toward her, and she ducked away. "Don't do *that*," she said.

"Why not?"

"Because this is somewhere I work. And I don't want people getting the wrong idea about you and me."

He stepped back. "What's the wrong idea?"

"That I'm fooling around with a client."

"That sounds like a pretty good idea to me."

"That's because you're the one who won't get called a slut for doing it. And it won't affect your professional reputation." She started walking toward the terminal.

Lucas moved with her. "So let's go somewhere away from this and talk about it. Because I'm sorry, Sara but I'm not giving up on you just yet."

"Don't you have an important dinner date or something?" she said, trying to sound casual. He had her stomach squirming and her pulse doing strange things. He wanted to have dinner with her. He wanted to see her again. It was amazing. And a disaster.

"This is it."

She jerked to a stop. "Excuse me?"

"I wanted to come to the city so we could have dinner," he said simply. "I figured you wouldn't want to on the island, given you grew up there. Not discreet enough."

She didn't know whether to be charmed or appalled. "You could have just asked me."

"Would you have said yes?"

"Probably not."

"That's why my way is better," he said. "C'mon, Sara. Just dinner. Let's talk. See what happens. You never know, we might bore each other senseless and then your problem is solved."

She really didn't think there was a possibility in hell that he would bore her senseless over dinner. Not that she was going to tell him that. She should say no. The simple and safe plan was to say no.

"Just dinner," he repeated. "You must be hungry. It's nearly eight."

He had that part right at least. She was starving. She'd been thinking wistfully of the red chicken curry takeout she'd planned for the evening ever since Lucas had told her of his change of plans.

Just dinner. How bad could it be?

"There's a diner a block or so west of here. Meet me there and we can catch a cab," she said.

"There's a taxi stand just outside the terminal," he said.

"Yes, but I'm not getting into cab with you in full view of everyone here. They all know me. And I'm guessing most of them know you." she said. "Go to the diner and wait for me. I've got to do a few things first." Not least of which was try to work out if she could make herself look like someone that Lucas Angelo might be taking out for dinner.

"What do you feel like eating?" he asked.

"I like food," she said. "You choose." She glanced

down at her uniform. "Nothing too upmarket. I'm not dressed for upmarket."

"You look great."

"Maybe, but that doesn't change the fact I'm not dressed for an expensive New York dinner."

"Okay." He paused, with his hand on the door. "You're not going to leave me standing out there in the dark, are you?"

"Well, that would be kind of dumb given I have to fly you home later," she pointed out. "So just go. I'll be ten minutes."

It was actually more like fifteen because the girls doing the admin with her were full of curiosity about Lucas. Apparently he was something of a frequent flier here at the heliport and had his own little fan club.

"What were you talking about?" Jenna asked. Of all the girls who worked here, Sara had known Jenna the longest. But she wasn't exactly a BFF and there was no way Sara was telling her she was going out to dinner with Lucas.

"He was telling me about one of his cases," Sara lied.

"Oh yeah. He's a surgeon, right?"

"That's right."

Jenna sighed. "A hot rich doctor. And you get to fly him around. Nice work."

"He's just another passenger," Sara said.

Jenna narrowed her eyes. "You have too many hot passengers if you think that man is just another passenger," she said. Her expression turned curious. "One of Ron Harris's pilots came through this morning. He said you had a gig flying for the New York Saints. So you get to fly with all three of the guys who bought the team. Is that true?"

No point denying it. "Yes."

Jenna actually squealed and clapped her hands. "That is so awesome! What are they like? Is Alex Winters as hot as he looks on TV? Dish."

"It's great. And no comment," Sara said with an apologetic smile. Then she signed the paperwork and fled before she could be grilled about anything else.

The restaurant Lucas directed the cab to was in the East Village. A tiny place that he told her served the best Greek food in the city. She was starting to feel like she could eat a horse, so she wasn't too fussed about the restaurant's credentials. She just wanted food.

Food would level out her blood sugar and then she wouldn't feel quite so floaty and silly every time she looked at Lucas, right?

She took a deep breath as the waiter directed them to a table and breathed in the scent of garlic and lamb and spices appreciatively.

Happily, the waiter reappeared with a basket of bread and a platter of dips so that she didn't start drooling while she waited for food.

She picked up bread, slathered it with the nearest dip, and bit into it.

It tasted divine—smoky and garlicky and decadent—and she closed her eyes for a moment, chewed, swallowed, and then took another bite before she opened them again.

When she did, Lucas was watching her, smiling.

"I like the way you eat," he said. "It's very . . . enthusiastic."

"I'm hungry."

"Me, too." He picked up bread and swished it through the dip. His eyes didn't leave hers as he took a bite and then licked his finger where the dip had blobbed onto his knuckle.

Sara thought her skin might just catch on fire as she watched his mouth.

Damn it. She made herself look at the menu but she couldn't concentrate. So she picked the first thing that her eyes settled on and tried to calm down a little. This was just dinner. She pretended to keep studying the menu but the waiter reappeared all too quickly and took their orders before disappearing again. Leaving her alone with Lucas.

Who was smiling at her again.

He looked somewhat like the cat who'd swallowed the canary. Pleased with himself. Which should have been annoying, but it was hard to be annoyed with a man who seemed to be delighted to be having dinner with her.

Still, it was a little unnerving to be under the gaze of those eyes. Small talk, that was what was needed. God. She had no idea what to talk to him about.

Then she remembered baseball.

"So did you make any decisions about the pitchers?" she asked.

"You're asking me about baseball? I thought you weren't interested?"

"I'm not."

"Ah. Then why did you ask?"

"It seemed polite," she said.

He laughed then. "Are you always this polite?"

"No." *Only with gorgeous men who make me nervous and could ruin my life.* "But those kids were kind of sweet. So talk to me about them. Anyone having their dreams come true?"

"Why?"

"Because I'm not ready to talk about other things with you yet."

That made his smile widen. "Do I make you nervous, Sara Charles?"

"A little."

"I swear, I'm harmless."

If he thought that, then he really had no idea how hot he was. "I find that very hard to believe."

"Why?"

She waved a hand toward him. "Just look at you. You're the kind of guy who leaves a trail of broken hearts in his wake."

"I'm really not."

"You want me to believe that women don't swarm around the good-looking rich doctor?"

He shrugged. "*Swarm* is an overstatement. I'm not a monk, if that's what you're asking. But neither am I a . . ." He trailed off, seemingly searching for the word.

"Womanizing jerk? Cad?"

"Cad?" He grinned again. "Are we in a Regency romance?"

That raised her eyebrows. "What do you know about the Regency?"

"I've read *Pride and Prejudice*."

"You have?" She was impressed. In the army she'd known guys who had her appetite for books but their tastes, on the whole, tended toward thrillers and mysteries and science fiction. She'd never met a guy who'd read Austen. Or one who admitted it, at least.

"High school?"

"English lit in college. It was compulsory. But I liked it."

"You did?"

"Yes. I even read *Emma* and *Sense and Sensibility*."

Now she was fascinated despite herself. "Which is your favorite?"

"Probably *Pride and Prejudice*. I like Lizzy. Emma's naive and Elinor's a bit stuffy. Lizzy is just trying to be herself and look after her family. What about you? Are you a Darcy fan?"

"I have kind of a soft spot for Knightley, actually." She was a Darcy fan, actually, but she wasn't going to tell him that. The perfect rich guy who seemed standoffish and then turned out to be a true gentleman and all-around good guy seemed a little bit too close to the reality at the moment. And she didn't want Lucas thinking that she wanted a rich guy to ride in and save her.

"Knightley." He studied her a moment. "Knightley sees Emma's faults and loves her anyway," he said. "Isn't that a bit foolish?"

"No, it's what love really is, isn't it? Loving the real person. Knightley saw what Emma could really be." She shifted in her seat, suddenly wondering if this conversation was revealing too much. "I thought we were talking about your baby pitchers."

"But you don't like baseball."

But I like you. She didn't say the words. Because she wasn't ready to admit it to herself, really, let alone to Lucas. He'd asked her to dinner, true, said he couldn't forget her, but it could all be a line. He could just want more sex and then he'd ride off into the sunset in his Mercedes or Porsche or whatever ridiculously expensive car it was that he drove.

The waiter appeared with their entrées and Sara waited while he arranged the plates in front of them. The bread and dip had taken the edge off her appetite so she didn't pick up her fork as he left them alone again. "So. Baseball. I don't know a lot about it. What I saw in Florida was okay. Maybe I'd like it if I knew more."

"I think people who like sports tend to know it."

"I've seen *Field of Dreams*," she offered. "Kevin Costner was hot."

He laughed again. "As much as my life would be easier if the Saints had a magic baseball park in a field of corn, the reality is a lot more prosaic."

"Damn, I only took the job for Kevin and James Earl Jones."

"Sorry to disappoint. But to come back to your

original question, no, we haven't made any final decisions. I like that Sam guy, though. He's hungry. And good."

"He's pretty young. Wouldn't coming to play for you mean dropping out of college?"

Lucas nodded. "Yes, but that's the nature of the beast. MLB doesn't leave a lot of time for things like studying on the side. That's the problem with dreams, sometimes you have to make sacrifices."

"Like commuting between New York and Orlando a couple of times a week? How do you do that and do your rich-doctor thing as well?"

"It's only for a few months." He speared a chunk of lamb and smiled at her. "And once you get to be good enough to be a rich doctor, there's a certain amount of flexibility in your schedule."

"I would have thought it just meant that you were more in demand than ever, if you're really good," Sara said.

"Yes, but I can control my workload to some extent." He frowned, and she got the feeling that he wasn't as blasé about doing just that as he was making out. She remembered how insistent he'd been on getting back to Manhattan to do his surgery on the figure skater. And how they'd cut the trip short this time. He was juggling things, that much was plain.

Did she want to be one more ball in the air for him?

One more ball that was probably the easiest to drop if push came to shove? It was clear he was a guy who was devoted to his work—both medicine and the Saints. Which didn't leave much room for romance.

And here she was jumping the gun again. Maybe he just wanted another night or two of sex. Maybe he thought they could burn each other out of their systems or something.

Though he could've just knocked on her hotel door back in Orlando if that was the case. But no. He'd waited. Asked her out for dinner. In a helicopter, true, and that made it clear he wasn't exactly your run-of-the-mill date. Of course, she'd already known that. But rich guys didn't have to play by normal rules. So maybe it really was just about scratching an itch.

"You're thinking very hard over there," Lucas said. He looked down at her plate. "And not eating. Is something wrong?"

"No." She forked up some lamb hastily, chewed, and swallowed. "It's great. I'm just . . ."

"Just wondering what my intentions are?" Lucas asked.

She nodded. "Don't get me wrong, I'm not expecting you to get down on one knee or anything, but this is complicated. So I want to know just how complicated it might be."

"You like to be in control, don't you?" He leaned back in his chair a little, lifted his wineglass, and sipped.

"I have a lot on my plate. Things are easier to deal with if I have all the facts."

"I'm not sure what facts come into play when you're talking about attraction. Other than the chemistry. I think we've already dealt with that part back in Sag Harbor. Our chemistry works just fine."

"Chemistry is the easy part." She and Kane had had chemistry. But once the initial heat had died down, there'd been nothing left other than that they were both pilots in the army. No commonality. And Kane had been someone a lot more like her than Lucas Angelo was.

"Why does there have to be a hard part?"

She frowned at him. "Because, like I said. This is complicated. You're technically my boss. You're rich. And I'm me. Not rich. Very far from rich." Their worlds were, well, worlds apart. It was like an Austen novel. Only she was the poor chauffeur and Lucas was the out-of-reach titled object of her affections.

"I don't care about that," he said.

"That's because you don't have to."

"No, I don't. So problem solved. Money isn't an issue." Lucas said. He took another mouthful of wine, and she found herself fascinated by the play of muscles in his neck as he swallowed.

Good grief. She was losing it.

"Okay," Lucas said. "Here are some facts. One. I don't cheat. If I want to sleep with someone else, then I'd tell you. Two. I don't want to be complicated. You don't need complicated. You need easy. You need some fun in your life."

"My life is fine," she said.

He shook his head and put down his glass. "I have a mother, a sister-in-law, and about twenty female cousins. Not to mention many aunts and about half a hundred female colleagues. Not one of them has ever used the word *fine* in that tone and actually been fine."

She scowled at him.

He laughed. "And that expression just proves it. People who are having fun do not scowl like that."

"I hardly see how your life leaves much time for fun, ether," Sara said.

"Ah, but you see, I love baseball. Sure, the travel is killer, and turning the Saints around isn't easy. That doesn't change the fact that it makes me smile every time I think about owning a baseball team. It's one of my childhood dreams come true. So it's fun. And surgery is fun, too."

"Cutting people up is fun?"

"Fixing people is. Seeing someone walk again or compete again because of me, that's better than fun. So here's what I'm proposing. You need some fun. You need something that makes you happy. I can help you with that."

"Oh, so you'll sleep with me to make me happy?"

"Well, based on past experience it will make me pretty happy, too. It's a win–win situation. But I'm not just talking about sex. You're so busy running around trying to fix everything for everyone and keep control. You need someone who wants to make your life easier for a change."

"You think you make things easier?"

"I think I can. And we can see what happens from there. So what do you say? Want to give it a whirl? Let me be your . . . guardian angel."

"Guardian angel?" Her eyebrows rose. "Trying to earn your wings, Dr. Angelo?"

"You're the one with wings," he said. "I just want to . . . make you smile. Give you some time out."

Make her smile. Make things easier. Damn. He certainly knew which buttons to push. "I don't think guardian angels sleep with their . . . um, what do you call it? Charges?"

"I'm a modern angel," he said with another smile. "Whatever it takes to make my girl happy."

"I didn't think guardian angels were quite so cocky," she shot back. And she didn't think they were hot, either. He was much more your basic fallen-angel model, tempting her onto the wrong path. Only it didn't feel wrong. It felt very, very tempting.

"I'm not cocky, I'm optimistic. After all, you haven't said yes, yet."

"And what happens if this all goes wrong?"

"Then I'd hope that I'd behave like any good angel and do the honorable thing. Bow out gracefully."

Which would be easy for him to do, because if things went wrong between them, it was likely that she'd be the one doing the one-way ticket to hell. She chewed her lip. "I like you, Lucas. You know that, but I can't lose this job."

"I will not fire you if you break up with me, Sara. And if you don't want anyone else at the Saints to know, I'll be the very soul of discretion. Angels are good at that. Trust me. I don't want to screw up your life."

"If you really meant that, then you'd walk away."

"I really don't want to do that," he said.

"Why not?" she asked.

He reached across and curled his fingers around hers. Her pulse skittered as the warmth of his skin spread across hers. When she met his gaze, his eyes had gone dark and hot.

"Because of that," he said. "And the thing is, Sara Charles, I don't think you want to walk away from that, either."

Chapter Twelve

When the whine of the rotors finally died, the silence in the helo was far too intimate for her liking. It wrapped around them, drawing them together like the candlelight had back in the restaurant. Making her think foolish, foolish thoughts. Making her wish she could be the girl that Lucas saw when he flirted with her.

But she wasn't. And this was a helicopter that Lucas was paying for and she needed to climb out of it and remember what her life was really like. No matter how seductive Lucas's argument had been back in the restaurant. Where she hadn't said yes. And she hadn't said no, either.

"Give me your home number," Lucas said softly.

Five little words. Six whole syllables. How much trouble could four little words cause?

A lot, part of her knew. You just had to listen to his voice in the darkness to know he was a lot of trouble waiting to happen. To her.

Oh but such good trouble, the rest of her retorted. *C'mon, you know you want to.*

Lucas leaned a little closer. Just a little. Just enough to make her want to lean in closer, too. She tried to remember why it was she hadn't just said yes already. "I—"

"Just your number," he said. "That's all. After all, a guardian angel needs to be able to get in touch with his charge."

She smiled then, against her will. "You already know my work cell. And I already told you, I don't need an angel."

"Maybe the angel needs you."

His voice was so low and delicious in the dim light that she really wanted to believe this could be true.

Her good sense cracked, just a little. She wrote the number down on the notepad she kept stashed near her pilot's seat and handed it to him.

"Just a number," she said. "It's not an invitation."

He smiled as he took it. "Whatever you say."

She was relieved when he climbed out of the helicopter and strolled off toward the car park.

Leaving without her.

He'd stop if she asked him to. He'd stay. He'd come home with her and demonstrate that expert anatomical knowledge again.

She went hot just thinking about it and shut down the thought as she finished shutting down the helicopter. The mechanics would have all gone home hours ago; they'd check it and prep it in the morning. Still, she lingered a little, walking a circle around the helo, running her hand over the metal skin, not quite ready to let go of the flight and the few stolen hours with Lucas.

Was it too much to hope that Lucas would have the good sense to leave quickly so she wouldn't be tempted to follow him into the night?

She reached her car, stowed the flight bag in the back, rolled her shoulders once to ease the slight stiffness caused by the flight, and then climbed into the driver's seat. The engine coughed to life as she turned the key and she headed out of the lot, trying not to feel like she was a complete idiot for letting Lucas leave.

She was halfway home when her phone rang. She hit the button for the speakerphone. "Hello?"

"It's me."

Lucas. Her stomach tightened, but she couldn't stop the smile that immediately stole across her face.

"Did you forget something?"

"In a manner of speaking."

He was doing that low and wicked thing with his voice again, and her mouth went dry. She had to take a breath before she could speak. "What?"

"I forgot to ask you to give me your address."

Her hard-won breath left her in a rush. He wanted her address.

Oh *yes*.

Every particle in her body shrieked it.

"We agreed the phone number wasn't an invitation," she said, managing to ignore them.

"I know," he said. "But you never said I couldn't use it to ask for an invitation."

"Lucas—"

"Sara," he said, mimicking her tone. "I'm driving in the dark and I swear I'm going to run off the road because all I can think about is you. Tell me you're not driving home in the dark thinking about me, too. Tell me that and I'll leave you alone."

"I . . ." She wanted to say it. The sensible part of her knew that she should say it. One little white lie and he'd leave her alone and she'd be safely back on solid ground. No Lucas Angelo disturbing and disrupting her.

Oh, but she wanted him to disrupt her. Wanted him to turn her world upside down and into something different. Wanted it enough that she knew it was a very bad idea to give in to that desire. "I—" she started again and then it happened. Instead of being sensible Sara Charles and telling him to keep driving, to leave her alone in the dark, she gave him her address in a rush of words that spilled out of her before she could think.

"I'll see you there," Lucas said and hung up before she could say anything else.

She realized that she'd stopped at a stop sign. She had no idea how long she'd been there. She peered through the darkness at the nearest street sign, suddenly unsure where she was exactly.

Hell, she was unsure who she was exactly. She'd just invited Lucas Angelo over to her apartment.

About the only thing she was sure of was that right now she wanted very badly to be home.

* * *

When she reached the drive of the little apartment block, her heart was pounding madly. But she couldn't see any strange cars and the pounding was joined by a sudden rapid swoop of disappointment.

She parked and sat for a moment. Had he not arrived yet? She had no idea where he'd been when he'd called her, of course. Or had he changed his mind?

Maybe he'd had a sudden fit of sanity and driven away. That would make everything infinitely simpler. But leave her here with her racing pulse and tingling skin and the heat traveling her body that had been growing fiercer and fiercer with every mile closer to home.

He had to be here. If he was a guardian angel, he was here to make sure she got what she wanted, wasn't he? And what she wanted right this minute was Lucas Angelo's hands on her body.

She gathered her things and walked toward the entrance to the block. A small faux porch surrounded the door to the lobby, and as she reached the first step Lucas stepped out of the shadow beside the door. She dropped her bags and flew up the steps and then his arms were around her and his lips touched hers and she would have sworn the world just melted around her as her blood went volcanic and every inch of her shrieked *More*.

She opened her mouth to him and pulled him closer. They kissed frantically, like they needed each other for oxygen, and he backed her up against the door. His hands went to work, unzipping her jacket and pulling her shirt free of her trousers, and then his fingers were sliding over the skin of her waist, which made her moan and arch toward him like a cat seeking the sun.

He muttered something against her mouth that might have been her name or might have been *God* but then his hand dipped lower and pressed between her legs and she moaned louder, moving into him, thinking, *There, there, there* and *Oh God, yes*, as colors exploded behind her eyes and pleasure streaked through her body.

He reached for her zipper and slid it down and even though she knew she was standing at the front door and any minute any of her six neighbors might see them, she couldn't care about anything but the feel of his fingers against her. She widened her legs and his fingers slid into her panties and curled into her precisely where she needed to feel him. She felt the world narrow to just that spot. Just the feel of him, and the taste of his mouth and the smell of him curling around her as she rocked against him, desperate for him and letting him do this completely crazy thing as the heat built and then surged and pulsed through her like the scream of a jet engine, and her mind went completely blank as she struggled not to cry out through the sheer perfection of it.

When she came back to herself, Lucas had eased away from her, his hands at her waist again, holding her steady while she tried to make her brain work. His fingers stroked her skin where they touched.

She lifted her head and smiled, drunk with pleasure.

"Hello," she said.

"Hello," he said, sounding only a little more together than she was. "Nice place you have here."

The pleased rumble of his voice made her smile grow wider. "You haven't seen it yet."

"I don't care," he said. "I like it." His head dipped and he kissed her and she felt everything start to go hot and blurry again. "Ask me in, Sara."

"Do you want to come up and see my etchings?" she said, giggling.

"Do you have etchings?"

"I'm not sure I even know what etchings are." She laughed again. "Want to come up and take my clothes off?"

"Hell, yes." He straightened then, suddenly all business. "Where are your keys?"

It took her a moment to remember what keys were, let alone what she might have done with hers. "Keys. Bag. Stairs." She gestured back down the stairs to where her things were sitting on the damp path—thank God it hadn't been snowing or she might have just done dire things to her laptop. Lucas turned on his heel, descended the stairs with three quick steps, and then rejoined her. He handed her her purse and kept hold of her flight bag.

"Keys," he said. "Now."

She grinned. "Bossy, are we?"

"Yes," he said. "Whatever it takes to get you naked."

* * *

It didn't take too much, as it turned out. They made it up the flight of stairs to her apartment and inside the door before the bags hit the floor again and then he was kissing her again with those fierce wild kisses that scrambled her brain. She tugged off his coat and he dispensed with her jacket and she toed off her shoes while he unbuttoned her shirt.

"Christ, that's pretty," he said, one hand tracing the edge of the lace of her bra before it moved down to cup her breast, long clever fingers dragging across her nipple.

"You're prettier," she managed to say before she lost her breath again. More clothes tumbled to the floor between kisses and hands discovering skin and then she was on the floor, the wool of her rug soft against her back and Lucas hard against the rest of her as she pulled him down and wrapped herself around him and almost sobbed as he moved into her with one sure and solid thrust that felt better than anything she could ever remember feeling.

Apparently the interlude on the porch hadn't done much to satisfy her need for him, either. The feel of him on top of her, inside her, moving with her sent her crazy and she nipped at his mouth and locked her legs higher around his body. "Harder," she said.

She didn't have to ask twice. Lucas growled in her ear and then did something that changed the angle between them, tilting her hips up before he moved again. Moved hard.

"Like that?"

"Yes." It was half a gasp as he did it again, the slide and shock of him making her skin even hotter even as she rose to meet him.

Lucas grinned above her, but neither of them managed to find any more words. Things went dark and hot in Sara's head and she could only think of him and how good he felt as he drove into her, his body solid and warm and slick against hers. The only sound was the harsh breathing and the slide of skin upon skin.

Sex. God, she'd missed this. Though she knew it wasn't just sex she'd missed, but sex with this particular man. This was what she had been trying to forget ever since Sag Harbor, and the pleasure spiking through her with his every move was evidence of exactly why she hadn't been able to do that.

He kissed her as he took her—or was she taking him, it wasn't exactly clear as they met each other like a clash of warriors. She found herself digging her nails into his back and biting at his shoulder as he moved on and on, the rhythm growing wilder and less controlled.

His hand moved to her clit and it was almost too much, the added sensation sparking through everything else. She dropped her head back and moaned.

"Come for me," he said, his fingers moving to just the right spot.

She shivered and opened her mouth to say she wasn't quite there when he changed the angle again and slid into her and she broke open, seeing stars as she dropped into the place where there was only the hot pulse of satisfaction as he called her name and came, too.

The sound of the curtains sliding open woke her. She bolted upright, trying to work out who the hell was in her apartment, but then as she caught sight of Lucas standing by the window, pulling on his trousers, she remembered. Remembered the whole very long night. They hadn't gotten much more than snatches of sleep between lots and lots of sex.

"Going somewhere?" she said.

Lucas looked up. "I have to get to the hospital. They need me."

"Oh," she said. She should believe him, there was no reason not to believe him, but she couldn't help the evil little sliver of doubt that suddenly stabbed her in the gut.

He must have heard something in her voice because he came back over to the bed, bent down, and kissed her. "Trust me, I wouldn't be going anywhere this early if I didn't have to."

The kiss chased the doubt monkey away temporarily. But only a little. She tried to remember what day it was. Friday. Which meant that she was going to have her first day at Saints headquarters.

Only now she was going to have to do it without Lucas there. "Any chance you need me to fly you into Manhattan?"

He shook his head, bending to slide his foot into a shoe. "No, I'll find my own way this time." Then he paused, twisting back to look at her as he tied the laces. "Are you nervous about going to Deacon? Gardner will introduce you around. And I'll come back, if I can."

She managed a smile. It wasn't as though there was an argument she could make other than *I'm nervous*. There hadn't been enough time the other day for her to meet anyone else at the Saints, and she'd sort of been counting on Lucas being there now. But that just didn't rate against someone who needed medical attention.

She was just going to have to suck it up. She could do it. If she could leave home and join the army, she could manage to deal with a new job.

That part was easier than dealing with the fact that she'd slept with Lucas again and that, during their very long night, it had become crystal clear that she wasn't ready to stop sleeping with him anytime soon. And he was her boss.

"I don't want anyone at the Saints to know about us," she said as he started to tie his other shoe.

Silence. He finished tying the shoe then straightened slowly. "Forever?"

"For now," she said. "Is that okay?"

"Mal and Alex won't care," Lucas said.

"Maybe not. But I will. I have to work with them. They need to trust my piloting skills if I'm going to be worth what you're paying me. So I don't want them thinking that you only hired me because I slept with you."

"Technically you weren't sleeping with me when I hired you."

"That's not the point."

"Mal and Alex are my best friends," he said. "It's not really feasible that I'm never going to mention you."

She pulled the quilt tighter around her. The heating in this apartment was temperamental and apparently this morning it hadn't yet kicked in, making the air chilly. "This is brand new," she said. "We have no idea if it's even going to last. So let's not do the friends-and-family bit, just yet. Okay? Just for a little while. That's all I'm asking."

"You getting ready to kick me out of your bed?"

"Right now, no," she said. "But like I said, this is new. In a few more weeks we might annoy the crap out of each other."

He cocked his head as he slid his heavy watch onto his wrist. "After last night, do you think that's likely?"

"I think last night proved we're good in bed. That doesn't equal good at life together. So let's keep it under wraps for now."

"You want me to be your secret boy toy."

She smiled. "Well, who doesn't want a secret gorgeous sexy boy toy?"

"Now you're just appealing to my male vanity."

"Is it working?"

His face was serious. "Maybe. But only for a while, Sara. I'm not going to lie to my partners forever."

She nodded. "That's fair enough. Just a month or so maybe. Which means, no sleeping together in Florida. I definitely do not want anyone catching you sneaking out of my hotel room."

He frowned. "Not sleeping with you isn't very appealing right now."

"You'll live. I hear cold showers work wonders."

"How about phone sex?"

She laughed. "I'll take it into consideration." She glanced at the clock. It was getting close to six thirty. She wanted to be at Deacon by eight. "You should get going, shouldn't you?"

"See, you are trying to get rid of me," he said, but he smiled and leaned over and kissed her again. The kiss had turned heated way too quickly when she finally pulled away. They stayed close for a moment, foreheads resting together, breathing heavily.

"Remind me why I have to go again?" he said, sounding hoarse.

"Something about a pesky Hippocratic oath and some idiots who've managed to smash themselves up."

"Right. That." He made a noise deep in his throat as he moved his hand off her breast. "I hate that."

"No, you don't. So go be a doctor. I'll be right here tonight."

"Tonight's a long time away."

"Operate fast then."

Chapter Thirteen

True to Lucas's word, once Sara flashed her pass at the security gate and drove through into the underground parking lot, Gardner was waiting for her by the elevator.

"Good morning," he said as she reached him.

"Hi." Nerves bloomed again as she stared at the Saints logo painted on the elevator door, fingers clamping around the strap of her purse. Nothing to be nervous about. It wasn't as though this was a job interview. They'd already hired her. "It's nice to see you again."

"You, too. I hope things went smoothly in Orlando? There was no problem with the helicopter we hired?" The doors slid open and he gestured for her to get in.

"It was great," she assured him. "Do I need to take anybody anywhere today?"

"Not so far," Gardner said, pressing the button for the fourth floor. "But that could change. Alex wanted to be here to say hello but he got called into Ice headquarters. So Maggie Jameson is going to give you the tour."

"Maggie Jameson? Whose dad used to own the Saints?"

"The one and only." Gardner smiled. "She insisted. Said she knows the place better than the rest of us. Which no one can argue with."

The elevator came to a halt. Sara took a deep breath.

Gardner looked sympathetic. "Trust me, Maggie's not scary. Well, not unless you're a Yankees fan." He frowned. "You're not, are you?"

"Definitely not," Sara said. Thank God he hadn't asked if she was a Saints fan.

"Good." The smartphone in his hand suddenly started buzzing. He looked at the screen. "I'm sorry, I have to take this. Do you mind finding your own way? Maggie's in Alex's office, it's the one at the end of this corridor. Just knock on the door."

Sara hesitated but nodded when Gardner lifted the phone to his ear. She was going to have to meet everyone eventually. Might as well start at the top. And she had to admit to a certain degree of curiosity about Maggie Jameson.

She'd managed to avoid the finer details—or most of the details, really—of baseball growing up, but it was hard not to know at least something about Maggie Jameson, who hadn't gone to school on Staten but was kind of island royalty, if there was such a thing. Maggie had been a year or two ahead of Sara at school and she'd been a topic of frequent speculation whenever she appeared in the news due to the Saints connection. Sara hadn't paid much attention but she knew a bit about her. That her mom had died and she'd been raised by her baseball-team-owning father.

She had a vague mental image of a very pretty girl with long dark hair and dark eyes, but who knew if that was right?

So meeting Maggie was kind of like meeting a celebrity . . . someone you'd heard about but never met.

Besides which, this was the woman who'd roped herself the golden, glowing Alex Winters. Anyone would be curious about that. The man was hot. Sara had read stories about his companies and their aeronautical research and she remembered the pictures of the man who accompanied the articles. Tall and chiseled with piercing green eyes and brownish-blond hair.

Of course, she leaned more toward near-black hair and blue eyes, but Lucas or no Lucas, she could appreciate other guys. Maggie Jameson was obviously no one to be underestimated if she'd scored herself Alex Winters.

It almost made Sara have second thoughts about the whole keeping-herself-and-Lucas-under-wraps thing. If anyone could give her tips on how to handle a man with piles of money like Lucas, it would be someone like Maggie.

Of course, Maggie had grown up with piles of money herself so maybe it was no big deal to her. Still . . . girl talk. With moving to back to Staten

Island and Viv settling into her new job, it had been weeks since she'd had any serious girl time. The brief chats with the women who worked at the various heliports didn't count. She couldn't let herself confide in them because the helicopter charter world was small and she had no intention of letting her private life be the subject of its grapevine.

So yes, she wanted to meet Maggie and talk girl for a little bit, if there was a chance to do so. She could talk girl without giving away the fact she was seeing Lucas. Of course, if Maggie was as baseball-mad as the rest of them, they might not have a lot in common, but Sara would cross that bridge when she came to it.

The corridor went on for a while, its path slightly curved. The white walls had rows of black-and-white pictures of both teams and individual players breaking up the space between doors leading to other rooms or offices. Sara didn't pass anyone coming in the other direction. Gardner had said the office at the end of the corridor so she just kept walking until she came to a set of doors marked CEO with a discreet silver plaque.

She pushed one of the doors open and stepped into a large room with another set of doors at its far end. Those would be the actual office, she figured. The room she was in had several cubicle-style desks that held computers and various knickknacks and pictures but were currently uninhabited. One of the doors across the room was open and light spilled out, along with the loud sound of guitars and drums.

Sara smiled when the drums faded a bit and a guy

started singing and she finally recognized the song. Springsteen. She'd grown up with Springsteen, Jamie having formed a small obsession with the man's music at an early age. Maybe she and Maggie had something in common after all.

She reached the doors and paused at the threshold. The office was big with an impressive desk centered against the far wall. But the decor was less interesting than the tall brunette wearing dark skinny jeans, battered pink Converse shoes, and a Saints hoodie, who was shaking her booty to the music as she studied a row of figures scrawled down a massive whiteboard.

As Sara watched, she executed a twirl when the guitar riff screamed into life then stopped when she saw Sara. She looked embarrassed for half a second then just laughed, her dark eyes bright. She pulled out a small white remote control out of her pocket and pointed it at the computer on the desk. The music died.

"That's what I get for getting my groove on." She tucked the remote away again. "I take it you're Sara?"

Sara nodded, wondering if she'd just put her foot in it by surprising Maggie. But she would worry about that another time. Right now she had to act like a normal person and make nice with Lucas's best friend's girlfriend. Who was also one of her bosses, in a way.

"Hi," she said. "Sorry to interrupt you. Gardner had to take a call."

Maggie shook her head with a smile and beckoned

Sara into the room. "Trust me, you aren't interrupting anything exciting. That's why I had the music on."

Given how intently Maggie had been looking at the figures on the whiteboard, booty shaking or no booty shaking, Sara wasn't sure she believed her.

She hovered near one of the leather chairs set opposite the desk. Maggie perched on the edge of the desk, tapping on her pink shoes. Her casual clothes made Sara wonder if she'd misjudged her outfit choice. She'd gone with a neat black pantsuit and white shirt with her usual black flats. But Gardner had been in a suit as slickly cut as any of Lucas's, so maybe not.

"Sorry about the outfit." Maggie must have noticed the uncertainty on Sara's face. "Mal wants to drag me around the bowels of the stadium later. I've learned it's safer not to wear heels and a suit for that." She smiled, but curiosity was plain on her face. "So you're our new helicopter pilot."

"Yes."

Maggie nodded approvingly. "Very cool."

"You like helicopters?"

"Absolutely. Dad had one for a while in the late nineties when he was running way too many companies. I used to love it. Being up so high, seeing everything laid out below you. I used to nag him into taking me on flights whenever I could." She grinned, looking nostalgic. "How did you become a pilot?"

Sara smiled at her, finding her enthusiasm contagious. "My dad is a pilot. So was my grandfather."

"Ah, the good old family business," Maggie said. "I know a bit about that. It can be hard when something's in the blood that way."

"Hard, but good," Sara said. "I love flying."

"Well, with the current state of crazy around here, there will be plenty of that."

"I'm happy to do other things, too," Sara said. "I already asked Lucas about it in Florida. I'm not very good at just sitting around, so if there's other stuff I can do for you when you don't need the helo, you should let me know."

"What sort of thing did you have in mind?"

"I did a lot of office work for Charles Air—that's the family company—so I know my way around a computer and admin-type stuff. The amount you're paying me, I want to be useful."

Maggie's expression turned approving again. "Well, there's always plenty of paperwork and stuff to be dealt with. And Lucas said you'd been in the army, so Mal might find a use for you with what he's doing with the security stuff."

"I just flew in the army, I didn't do anything too exciting," Sara said.

"Flying in war zones sounds plenty exciting to me." Maggie slid to her feet. "Anyway, how about I start by showing you around and then we'll figure out how best to put you to work. And you can tell me how you met Lucas."

Sara's stomach curled slightly. She'd expected the question, knew damned well that Maggie was likely to ask about Lucas, but that didn't mean she had to give anything away. And hey, that would just give her the opportunity to grill Maggie in return. So she was going to grab the opportunity while she could.

"There's not much to tell," she said. "He hired me to take him to Newark. Pretty standard."

Maggie waved a hand toward the door. "You must have done a good job. He was the one who pushed to hire you. Lucas doesn't impress easily."

She headed toward the outer office, and Sara followed her.

"We'll start with the stadium," Maggie said. "That's the fun bit, that and the training complex. Then I'll show you where everything is back in here." She reached out and hooked a scarf and gloves off a shelf near one of the desks. "Will you be warm enough outside?"

"I have a scarf and gloves in my purse," Sara said.

"Well, leave that here and bring those."

Sara did as she was told.

Maggie set off again. "So," she said as they walked, "being a pilot must mean lots of travel. What does your boyfriend think about that?" She smiled innocently at Sara.

Sara sent an equally innocent smile back. "No boyfriend. Just a dog. And he stays with my folks when he needs to."

Maggie's expression softened. "A dog. What kind?"

"He's a big black Lab. A big softy." Most of the time.

"What's his name?"

"Dougal. Do you have a dog?" Sara asked. Safer

to talk about innocuous things to start with. Like dogs. Not Lucas.

Maggie shook her head. "My mom had a gorgeous Border collie when I was little, but he died. And after my mom passed away, there never quite seemed to be the right time to get another one. Dad was always traveling a lot and he didn't want me to have to take care of a dog by myself. Or at least, that was his excuse. I think dogs remind him of my mom."

"How old were you when she died?" Sara asked.

Maggie smiled, a little wobble in the expression. "I was twelve. Too young. But Dad was great. He's still great. How long have you had Dougal?"

"He's six and a bit," Sara said. "And I got him when he was a couple months old." She didn't add the part about Jamie dying and the grief that had driven her to want a dog so badly.

"Lucky you," Maggie said. She paused at a doorway and threw the door open. "This is the conference room," she said. "It's got the best view of the complex." She walked over to the floor-to-ceiling windows that made up the far wall and pulled up several sets of blinds. "Come have a look."

Sara walked over her and peered out the glass. They were looking not at the stadium itself but at what lay behind it. Which consisted of several small baseball fields, a row of caged enclosures, and a couple of other single-story fairly nondescript-looking buildings. NEW YORK SAINTS was painted in bright-yellow letters across the flat roof of one of them.

"I never realized all this was here," Sara said. "I've

only ever driven past the stadium. You don't see all this from the road."

Dark eyebrows lifted. "Lucas said you were a local. You've never been to a game here?"

Damn. Her dirty secret was about to be out. Again. Maybe it would be easier to have a T-shirt printed with SORRY, I DON'T LIKE BASEBALL. Save the explanations.

"I was more interested in helicopters than sports, growing up," she said.

"Not even a school tour?"

"Not that I remember." She was pretty sure there'd been a field trip to Deacon Field at some point, but she'd played hooky.

"Huh," Maggie said. "So you're not a baseball nut then?"

"No, sorry."

"Don't apologize. It makes a nice change," Maggie said. "We need some sanity around here." She waved at the buildings out the window. "Training facilities. Mostly. We use the fields for some of the community leagues we get involved in, too, but mostly for practice. Gotta keep those players on their toes."

"It's bigger than I thought," Sara said.

"Yeah, we're like an airport that way. The public only sees half of what goes on. Thank goodness." Maggie stared out at the buildings. "It's bad enough running security for the stadium on game day, so we limit access to the rest of the complex. Less potential for chaos. As much as that's possible in the majors. So what has Lucas told you about the place?"

"Not much," Sara said. "There hasn't been that much time. He's always reading stuff on his laptop when I fly him places."

"Yeah, his schedule is pretty nuts. Mal's and Alex's, too. But yay, you're a Saints history virgin." She rubbed her hands together. "I can tell you all about us."

"Ollie Shields told me a little bit about spring training when I was in Orlando."

Maggie rolled her eyes. "Let me guess, he did it while flirting madly."

"Yeah. Don't worry, I figured he pretty much flirts with anything female."

"It is kind of instinctive with him," Maggie said. But her expression was fond exasperation, not annoyance. "He's a good guy, though. Just needs the right gal to sort him out, maybe."

Sara held up her hands. "Don't look at me, I don't think I'm any athlete's ideal mate. He needs someone who at least understands the game. Like you. You must know it inside out."

"Yup. Hopeless baseball nerd. Always have been. In the blood, like we said. But despite that, I'll leave Ollie to someone else's capable hands, thank you very much. He and I work best as friends."

There was a story behind that, Sara thought. But she wasn't about to ask the woman about her love life on their first meeting.

"Okay, enough about Oliver," Maggie said. "He's already got a healthy enough ego without us boosting it vicariously. Let's go touring."

They made their way out to the stadium via

another trip in the elevator and a confusing series of turns and corridors that ended in a locked fire door. Maggie produced a security card, swiped it, and the door opened. They stepped out into a concrete tunnel that looked pretty much like the ones in every stadium where Sara had ever gone to a concert. There were stripes in Saints colors running horizontally along the walls but that was about the only distinguishing feature.

Maggie kept walking. "I always thought it must be pretty cool to know how to fly a chopper. Just never had the time to learn."

"Well, it's never too late. And helicopters are more fun than planes. Most of the time."

"Maybe after this year's season is done," Maggie said. "Things might have calmed down a little by then. Then you can show me the basics."

"Sure. And if I fly you anywhere, you can sit up front with me and I can explain some of it to you."

"That would be cool." Maggie stopped as they reached a security screen. This time she pulled out a key and dealt with the chain and padlock that secured it. "Better put on those gloves . . . this is where we get into the stands."

Sara pulled on her gloves. "So do you travel as much Lucas does?"

Maggie shook her head. "His schedule is the worst," she said. "Alex's is bad enough but now that they've dumped Lucas with spring training, he's got the short straw." She paused. "You know, I'm not sure that he even likes flying. We did quite a few plane trips when the deal was being approved. He always goes quiet and works through the whole flight, like you said."

Sara nodded. "Yes, I got that impression, too. Though he's pretty good at hiding it, if he really is bothered by it. Which is better than the ones who white-knuckle the whole thing. Or barf." She wrinkled her nose. "The barfing is the worst."

Maggie grimaced sympathetically. "Ugh. That's bad enough on a big plane. So Lucas has never tossed his cookies on your helo? Too bad, that would give me something to tease him about. Dr. Gorgeous shows a weakness. He's kind of a little too perfect, that one. Makes you want to rumple him up a bit. Or it would if I didn't have Alex," she added with a wink as she dragged the screen back. It made a rusty protesting whining noise as she did and she frowned at it, obviously making a mental note.

Sara decided to ignore the rumpling comment. "No, no barfing. How long have you known him, or them, I guess?"

"Not long," Maggie said as she started walking again. "I only met the three of them when Dad sold the Saints."

"And you and Alex?"

"Yeah." Maggie rolled her eyes. "It's kind of ridiculous. I should hate the man. After all, he kind of stole my baseball team . . . but, well, you've seen him?"

"I have," Sara said. "He's pretty easy on the eyes."

"Well, so is Dr. Gorgeous. And Mal, for that matter. Though easy on the eyes isn't always easy on the heart . . ." Maggie trailed off.

"So I hear," Sara said. She stopped to take in the view before her. They were standing about halfway up one of the empty stands, looking down on the field. The stadium arced around them, the stillness kind of eerie. "This is pretty cool." Not as cool as being up in the air, but somehow the emptiness gave the same feeling of space.

Maggie smiled. "I think so. You'd better be careful. Baseball kind of sneaks up on you when you least expect it."

Sara wondered if she was talking about baseball or the men involved in it. But she refused to take the bait. "I'll keep that in mind, too," she said. "But why don't you tell me about it anyway?"

By the time Sara got home, Dougal in tow and bouncing all over the place with delight at being back with Sara, she was beginning to feel the lack of sleep.

Maggie's tour of Deacon had been both comprehensive and informative. It had even included a tour of the tunnels in the depths of the stadium, where Maggie had introduced Sara to Malachi Coulter, who like his partners was startlingly attractive. In Mal it was more a tawny, rangy, slightly-too-long-hair-and-tattoos sort of way. He was unmistakably ex-military, though; his bearing and the way he scanned any space they entered gave that away. She'd ferried him to Manhattan and back later in the afternoon, and his ease and familiarity with the helo—not to mention the fact that he called it a helo—were further proof.

But she didn't ask him where or whom he'd served with. He didn't offer, which meant she'd judged right and he was the doesn't-want-to-talk-about-it type. Instead they'd talked a little more about the stadium and the security upgrades Mal was making. Fascinating, even if it was over Sara's head.

And now she was back home and waiting for Lucas to arrive. She fed Dougal then showered and changed into jeans and a deep raspberry V-neck sweater and her favorite black boots. It was, at least, more female than her uniform. She had no idea if Lucas would want to go out for dinner or something so anything dressier felt like overkill. There was very nice red lace underwear underneath, so that should distract him if she'd judged the outer layers wrongly.

Her stomach was rumbling by the time the intercom buzzed, which sent Dougal padding toward the door, with a woof of alert.

Damn. Dougal. She hadn't thought about Dougal when she'd agreed to have Lucas come over again. Or how Lucas might feel about a large dog who was going to be expressing his displeasure at Lucas's presence any second now.

Too late now. She ordered Dougal back onto his spot on the rug in front of the TV and pressed the intercom to let Lucas up.

The sound of his footsteps in the hall outside made Dougal bark and raise himself into a sit. Sara hushed him with a signal, sending him back into a downstay.

She was rigorous with his training and made sure her parents were, too. That way, while he still might bark his head off when they encountered men, he usually didn't do anything more if they told him not to.

Dougal made a grumbling growl, and Sara kept half an eye on him when she went to open the door.

Lucas had a bouquet of hot pink lilies in one hand and a pizza box in the other. "Hello," he said.

"Hi." Sara said, but she didn't step back to let him in. "Look, I forgot to mention my dog isn't a big fan of men."

Lucas's brows drew together. "Dog? Oh right, you mentioned him. Where was he last night?"

"With my parents. But he's here now. And he's going to start barking his fool head off once you step over the threshold. He won't do anything more than that, I won't let him, but I wanted to warn you."

"What kind of dog did you say he was again?" Lucas asked. To his credit, he didn't look overly concerned with what she'd just told him.

"He's a black Lab." From behind her she heard Dougal bark, and she turned to hush him again.

"Big guy, huh? I thought Labs were marshmallows."

"He is. Just not if you're tall and male. Don't ask me why, I've had him since he was a puppy, but at some point before I got him, a guy did him wrong. And he hasn't forgotten."

"Does he like any guys?"

"He's okay with my dad. Now."

"And how long did that take?"

"About six months until he didn't growl at him every time he saw him. Maybe a year until he would let Dad pat him for more than a second or two."

"Does he like pizza?" Lucas said.

"Yes. But bribes won't work. We've tried that."

"Oh well," Lucas said. "He's just going to have to get used to me, too."

She liked his optimism. Even if it was misplaced. "Come on in then." She stepped back and then turned to face Dougal. He was, as usual, watching the door intently, making little growling noises in the back of his throat.

Lucas moved into the apartment behind her. She braced herself for Dougal to go nuts.

Instead he gave a single short bark and then sat there, ears pricked, eyes on Lucas. His tail started to thump against the floor.

"Am I missing the savage-beast part?" Lucas said. "He doesn't look so scary to me."

"This isn't how he usually reacts," Sara said, staring at Dougal. No, this was how he acted with people he liked.

"Told you I was charming," Lucas said. He took a few steps closer to Sara. "Hey, buddy," he said to Dougal. Dougal tilted his head and panted before barking once. His tail still thumped the floor.

"Stay," Sara said warningly.

"Hold the pizza," Lucas said. He held out the box. Sara took it. Lucas walked halfway between her and Dougal. Dougal whined a little and looked at Sara.

"So far so good," Lucas said. He took another couple of steps, bringing him within arm's length of Dougal. He crouched down and held out the back of his hand. He was obviously used to dogs. "Hey there, Dougal," he repeated. "What's happening?"

Dougal, after a quick look at Sara, stretched his head forward and sniffed Lucas's hand. And then he whuffed happily and shoved his head under Lucas's palm, clearly angling for an ear rub.

"Yeah, this one's a killer," Lucas said as he obliged.

Sara still couldn't quite believe what she was seeing. Of all the men in the world that Dougal could choose not to hate, he was picking Lucas?

Why? It wasn't like Dougal could tell Lucas was gorgeous. That, Sara kept telling herself, was the reason she had let him back into her bed last night. "He's never done that with any strange man before. What are you, an orthopedic dog whisperer?"

Lucas twisted back to her, looking smug as he continued to pet Dougal. Dougal looked kind of smug, too. Smug and blissful. "He's no dummy, he can recognize a guardian angel when he sees one."

Chapter Fourteen

Sara still wasn't sure how she felt about Dougal adoring Lucas when she set the helo down at the Vero Beach stadium two days later. It was kind of ridiculous. Each night when Lucas arrived at her apartment, Dougal's wriggling, yipping welcome became even more ecstatic.

True, she did kind of feel like wriggling in ecstasy every time Lucas put his hands on her too, but she was trying to keep hold of some degree of sanity. She and Lucas were temporary. She knew that deep down.

Dougal was not going to be happy when Lucas finally bailed. Neither was Sara.

"Thanks, Sara." Maggie's voice came through the headset and Sara turned to smile at her. Maggie had taken her under her wing and, as a result, she now knew almost everyone who worked for the Saints who wasn't in Florida. She suspected she would know the rest of them by the end of this trip.

In between introductions, Maggie had found her
a job helping Shonda, Alex's PA, with various tasks.
In the spare moments when Sara wasn't doing that
or ferrying Alex, Mal, or Lucas between Staten Island and Manhattan, Maggie kept giving her the
potted history of the Saints with enough juicy gos-
sip interspersed with the facts and figures to make
it interesting.

She watched Lucas climb out of the helo and
then hold out a hand to help Maggie out. Maggie
grinned down at him, and Sara felt a wholly unreasonable twinge of envy. She wasn't going to be able
to touch Lucas for two days while they were here in
Florida. That thought already made her skin itch.
So it hardly seemed fair that Maggie got to.

Which was ridiculous. For one thing, Maggie was
madly in love with Alex—that was blindingly obvious to anyone who saw them together. And for another, Sara had had orgasms aplenty in the last few
days. She didn't have any excuse to be as horny as
she felt now watching Lucas walk away.

As he and Maggie headed toward the stadium
buildings, Sara looked back down at her instrument
panel, just in case Maggie turned around.

She didn't want to be caught staring at Lucas.
Maggie hadn't done any more outright probing
about Sara and Lucas, but Sara wasn't stupid. She
knew Maggie had her suspicions. Sara had caught
Maggie looking at Lucas when he spoke to Sara a
time or two. Which meant she had to keep her nose
clean.

Maybe she should find Ollie Shields and flirt with him shamelessly in front of Maggie or something.

Though that might backfire if Lucas thought she was serious.

She sighed as she settled back in her seat. She had to deliver the helo to the airfield where it belonged. Then she'd come back and worry about fooling Maggie Jameson when she had to.

Lucas heard the chopper's now familiar takeoff behind him but made sure he didn't look back to watch Sara fly away. Sara had warned him that Maggie had asked questions and, as much as he'd be happy to tell Maggie about Sara, he had to respect what Sara wanted. He wasn't going to keep them a secret forever but a little time for Sara to get comfortable with the situation was reasonable enough.

He hid a yawn as they walked toward the stadium entrance.

Beside him, Maggie turned her face up to the sun. "Sunshine! I'd forgotten how nice this is."

"Are you wearing sunblock?"

She laughed. "Yes, Dr. Gorgeous. I am enjoying my UV rays responsibly. I have no desire to fry. Just to be warm and not have to wear seven layers of clothing."

Lucas couldn't argue with that. The New York winter had been long and cold so far, and there was no sign of it letting up. It was almost March. There should at least be some hints by now that spring might happen eventually.

Of course, with his current workload, he wouldn't have much time to enjoy nice weather in New York even if there was any.

"So are we going to see this Sam Basara that Dan keeps telling me about?" Maggie said.

"That's the plan. Dan's going to give him a trial in the game today. See how he goes. He's sent a couple of them home already, so pressure's on."

"Thank God I don't actually play baseball," Maggie said. "I've never liked this part. I mean, it's fun to look at stats and try to work out who's undervalued and go with the scouts and study the guys playing. But it's harder when you get to the part where you have to crush their dreams."

"I don't think anyone aspires to crush dreams," Lucas said. "But we can't hire everyone."

Even if he wanted to. It had been hard when Dan had told him he'd already cut Walsh and the other two older pitchers who'd been after a contract. He agreed with the assessment on the older guys, they were about done, but Walsh had been a good strong candidate. Sadly for him, not as strong as his friends. Or the pitcher from the Preachers who was still hanging in there. But Walsh was going back to his college team and had a few more years to prove himself and get a shot.

Maggie was swarmed by the players sitting in the bleachers as soon as she walked out into the stands, so Lucas continued on alone to find Dan. He saw

Sam sitting alone in the stands, down near the fence line, and decided to make a detour.

"Hey, kid," he said. "How's it going?"

Sam looked up and pulled off the shades hiding his eyes. "Mr. Angelo," he said, sounding nervous. "Okay, I think."

"It's Dr. Angelo," Lucas said. "Or Lucas, outside hours. You're still here. That's better than okay."

Sam nodded. "I know. And I'm happy about it." He didn't sound all that happy. He sounded stressed. Working himself up in his head. Lucas knew about that particular monkey. Maybe Sam needed another trip in Sara's helo. For that matter, maybe Lucas needed another trip in Sara's helo. One where she took them somewhere secluded so he could put his hands on her. It had only been a few hours and he was already going nuts thinking about when he could be back in her bed.

And that was a line of thought that wasn't going to help him make a nervous kid less nervous. He tried to push Sara to the back of his mind. They needed pitchers, and this kid was the best of the bunch. So it was time to think about him.

"I heard about Walsh," Lucas said. "That's tough. But he'll be okay. He's talented, he'll find a home. Coach tells me he's thinking of giving you a start in today's game. So concentrate on that."

"I am," Sam said. His forehead wrinkled. "Coach said you were a pitcher. Played for U of T?"

"Yeah, I did," Lucas said.

"What happened? Did you blow it?"

Lucas shrugged. "No. Didn't end up getting a chance to take my shot. I got hurt. In an accident. Screwed up my shoulder, and it was never going to be stable enough for pro ball. So I became a doctor instead."

"Do you miss it?"

"Baseball?" He grinned. "Why do you think I bought a team? This game gets into your blood. But I don't have to tell you that. So you need to take care of that arm of yours, okay? No doing anything stupid." Like running into burning stadiums. Not that he could regret saving lives or that he'd do anything differently if he had to do it again. But he would do his best to make sure that this kid and anyone else on his team never had to make that choice.

"I will," Sam said. "I'm doing everything they tell me to."

"Good. And tell you what. If you do okay, I'll see if Sara can take you for another spin in the chopper. How about that?"

"That would be cool. Could Tico come, too?"

"As long as he doesn't do anything stupid," Lucas said. "Is he getting a chance this game?"

Sam shook his head. "Coach says next time."

"How'd he take that?"

"Okay," Sam said, but the words came a little too quickly.

Not so well, was what that translated as. Lucas made a note to check on Tico. There was something a bit wild about him, and he had the kind of attitude that suggested a chip on his shoulder about something. He reminded Lucas of Mal in some ways, and

Mal had always been the wildest of the three of them. He didn't want Tico losing his chance because he cracked and did something dumb under pressure.

"You'd better go join the others," Lucas said. "You can meet Ms. Jameson."

"Okay, sir. Are you coming to the game?"

"Wouldn't miss it."

For this to work, Lucas decided much later that night when he was finally alone in his hotel room, the cold water in his shower needed to be a lot colder. At this stage, maybe a walk-in freezer would be required. The cool water might have temporarily killed the inconvenient hard-on but it couldn't kill the thoughts of Sara that plagued him. Even through the postgame celebration dinner—they'd actually won—he'd been distracted by her.

All that softness and smooth skin and laughter. Lying in her bed just a few doors down the corridor.

But she might as well have been on Mars. They'd agreed no sex in Orlando, too risky.

He rested his forehead on the slick cool tile. He really didn't like hiding things from Alex and Mal. But Sara wasn't ready. So he had to wait. Though he was pretty sure that Maggie, as Sara had said, had some fairly serious suspicions.

All the more reason why trying to sneak down the hall was lunacy.

He turned the water pressure on harder but that didn't help.

He wanted her. Wanted sex and the smell of her

on his skin and the sound of her voice in his ear as she told him what she wanted.

Damn.

He killed the water with a savage twist of the faucet and stepped out of the shower. Even as he toweled off, his hard-on rose again.

Maybe he should just take care of things. Then he might have some chance of getting to sleep at some point during the night.

He wrapped the towel around his waist and stalked out of the bathroom over toward the bed, flipping on the lamp as the sole source of illumination in the room.

Just as he was about to lie down, his cell buzzed to life on the nightstand.

He picked it up, ready to snarl at whoever was calling him at this hour of the night, but the caller ID read SARA and irritation turned to anticipation in a second. He hit the ANSWER button so hard it was surprising the screen didn't crack. "Hello?"

"Oh good, you're awake," she said.

Her voice was soft and a little husky over the phone. He felt his cock go harder still.

"Having trouble sleeping?" he asked.

"It's a very big bed," she said. "And it's half empty."

"Don't blame me for that," he said. "You're the one who wants to keep this a secret."

"I know." She sighed, and there was a world of frustration in that sound. "I do. But . . ."

"But this is insane and you want me to come right over?"

"No. I want you to stay there and come."

The breath left his chest in a rush and the room spun for a second as most of the blood left his head equally fast. "Phone sex? Really?"

"You got a better idea?"

Well, yes, he did, but it wasn't one that Sara would go for. "Not right now."

"Good. So, what are you wearing, big boy?"

He looked down at the towel, which was currently tented with the force of his hard-on. "A towel."

She laughed, throaty and delicious. "Seriously? Or are you just saying that?"

"Scout's honor," he said. "I just got out of the shower when you rang."

"A cold shower?"

"Definitely."

"Oh good. Me, too."

"You're wearing a towel?" He flopped back on the bed, put his arm over his eyes for a moment while he pictured it. Sara with wet hair curling around her shoulders. Smelling like soap and warm woman. Ker-riiiisst.

"Well, I was, but then I took it off so I could put some lotion on."

Warm, slippery woman. "You're trying to kill me, aren't you?"

"Is it working?"

He focused on the aching heat in his groin. "Definitely."

"So maybe you should take that towel off."

He couldn't argue with that. He tossed the towel across the room. Then moved up the bed so he could lie against the pillows. "One towel gone."

"Mmmm," she said. "I like that image."

"You know, we both have smartphones, you don't have to imagine."

"Ah, but imagination is sexy, Dr. Angelo. Don't you know the research that says the brain is the biggest erogenous zone? Like right now. Right now I'm imagining you lying there, naked. Hard."

His mouth went dry. "You are?"

"And I'm imagining what I'd do if I was there with you."

"Are you going to tell me what that is?"

She sucked in a breath. Then he heard a rustle, like maybe she was settling back into the pillows, too. "Does that mean you're up for phone sex after all?"

"I am one hundred percent in favor," he said fervently and lay back to see where Sara's imagination might take him.

Sara smiled as she watched the cab pull up outside her apartment two weeks later. Sneaking around seemed to be working pretty damned well. Even if she did say so herself.

Several nights a week, Lucas arrived on her doorstep, they had incredible sex, and then he left before daylight. Okay, so that part wasn't quite so good, but she could live with the incredible-sex part.

Even better, they continued to rack up the frequent flier miles. So far they'd flown to Florida and back six times in that same two weeks and she'd delivered him to and from JFK each time.

So she was getting flight time. Not quite as much as she would have with Charles Air, but more than she would with no helo. Air time and hot sex. What more could a girl ask for?

Beside her Dougal woofed and bounded toward the door, delighted, as usual, that his new idol had arrived.

Which could maybe be attributed to the fact that Lucas was smart enough to always arrive with jerky or dog biscuits or, once, a truly gross pig's ear to keep Dougal occupied while they did other things.

Just as Dougal began to bark with more enthusiasm, the buzzer sounded and Sara darted over to let Lucas in. She made Dougal sit, which he did with one of his protesting little whining grumbles that sounded as if they should be coming from something the size of a Pekingese, not a Lab.

And then she opened the door and Lucas stepped through. Beside her, Dougal started whuffing with happiness.

She was about to throw her arms around Lucas and kiss him hello when she realized he was carrying two grocery bags.

"What's this?"

"I thought I'd make dinner," he said. "We've been eating in hotels and restaurants and airports for two weeks. I want real food."

"You cook?"

"I do," he said gravely.

She shook her head. "You really are trying for the too-good-to-be-true award, aren't you, Dr. Angelo?"

"Am I in the running yet?"

She took one of the grocery bags and carried it through to the tiny kitchen. She cooked well enough to ensure she didn't starve or blow all her money on takeout, but a well-appointed kitchen hadn't been high on her list of priorities when she'd been hunting for an apartment here on the island and she hadn't really put the kitchen through its paces yet.

It was easier sometimes to just go to her parents' and eat there while Dougal ran around the backyard in the dark. She put the bag down at the counter. "It's not the greatest kitchen in the world."

"Does the stove work?"

"Yes." She'd made scrambled eggs, grilled cheese, and stir-fries, so she could at least vouch for the burners being in working order.

Lucas put his bag next to the one she'd taken and then leaned down to kiss her. "Then we're in business."

He started to draw back but she pulled him closer. It was nearly six hours since she'd delivered him to Deacon Field after their latest trip to Florida. Two nights since she'd had him in her bed. She wanted a taste of him more than she wanted dinner. He seemed to feel the same way. His hands came down to grip her butt and pull her closer as their mouths met and she pressed into him, glorying in the feeling.

Dougal's patience finally broke and he got to his feet and shoved his nose between them.

"Ow, quit it, dopey dog," Lucas said, breaking off. He grinned down at Dougal, and bent to rub the dog's ears. Which led to the two of them wrestling around the apartment for a minute or two, Lucas looking just as delighted as Dougal. Damn it. It was hard to resist a man who loved her dog.

"Did you have a dog when you were a kid?" she asked when he came back to her and Dougal followed to come and lean against her legs.

"No," Lucas said. "My mother isn't a fan of dogs."

Every time he mentioned his family, his eyes went flat. Time to change the subject.

"So, dinner?" she said.

Lucas's face eased. He nodded and turned toward the grocery bags, Dougal bouncing around his legs.

"Bed," she said to Dougal, who looked dejected but trotted immediately to the ratty dog bed that lived in the corner of the small living room, circling a few times before dropping down with a whuff. Sara laughed but didn't relent. There wasn't enough room in the tiny kitchen for two adults and Dougal. Not if any of them wanted to move.

Lucas kept unpacking the bags. With each package or can or bag that hit the counter, Dougal whined.

"I think you have a volunteer for assistant chef," Sara said.

Lucas grinned and opened her fridge. "Your dog thinks I'm awesome."

"He's a dog, I wouldn't rate his opinion too highly." Though she did, to an extent. She'd give anything to know what made Dougal like Lucas so much.

Lucas folded his arms, grin widening. "You're just jealous."

She didn't dignify that with a response. "You're

early," Sara said. It was Saturday and he'd told her he'd probably be at Deacon until eight-ish. It was barely six now.

"Mal had something to do back in the city," he said. "So Alex let us out early. In fact, because I'm early, I thought maybe we could do something before we ate."

"Oh yes?" She grinned at him. "What exactly did you have in mind?"

He opened his mouth to answer but then her phone started to ring. Landline, not cell. Which meant it was probably her mom. "Hold that thought," she said and looked around to figure out where she'd left the phone.

She spotted it on the kitchen table and scooped it up. Sure enough, it was her mom.

"Sara, honey," Liza said. "I wasn't sure you were home tonight."

Sara's stomach tightened at the too-bright tone in her voice. She sounded . . . brittle. Sara knew that voice. It meant her dad was having a bad day. "Hey, Mom. Yup, I'm home. Is something up?"

"I was just wondering if you wanted to come over for dinner. I made lasagna."

Lasagna. Her dad's favorite food. Which meant that her mom was definitely trying to either get him to eat or coax him out of one of his down days. She looked over at Lucas, who raised his eyebrows in question. "I'm not . . ." She hesitated.

"Oh, did you have plans?" The tension in her voice didn't do anything to ease Sara's stomach. Damn it. Something was going on and she couldn't just abandon her mom and let her deal with it on her own.

"Not really," she said.

"That's okay, I—" Liza continued in a rush.

"No, Mom, it's fine. I'll come. Only, do you mind if I bring a . . . friend?" She tilted her head at Lucas, and he just nodded. Apparently a surprise meeting with his secret lover's parents wasn't enough to throw Dr. Gorgeous. Which made sense, given he wasn't the one who wanted to keep them a secret.

"A friend? Honey, you didn't tell me you were seeing someone. That's wonderful. Of course he can come. It'll be ready in about an hour. Bring Dougal, too. And . . . what is your friend's name?"

Sara bit back the groan that rose in her throat. "Lucas. His name is Lucas, Mom." Maybe it wouldn't be so bad. After all, her parents didn't exactly run in the same circles as Alex and Mal, and they didn't have anything to do with the Saints. Even if they knew about her and Lucas, keeping it quiet at work should still be doable.

"I always liked that name," Liza said. "So we'll see you and Lucas around seven?"

She hoped. "Sure, Mom, see you then. Love you." She waited until her mom hung up and then turned back to Lucas.

"So, I guess you heard that."

"I got the gist."

"And you don't mind?"

"Meeting your parents. No, of course not. I'll cook you dinner tomorrow night."

"My mom's making lasagna. It's pretty good." She

smiled at him. "Though maybe not as good as your mom's."

"Trust me, I've never had lasagna that my mom made from scratch."

"You haven't?"

"My mom leaves the cooking to the housekeeper," Lucas said.

Right. She'd forgotten how he'd grown up for a moment. "Well, in that case, you're going to love it." She stopped. "You know, it's okay if you don't want to come."

Chapter Fifteen

"Why would I not want to eat your mom's lasagna?" Lucas asked, wondering why she looked worried.

Sara's face didn't relax even though she shot him something he thought was supposed to be a smile.

"Is there something wrong?"

She shrugged, mouth twisting. "I'm not sure. Mom sounded . . . tense. I think maybe Dad's having a bad day."

"His leg?"

"Yes. I think it hurts him more than he lets on. And he doesn't seem to be progressing like he did at first."

"Sometimes things are never quite the same," Lucas said. "Surgery isn't perfect. Sometimes there's just too much damage."

"Or maybe his doctors are screwing up," Sara said. She hesitated. "I know I don't have the right to ask you this, but do you think you could talk to him? He might listen to you, you're a surgeon."

A surgeon who was sleeping with his daughter. If Sean Charles was anything like the fathers of most of the women he'd dated, then taking Lucas's advice about medical issues on first meeting wasn't necessarily likely to happen. "Let's see what happens."

Sara's face fell. He walked over and pulled her close. "I didn't mean I won't talk to him, just that tonight might not be the perfect time. I mean, they didn't even know I existed until a few minutes ago, did they?"

"No." Her voice was somewhat muffled against his chest. "You're right. I'm just worried about him. It'll kill him if he never flies again. He needs two good legs to fly."

"It'll be okay," he said. He wanted to make it okay. Wanted to chase that fear out of her voice. And the ferocity of that emotion startled him. He thought he'd been keeping himself back a little. Trying to play it smart, given that she didn't seem to be sure about him.

But apparently she'd wriggled her way into his heart deeper than he thought.

And breathing in the smell of her hair as she held on to him, he couldn't bring himself to feel too upset about that.

Sara was worth getting attached to. He admired her determination to work hard and solve her own problems. He admired her guts—she'd flown in war zones, for Christ's sake—but the fact that she was strong didn't mean she couldn't use a hand now and then. He could make things easier for her.

Don't bring home strays, Lucas. He could almost

hear his mother's precise tone in his head. His parents had never understood his impulses to try to save baby birds and feed the feral cats that he'd found hiding out under one of the garden sheds any more than they'd understood his love of baseball.

Odd when his mother was so big on charity work. Though Lucas had come to think, perhaps unfairly, that his mother did charity work because it was expected and because, in the world of the Angelos, the men ran the business and the women ran the home and made sure some of the money went to good causes so that they could all sleep easier at night. It was stupid and antiquated and yet another reason why he'd run like hell into the arms of first baseball and then medicine when he'd gotten the chance to get out.

Maybe after all, it was the fact that his mom didn't really like anything that took his attention away from the things she thought were important. Which didn't include saving strays.

All the more reason to help Sara out. Because she wasn't a stray. She was his. She deserved a life that wasn't a struggle all the time.

As Sara took the plate from in front of Lucas and he smiled at her, her father pushed his chair back and rose from the table.

Lucas didn't miss the wince that crossed his face or the unevenness of his gait as he carried the salad bowl into the kitchen, following his wife.

Beside Lucas, Sara stilled as her eyes tracked her dad's progress.

"How recently has your dad seen his surgeon?" Lucas asked, keeping his voice soft so Sean and Liza wouldn't hear.

"It's been months," Sara said. "He's been doing physical therapy mostly."

"And he's not improving?"

He reached for the lasagna dish and saw Sara bite her lip.

"He was at first but he's been like this for a while now. Though today seems like it's a bad one."

Lucas couldn't argue with that diagnosis. Sean Charles was too thin for a man of his height, and there were light-gray patches in his brown hair that Lucas suspected were new. The dark circles under his eyes meant he wasn't sleeping well. He hadn't eaten much of his wife's delicious lasagna but he had downed two beers. Plus another during the somewhat awkward small talk they'd all exchanged before dinner. The man was obviously in pain.

Something wasn't right. Discomfort was to be expected from a major injury—hell, even his shoulder ached now and then when he overdid it, and that was from nearly twenty years ago—but the type of pain that required self-medicating with three beers before eight p.m. was something else. "He should go back and see his ortho guy."

"I've tried to get him to," Sara said. "But he's worried about the money."

"Who was his surgeon?"

"Garth Nixon. Do you know him?"

Lucas nodded. He'd met the guy a couple of times. Nixon was competent but hardly brilliant. He didn't work at Lucas's level. And from what Lucas had seen of Sean Charles, he hadn't brought his A game to this particular case. "He's good," he said. But just good. And in Sean Charles's case, maybe just not good enough.

"But you're better?" Sara said softly. "Do you think you could talk to Dad, convince him to get it looked at again?"

He didn't think Sean was ready to take any advice from him. The looks he'd been getting from the older man over dinner had confirmed his earlier suspicions. Sara's dad wasn't impressed with the hotshot doctor who was screwing his little girl.

Lucas couldn't blame him for that. If he ever had a daughter, he'd probably want to wring the neck of any male who tried to put a hand on her. But Sara was looking at him with hope in those gorgeous blue eyes. So he had to try.

"I'll try," he said. "But if he's as stubborn as his daughter, then I'm not making any promises."

"Just try," she said. She took the lasagna dish from him and balanced it on top of the stack of plates. "I'll send him back out here."

Sure enough, a minute or so after she disappeared into the kitchen, Sean reemerged, looking grumpy. A blue checked dish towel was flung over his shoulder. "Sara has suddenly expressed an irresistible urge to dry the dishes. I expect that means she wants us to do some bonding or something." He looked Lucas up and down. "Come into the den, we can have another beer."

"I wouldn't say no," Lucas said. He'd only had one. So another wouldn't hurt. Manly and responsible, that was the impression he needed to give. So he would have one more beer and then switch to coffee.

Sean led the way, still limping, and Lucas studied him from behind, walking slowly to accommodate the older man's halting walk. The den was small but Sean had managed to squeeze in two well-stuffed brown leather recliners that looked well used along with a reasonable-sized flat-screen TV. The walls were lined with photos of helicopters and grinning men who were obviously former generations of Charleses.

There were several of Sara, too, both alone and with a young guy who looked like a more rugged version of her.

He walked over and took a closer look.

"That's my son, James," Sean said with another wince as he lowered himself into the left-hand recliner.

Lucas didn't think the wince was entirely due to his knee. "Sara hasn't mentioned a brother."

"He died."

Ah. "I'm very sorry to hear that, sir," he said. "That's a hard thing."

Sean nodded, hand rubbing at his thigh. "He was a good kid." His jaw clenched.

Time to talk about something else. It wasn't going to win him any brownie points to poke at the man's emotional wounds. No, he should try to stick to the ones he might actually be able to do something about.

"Sara told me about your crash," he said as he took a seat in the other recliner. "Does your leg still bother you?"

"Sometimes," Sean said. "My physical therapist said it will get better."

"Do you mind if I ask what the injury was?"

Sean's eyes went narrow. "Sara ask you to talk to me about this?"

"No, sir," Lucas lied blandly. "Call it professional interest."

"Right, you're a bone doctor, aren't you? Well, the technical term was something like compound fracture of the tibia and a shattered patella."

"That's an impressive way to screw up your leg," Lucas said.

"You try being thrown from a helicopter and see how well you do," Sean said.

"I'd rather not, if you don't mind. That's a nasty injury. I'm guessing there's quite a bit of hardware in there."

"Enough to annoy the metal detectors at airports, that's for sure," Sean said.

"And you still get pain?"

Sean grimaced and made a dismissive gesture. "There's a fridge in that cabinet beneath the TV. That's where the beer is."

Lucas rose and found two beers and a bottle opener. He passed one to Sean and sat back down. Sean took a swallow or two then sighed gratefully.

"You were going to tell me about the pain?" Lucas prompted.

"Was I?" He shook his head. "I'm guessing if I don't tell you, Sara's just going to keep sending you at me until I give in? She's like a dog with a bone, that one. Doesn't give up easily. Yes, my damned leg hurts." He drank more beer.

Lucas sipped his more slowly. "Patellas can be difficult when it's a bad fracture. Is it your thigh that hurts?"

"Thigh, knee, lower leg. My damned left hip."

"That's from the limping," Lucas said.

"So my physical therapist tells me." Sean swallowed more beer.

Lucas eyed the level in the bottle. It was going down fast. Beer might be better than narcotics but it would do almost as much damage in the end. Sara didn't need a dad who was drinking too much. Not too mention Sean was likely to fall and just screw his knee up even more badly if he spent his days half drunk.

"Do you mind if I take a look?" Lucas said.

Sean eyed him. "Son, you might have charmed my daughter out of her pants but I'm not there yet."

Lucas almost choked on his beer.

Sean laughed. "So you are sleeping with Sara."

"I think that's between Sara and me, sir," Lucas said.

The smile vanished from the older man's face.

"She's my daughter. I don't want to see her hurt."
Sean swigged the beer again.

"I don't intend to hurt her," Lucas said.

"The road to hell is paved with good intentions."

"So I hear. That doesn't change mine."

"Why are you even messing around with someone like Sara?"

"What does that mean?"

"I know who you are," Sean said. "Sara's not much on baseball and, honestly, neither am I, but with this goddamned leg there's not much I can do every day and I had plenty of time to read all about you and your pals when you bought the Saints."

"Don't believe everything you read in the papers."

"I don't. But I doubt they got the part about your family wrong, did they? You come from money, don't you? The big old kind of money?"

"My family has money, yes." Lucas said. "But I don't see what that has to do with me and Sara."

Sean's eyes—a steelier version of his daughter's—narrowed. "You said Sara didn't tell you about Jamie? About the way he died?"

"No, sir." Lucas braced himself. He got the feeling he wasn't going to like this part of the conversation.

"Jamie was a pilot, too," Sean said. "Damned good one. Though Sara could probably outfly him now. She learned some tricks in the army. Sneaky stuff."

"She's an excellent pilot," Lucas said. "That's why I hired her."

"Yes. Well. So was my son. And he used to work

for me as well. Doing the tourist runs over Manhattan. Flying rich types around."

"Isn't that what charter pilots do?"

"Yes it is. But what they shouldn't do is fall in love with their clients. Or in lust. Whichever." Sean waved a hand in the air. "Jamie got involved with a girl whose dad used to charter us. He hid it from me, knew I didn't agree with mixing business with pleasure. I don't know whether Sara knew."

"How old was he?"

"Twenty-two."

"That's pretty young," Lucas said. "Everyone does dumb things when they're young."

"I know. I did my share of idiotic crap when I was his age. But I survived it. Jamie didn't."

The bleakness in his voice made Lucas wince. He had his ups and downs with his family, but he definitely didn't want to think about losing any of them. "Do you mind if I ask what happened?"

"He was out with this girl—Callie, her name was—and they were drinking. She ran her fool Porsche convertible off the road. And the car flipped. She was thrown free. Jamie wasn't. His neck broke."

"He died."

"Not straightaway. There was someone driving right behind them. They called the paramedics and both of them made it to hospital. She broke some bones, too, but nothing serious. Jamie—" Sean broke off, lips pressed together. Then he drained the rest of his beer. "Jamie never woke up. Traumatic brain injury, they call it. Along with the neck. We turned off the life support after a few weeks."

"And the girl?"

"She went home after a week or so. As far as I know, she was fine."

"Did she get charged with anything?"

"Reckless driving. But her family lawyered up and she got off with community service. Seeing as she was so young and all. No priors, apparently."

"That's horrible," Lucas said. "An injustice."

"Well, that's how it goes, isn't it? If you can afford the lawyers and can put some pressure on the DA, you're more likely to get off."

"That doesn't make it right." Lucas felt his hand tighten around the beer bottle. This was the sort of crap he'd wanted to get away from by stepping away from his family. The we're-better-than-them mentality that he'd come across too many times. "Did you get compensation?"

"We talked to an attorney but it was going to cost a fortune to sue them. I couldn't afford it. The medical bills were bad enough. The health insurance I could afford for Charles Air was pretty crappy. They didn't cover much. Not enough for three weeks on life support in intensive care, anyway. It took me a few years to pay the bills. Which is why we don't have many helos."

And why his daughter didn't trust people with money. People like him.

Fuck.

"So you can see why I'm not thrilled to find Sara sneaking around with a guy like you," Sean said.

"What makes you think we're sneaking around?" Lucas asked.

Sean snorted. "I see you in the papers all the time, son. You and your two friends. Your buddy Winters has the Jameson gal with him more often than not lately. But you and the other one. I haven't seen either of you with any women. So I figure you're sneaking around. Otherwise you'd be showing Sara off."

"I'd be more than happy to show her off," Lucas said. He might not be able to do much about being wealthy, but he wasn't going to take the rap for not going public with their relationship. "But Sara is the one who doesn't want to. Not yet. So I'm respecting her wishes."

"Is that so?"

"Yes, sir, it is. Like you said, once she makes up her mind about something, it's difficult to change it. But I'm trying. I'm sure it doesn't mean a lot to you, but I care about Sara. I'm not looking to hurt her."

"If you weren't looking to hurt her, you'd walk away."

"Why? Because she and I have different backgrounds? I'm more interested in the things we share."

"And what are those? Other than sex?" Sean asked. "She's not exactly a baseball fan, my daughter. No quicker way to get her to leave the room than to turn on a game. So, what? Are you a helicopter fan?"

"I spend a lot of time in the air," Lucas said. "But that's not what I like about Sara. I like who she is. She makes me laugh. She's smart and talented and beautiful. Why wouldn't I like her?"

"I'm not saying you shouldn't like her, just that you should think about how this is going to end.

You're her boss. You're wealthy. That's not a story that often ends well for the woman involved."

"Well, you'll just have to take my word for it that I'm not going to hurt her," Lucas said. "I don't mean to be rude but you don't know me, Mr. Charles, so don't lump me in with whatever it is you think guys like me do."

Sean's mouth curled upward briefly. "Well, you stand up for yourself, so that's a start. And hell knows, Sara isn't going to listen to me about this, so it's going to be her mess to deal with."

"Like I said, I'm trying to make sure there is no mess. I want her to be happy." Lucas swallowed the last of his beer, which was growing distinctly warm. "And speaking of making her happy, I'd be grateful if you'd let me take a look at your leg. Not here. But I'll get my office to call and set up an appointment."

"You think it can be fixed properly?"

"I can't promise that," Lucas said. "Not without seeing what's actually going on with it. Maybe not even then. But I can promise you that I'll do whatever I can to get it as good as it can be for you."

"No bullshit. I like that." Sean saluted him with his empty bottle. "All right, son, you've got yourself a deal. I'll let you poke and prod at me so Sara gets off your case. Now how about you get me another beer and we watch some damned baseball?"

Chapter Sixteen

"Don't you think you've left them alone long enough?" Liza said as Sara picked up the last plate from the dish rack.

Sara almost dropped the plate. "What do you mean?"

"Honey, I might be old but I'm not stupid. You sent Lucas in there to check out your dad's leg, didn't you?"

"You're not old," Sara said.

"Flattery won't get you out of the fact you're scheming. You know your dad doesn't like to be managed."

Sara flapped the dish towel at her mom. "I don't care. His leg is hurting him and it's stressing you out. And he's drinking too much. Lucas is one of the best orthopedic surgeons in New York. Probably in the country."

"He's pretty handsome, too," Liza said.

"I'd noticed," Sara said drily. "But I don't think that makes him a better doctor."

"Can't hurt with his female patients."

"Not going to help with Dad, though," Sara said.

Liza sighed as she stripped off her rubber gloves. "No, your father is stubborn. And not inclined to like the men you sleep with."

Sara froze. "Who says we're sleeping together?"

"Honey, if you're not sleeping with that man, then I'm sending you to the doctor to get your hormones checked out." Liza winked and fanned herself. "Those eyes with that hair. You sure he's not Irish?"

"Pretty sure that Angelo is an Italian name, Mom," Sara said, trying to ignore the fact that her mom thought Lucas was hot.

"Well, you know what they say about Italian men."

Sara put her hands over her ears. "La la la, not listening."

"Your generation didn't invent sex," Liza said. "And I might be old and married but I'm definitely not blind."

"Mom, can we change the subject, please? Yes, Lucas is hot. Yes, I'm sleeping with him, but no, I'd rather not discuss that with you. And I definitely don't want to talk about it with Dad. Lucas is a good guy, not just some walking, talking piece of man flesh."

"Well, that's good to know," Lucas's voice said from behind her.

Floor, swallow her up. Nope, didn't seem like that

was going to happen. She turned around, well aware that her cheeks were flaming.

Liza started laughing. "You should see your face, honey. You've got it bad."

"Mom!"

Lucas leaned against the door frame, a broad smile on his face. "No, you should listen to your mom. She's very wise."

Liza beamed at him. "I can see why she likes you," she said.

Lucas straightened. "I like her, too, Mrs. Charles."

"Is there something I can get for you?" Liza said.

"I thought maybe some chips or something? We're watching the game."

Something to soak up some of the beer, Sara thought. At least on her dad's part. Lucas had eaten two helpings of lasagna and salad and garlic bread, so he couldn't possibly be hungry. But her dad hadn't eaten much at all.

"I'll get it, Mom," she said. "Why don't you go pick out a movie or something? If these two are doing male baseball bonding, I'm guessing we'll be here awhile."

"I'll take Dougal out first," Liza said. "He's practically drowned himself in drool all through dinner. I'll give him a couple of biscuits."

"You spoil him," Sara said.

"That because he's the best dog," Liza said. She bent over and patted her leg. Dougal pricked his ears from his spot in the dog bed in the kitchen. "C'mon, handsome," Liza said. "Who wants a biscuit?"

She walked out of the kitchen with Dougal on her heels, eyes firmly fixed on the dog biscuits in her hand.

"I like your mom," Lucas said.

"I do, too," Sara said. She opened the pantry trying to see what suitably manly carbs might be lurking within. Corn chips, check. Salsa, check. Some of the disgusting beef jerky things her dad liked. And a bag of pretzels. That should do the trick.

"I'm not so sure your dad likes me, though," Lucas said.

"If he's watching sports with you then he's decided you're not too terrible." Sara found bowls and started opening packets. "Did you talk to him?"

"Yes. He's going to make an appointment to come see me."

"He won't—"

Lucas held up a hand. "By which I mean I'm going to leave all my details with your mom and get her to make the appointment. And if she doesn't do it first thing Monday then one of the assistants at my office will call her. I know guys make terrible patients. I've been doing this awhile."

She suddenly felt a couple of inches taller, like something had been weighing her down and had suddenly tumbled free. Lucas was going to see her dad. He'd figure out what was wrong and then he'd fix it and everything would be back on track. She beamed at him over the salsa. "You are so getting lucky later on, Angelo."

* * *

Sunday morning brought with it a few pale rays of sunshine, the first faint hint that spring might be coming at some point. Sara stared out the window, contemplating how to fill up her day. Lucas had headed back to Manhattan to check in on patients and repack his bags. They were flying back to Orlando in the early evening, which meant Sara had to go and collect the helo and get organized, too—but there was plenty of time for that. She'd done her laundry and cleaned the tiny apartment yesterday when she'd been waiting for Lucas.

She looked at Dougal. Maybe she'd take him out. The weather had been too awful for taking him on long walks lately; besides which, she'd been spending too much time away from him. He liked staying with her folks but she knew he was a handful for her mom to walk on her own. He behaved for her dad and didn't try to warn off all the men he encountered, but her dad's leg didn't let him take a Lab for several-mile walks right now.

So a hike with Dougal it was.

It was a plan. Quality dog bonding time then a stroll past her favorite bakery for a doughnut or something before she came back to pack. As good a way to spend a Sunday as any if she couldn't spend it with Lucas.

But as she opened her closet to find her coat, her cell started to ring. The generic ringtone rather than one she'd assigned to anybody.

She picked it up but didn't recognize the number. "Sara Charles."

"Hey, Sara, it's Maggie. Maggie Jameson."

"Maggie? Hi. Did you need the helo?" She couldn't think of another reason why Maggie would be calling her on a Sunday—and there was that pesky clause in her contract with the Saints that said she was essentially on call twenty-four seven.

Maggie laughed. "No. To be honest, I was hoping you'd be home. I'm at Deacon and Alex had to go back to Manhattan and I've had all the paperwork I can stand for one week. I thought you might want to come over and hang out. I was going to go hit some balls in the batting cages. I can teach you how to swing a bat. Give you some extra baseball cred points."

"I have zero baseball cred points," Sara said. "And terrible hand-eye coordination."

"Rubbish. You fly a helicopter. You've got to have good reflexes. You just need practice. And this way, you'll be able to play when we have a staff game."

"Do I have to?" It popped out before she could stop herself.

Maggie laughed again. "No. But give it a shot. Maybe you'll like it. C'mon, Sara. My dad's away and there's nobody here for me to play with. You could bring your dog. It's actually a decent day and he can run around."

"Are dogs allowed?"

"Not normally and definitely not in the stadium," Maggie said. "But the batting cages are in the training complex. You've seen it. There's not much there that can be ruined by a dog peeing on it."

Hanging out with Maggie did sound like more fun than walking alone. And with the team in

Florida, there weren't likely to be many men for Dougal to object to. It was hard to find new places for him to explore that met that criterion.

"Okay," she said. "I'll be there in about twenty minutes. But I'm not lying about the hand-eye co-ordination thing."

"I'll make sure I find you a helmet," Maggie said. "And if you're really bad then we'll try pitching. Failing that, I have some of Shonda's cookies and plenty of soda and stuff in my office. We can eat sugar and veg out before the guys get back and raid my stash."

Cookies—particularly Shonda's, which were so good they were probably illegal—sounded better than trying to hit a baseball. But Sara wasn't going to give up without even trying.

If she was still as terrible as she remembered being in school then she would have proved it to Maggie in private rather than humiliating herself in public at a staff game. Plus she could get Maggie to vouch for her complete lack of sporting ability and get her out of having to play. "Twenty min-utes," she repeated and hung up.

As Sara followed Maggie toward the row of bat-ting cages, juggling a bat and a glove in one hand and Dougal's leash in the other, she started to have second thoughts about the sanity of this particular idea.

Maggie was carrying a bat and a glove, not to mention two helmets, a large tote bag, and a bucket

of balls—which should have required an extra hand
or two but she obviously had the knack of toting
baseball gear around. Despite all of that she managed to gesture toward the cages as they approached.
There hadn't been snow for a few days now, and the
grass surrounding them actually looked green in the
weak sun.

"Good, yes?" Maggie said.

Dougal certainly agreed with her. He strained at
the end of his leash, sniffing rapturously in the direction of the grass. Though maybe it was the faint
smell of hot dogs and spilled beer that had him so
excited.

It was an odd combination but one that she was
getting used to the more time she spent at Deacon.
Combined with the cool air, it was strangely pleasant.

When they reached the cages, Maggie piled everything on a row of painted wooden benches placed
off to one side. Hands free, she bent down to pet
Dougal and he rolled over to let her rub his belly,
panting happily. Maggie bent closer. "Who's a good
dog? Dougal? Are you a good dog?"

As if in reply, Dougal bounced to his feet and
swiped her face enthusiastically with his bright pink
tongue.

Sara tightened her grip on the leash, but Maggie
seemed to have a sense of humor about doggy kisses.
She just grinned, wiped her cheek with her sleeve,
and then patted Dougal again.

"Do you want to let him off his leash? There're
no gaps in the fence around the cages," Maggie said.

Sara looked down at Dougal, who was practically vibrating with excitement. "You're sure it's okay?"

"Sure." Maggie paused. "He's not going to dig, is he?"

"No," Sara laughed. "He's never been a digger." Dougal sniffed politely at her mom's flower beds but he hadn't actually dug anything up since he'd been a puppy. Even then the worst damage he'd ever managed was demolishing a pot of pansies one afternoon when they'd left him home alone for what he'd apparently decided was far too long. "He might pee on a few things."

"Well, like I said, that's not going to hurt anything." Maggie turned back to the stuff she'd left piled on the benches.

"Are any of the grounds staff around?" Sara asked, adding her stuff to the pile.

"No," Maggie said. "A couple of security guys are here but I already told them I was coming to the cages, so it's unlikely they'll come by. Why?"

Sara nodded at Dougal. "He's not a fan of strange men. He won't bite anyone"—at least, he hadn't so far—"but if there are going to be guys around, it might be better to keep him leashed."

"It will be okay," Maggie said. "I'll call the guys, tell them not to come over here. Let him go."

"Are you sure?" Sara asked.

Maggie nodded. "It's not fair to bring him out here and not let him run around some. Why doesn't he like guys?" she asked as Sara bent and unclipped Dougal's leash.

"That's kind of a mystery. I got him as a puppy

and no guy's ever hurt him that I know of. Took him forever to warm up to my dad."

Dougal bounded off, running in widening circles for a minute before he stopped and starting sniffing at things instead.

"What about boyfriends? Doesn't that make it kind of tricky?"

"The last couple of guys I dated were when I was in the army," Sara said. "He never met them. And there hasn't been much time for dating since I was discharged. I've been busy with Charles Air."

"Right," Maggie said. "Your dad."

Sara hoped she'd cut off that particular line of questioning. "So, how about we get this over with?" She waved a hand at the baseball cages.

Maggie laughed. "Gee, you sound so enthusiastic. Don't worry, it'll be fun." She handed Sara a bat. "Have you ever actually played baseball?"

Sara studied the bat. It looked well used, the Saints logo painted across its widest part faded and chipped in places. "I think maybe softball a couple of times in grade school."

"Well, same general principle." Maggie picked up the other bat. "Hold it like this." She demonstrated the grip, curling her fingers around the bat like it was part of her.

"Let me guess, you used to play," Sara said.

"Yeah, I did in school. I was never a superstar. But it was fun. And these days, well, knocking a few balls around can be kind of therapeutic."

"I prefer chocolate," Sara said. "Or a good martini."

"Oh, I do those, too." Maggie bent forward and examined Sara's grip on the bat. "That's close enough. Now, headgear." She picked up a helmet and passed it to Sara.

Sara leaned the bat against the edge of the cage and put the helmet on, turning to check on Dougal. He was sniffing happily around the enclosed grass.

"Do I need to call him back in?" she asked Maggie.

Maggie shrugged. "He's probably okay. Does he like fetch? Maybe he'll bring the balls back for us." She picked up one of the buckets of balls.

Sara eyed them doubtfully. "A baseball might be kind of a mouthful. And hard on the baseballs." Though Dougal would probably manage it if he could. He was kind of ball-crazy.

"Hard to hurt practice balls too much," Maggie said. "And one thing we're well stocked up on here is baseballs. Okay, let's go. I'll pitch. That's easier than using the ball machine."

That sounded good to Sara. She took up position at the far end of the cage. Maggie walked backward with the balls then plucked one out of the bucket. She took up a stance that Sara thought looked a little too good based on what she'd seen in Orlando.

"Go easy on me," she said. "Complete idiot here, remember?"

"Sorry." Maggie adjusted her stance to something a bit more relaxed. "Force of habit."

"Let me guess, you were a pitcher?"

Maggie lobbed the ball underarm and Sara swung

at it. To her surprise, she actually connected. But the ball didn't go very far. She grimaced.

"It's a start," Maggie said. "And I was kind of an all-arounder. I batted mostly but I could pitch a bit if I had to. But like I said, I was no superstar." She smiled suddenly. "You know, if you want to learn to pitch, you should ask Lucas to teach you." She lobbed the ball again.

Sara swung without thinking about it. "L-Lucas?" The bat connected again, this time with a more solid *thunk*, and the ball headed back in Maggie's direction. Maggie stuck out her glove and caught it easily. Dougal, attracted by the noise, came trotting over to investigate and sat by Maggie's feet.

"Did Lucas play baseball?" Sara asked, then wished she hadn't when she saw Maggie's smile turned smug. Damn, she'd taken the bait.

"Sure did," Maggie said. "All three of them played in college. That's how they met. Didn't he tell you that?"

"It's not the kind of thing we talk about," Sara said.

"Oh? What do you talk about?"

"Mostly flight times and fuel bills," Sara said firmly. "Let me try again."

Maggie shrugged and pitched another.

Miraculously, Sara hit it for the third time in a row.

"Lucas was a great pitcher. I've looked at his stats. He probably would've made it to the majors," Maggie said, watching the ball sail past her.

Don't ask what happened, don't ask what happened. Sara bit the inside of her cheek.

"You don't want to know what happened?"

Sara forced a shrug. "Not really my business."

"Really?" Maggie looked skeptical as she scooped up another ball.

"Really. Throw another one."

"The correct term is *pitch*, not throw."

"Pitch it, then," Sara said.

Maggie stared at her a moment and then nodded. "If that's what you want. I'll go a little faster this time."

At the end of another forty minutes or so, Dougal was sound asleep in a sunny patch near the benches and Sara's arms were starting to ache. "Time out," she called. "Or whatever they say in baseball."

"Time out is right," Maggie said. She jogged back toward the benches, opened the tote bag, and produced two bottles of water and a plastic container of the promised cookies.

Sara swigged water gratefully then took a cookie.

"You know, you're not so bad," Maggie said. "We'll have you trained up in no time. You'll be the star rookie in the staff game."

"Only if you bribe me with a lifetime supply of these."

Maggie offered her the box. Sara took another one. Pecan and caramel and chocolate exploded on her tongue.

"You know, if you really don't want to play, that's okay. We do other things, too. Like next weekend.

There's a big fund-raising ball for our youth program."

"A ball? Tuxedos and gowns and dancing?" She knew that expensive charity events were a thing but somehow she didn't associate them with baseball.

"Yes." Maggie took another cookie. "It's going to be great. I have a kick-ass dress. Maybe so kick-ass that I shouldn't eat this." She bit into the cookie, chewed, and swallowed. "Then again, life's too short not to eat cookies. And I fully intend to ply Alex with alcohol after the official part and get him to relax for a night." She grinned happily while she contemplated that prospect.

Sara felt a twinge of envy. That part sounded nice—the relaxing-with-a-hot guy part. She wasn't sold on frocks and tuxedos and lots of attention. But she couldn't help asking about Maggie and Alex. "So how did you and Alex get together anyway? I would've thought that you'd hate the guy who bought your team."

Maggie laughed. "It wasn't exactly love at first sight. But somehow chemistry has a way of sneaking up on you. Alex is . . ." She paused, looking suddenly lost in thought. Then she shook herself and smiled again. "He's Alex and apparently that's it for me. He's a great guy. All three of them are. You know, if you want some more lessons in this—" She waved at the batting cage. "—I'll get the guys to teach you. You can learn from the best."

"Wouldn't the best be the actual players?"

"Yeah, but they're not here. Ollie might, if you asked him nicely next time you get to Vero Beach."

"Not sure my kind of asking nicely is Ollie's kind," Sara said. She'd bantered with Ollie a few more times since their first meeting and was starting to figure out that there was a good guy beneath the swagger. Not her kind of guy, but not the big-man-on-campus superstar sex-god baseball player he played, either.

"Well, that leaves you with Alex, Mal, and Lucas," Maggie said.

At her feet, Dougal suddenly clambered up and starting barking, the fur on his back bristling. Crap. Sara grabbed for his leash, looking around to see what had set him off. And saw Alex walking toward them with Lucas. Dougal must have spotted Lucas as well, because his barks eased back a little.

"Speak of the devil. Or two of them at least," Maggie said.

"I thought we'd agreed I wasn't the devil," Alex said as the guys reached them.

His voice set off Dougal into a storm of barking and Sara jumped half a foot, making an embarrassing little squeaky noise before she regained her composure. Her pulse went into overdrive, pounding in her ears, and she had to suck in a deep breath or too to calm down.

Ever since she'd gotten home, she'd been a little too quick to leap at noises and startle at things that were perfectly innocuous. Combat stress, her therapist said, and taught her some techniques of managing the adrenaline spikes. She mostly had the reaction under control now but apparently not today.

She tightened her grip on Dougal's leash. "Dougal. Quiet," she said firmly, looking apologetically at Alex. Only an inch or two shorter than Lucas, who stood beside him, he wore his usual jeans and a white business shirt with the collar unbuttoned. He looked tan, even at this time of year, and the sunshine made his hair glint golden. Very green eyes were regarding her, looking unconcerned at Dougal's lack of welcome. Unconcerned and kind of ridiculously handsome. She looked from him to Lucas—who stood a few feet behind him—and back again. "Sorry," she said. "Dougal's a little nervous around men." At her feet, Dougal was growling softly, the rumbles interspersed with whines as he watched Alex and Lucas.

Sara kept her eyes on Alex.

She still hadn't gotten quite used to the level of hotness of her bosses. Together, Alex and Lucas could have stepped out of a magazine spread. All-American god versus Italian suave god or something. All that was missing was Mal's slightly more rugged, slightly scarier but no less hot war god.

Alex didn't come any closer. "He's doing his job. Hey, Dougal," he said.

Dougal barked wildly.

Sara tightened her grip. "Friend," she said firmly. Then to Alex, she said, "He's harmless, truly. Definitely a case of his bark is worse than his bite."

Behind Alex, Lucas was watching the exchange with his face carefully neutral. "Nice dog," he said.

At the sound of his voice, Dougal sprang forward, hard enough to yank the leash free. He dodged around Alex and came to halt next to Lucas, pushing his head into Lucas's hand and wriggling happily. It was perfectly obvious that he liked Lucas. That he *knew* Lucas.

Sara froze. Oh crap. Where was the black hole to swallow you up when you needed one?

"I thought you said he doesn't like men," Maggie said slowly.

"He doesn't," Sara said, trying to sound surprised.

"Animals like me," Lucas said. He looked at Sara then away. Was he waiting for her to say something? She couldn't think, feeling certain her face must be flaming and giving her away. He bent down and grabbed Dougal's leash then steered him around Alex back to Sara's side. He passed her the leash.

"Thank you," she managed. Then, inspiration struck. "What are you two doing here? Did I get the time wrong for the helo?" There, a perfectly innocent way to change the conversation. Because she really didn't want to have to explain to Maggie and Alex why her dog loved Lucas.

"I got done with my thing earlier than I thought. Then Lucas called and said he was done, too, so we came back together," Alex said with an easy shrug. He walked over to Maggie, looped his arm around her shoulder. Which put him farther away from Dougal. "Did you miss me?" The grin he directed at Maggie was wicked.

"Maybe," Maggie said, her answering grin so

blatantly delighted in him that Sara once again felt a twinge of envy. "Depends whether you came to try and raid my cookie stash."

"We had pizza for lunch," Alex said. "No cookies required. Yet." He nodded at Sara. "And what brings you and your dog to Deacon this fine day, Sara?" he said with a glint in his eyes that told Sara he was enjoying himself.

She pretended not have noticed that Dougal was now lying against Lucas's legs. "I—"

"I was giving her a batting lesson," Maggie interjected. "Having fun. Unlike you two workaholics."

"Fun?" Alex said. "I think I remember that."

Sara snuck a sidewise look at Lucas. He was ignoring Dougal, too, apparently just listening to the banter, but she thought there was a little too much tension in his stance.

"You should ask Mal to teach you to hit," Alex said. "He's quite the slugger. And if you want to learn to pitch, then Lucas here can show you the ropes."

"That's what I told her," Maggie said. "That Lucas would be happy to give her a lesson or two."

Sara purposefully didn't look at Lucas.

"I'd be happy to," Lucas said neutrally.

"Oh for Pete's sake," Maggie said, throwing up her hands. "You two are hopeless."

Crap. They were about to get called on their pretense. Damn it. She knew Maggie had figured it out. "What?" Sara said, trying for bewildered.

"Give it up, Sara. Dougal has blown your secret,"

Maggie said. "Besides which, the two of you are not going to win any acting awards."

"Not to mention," Alex said with a grin, "I can practically feel the steam rising off you both. 'Fess up, you're seeing each other."

Chapter Seventeen

Sara's stomach went cold. Her eyes locked on Alex. Oh God. They knew.

Instinctively, she turned to Lucas, whose face had gone locked down and unreadable.

Alex laughed. "You two look like deer in the headlights."

"Maybe that's because we were just ambushed," Lucas said in a very cool voice. "And last time I checked, my private life wasn't your business."

The laughter in Alex's face dimmed a bit. "We've had this discussion before. It is my business and Mal's business if it involves an employee. So does it?"

God. She was going to get fired over this. Lucas looked at her, an eyebrow raised, as if to say *Up to you*.

Might as well get it over and done with. If their pretense was so flimsy, it was better just to come out with it. She lifted her chin. "I don't remember anything in my contract about not being able to date anybody at the Saints."

"That's because there isn't anything in your contract about that." Maggie stood and went over to Alex. "Because that would be pretty hypocritical of us." She dug her elbow into Alex's ribs. "You're scaring Sara, she thinks you're going to fire her."

"No one's firing anybody," Lucas growled.

Alex held up his hands. "Of course not. I just want to know the truth. Are you two together?" He looked down at Dougal, who whined and licked Lucas's hand. "Or is Lucas suddenly a miraculous dog whisperer?"

Once again she looked at Lucas, and this time he shrugged. Alex snorted softly.

Sara made an effort to relax, but her shoulders felt like they were up near her ears. "We're . . . well, I don't know if we have a definition yet."

"Yes!" Maggie whooped. "Good going, Sara." She grinned at Lucas, who shook his head at her. Or maybe at all three of them.

"Happy?" Lucas said. "Is the interrogation over?"

Maggie held up her hands. "I won't shine bright lights in anybody's eyes, I promise." Her eyes were laughing. "Though I'm thinking some quality girl talk might be required. Everyone will want to know about the secret life of Dr. Gorgeous here."

Lucas shook his head and put his arm around Sara's shoulder. She wriggled closer, her heart still beating too fast, head spinning from the big reveal.

"I have no secret life. You guys don't leave me any time for a secret life," Lucas said.

"You found time for Sara," Alex said. "Which is a good thing," he added when Lucas stiffened.

"All right, so now you know," Lucas said. "Can we change the subject please?"

Alex nodded but Sara suspected that Lucas hadn't heard the last of this just yet. Well, that was between the two of them.

"Sure," he said and turned his green eyes on her. "So Sara, has Maggie turned you into a batting champ yet?"

"No, I'm pretty bad."

Maggie wagged a finger at this. "Actually, no, for someone who hasn't done this before, you did good."

"Careful, Maggie will infect you with baseball cooties before you know it," Alex said.

Sara smiled. "It's . . . not so bad."

"She sounds underwhelmed," Alex said to Lucas. "You've obviously been slacking off. You're meant to show off more. Impress her with your baseball team and big stadium."

"She's already impressed with me, she doesn't have to care about baseball," Lucas said, his voice more easy.

Some of the tension dissolved from Sara's shoulders. "Don't pick on Lucas. It's not his fault I don't know much about baseball. Besides, I've been learning lots at spring training."

"Don't learn too much," Alex said. "It might be refreshing to have someone not affected by baseball insanity around here. And you must get along like a house on fire with Lucas's family if you don't like baseball."

Lucas went stiff again. She looked up to see him looking oddly uncomfortable.

"Ah. I take it you haven't met the Angelos yet?" Alex said. "Lucas, are you keeping Sara a secret from everybody, not just us?"

"I'm not keeping secrets," Lucas said coolly. "Some of us like a bit of privacy. It's not like you and Maggie would've announced your relationship so soon if your hand hadn't been forced."

Alex held up a hand. "I was joking. Ease down."

Sara felt her teeth catch at her lip. "We're just taking things slowly," she said. "It's only been a few weeks." Beside her, Dougal whined softly, his ears lowering.

"I'm not going to get into this right now," Lucas said. "Look, Sara needs to get ready for the flight later. So I think it's time we got on our way."

Maggie looked unhappy. "Lucas, don't go. Alex is being his usual idiotic self. If you and Sara don't want to be public yet, then we'll keep our mouths shut. But you need to think about this. The press has been leaving us alone here for the moment while the team is in Florida, but that's not going to last forever. And it only takes a picture at the wrong moment and everyone will know."

"I'll worry about that when I have to," Lucas said. But he didn't look quite so defensive, and he smiled crookedly at Alex. "Sorry, A. It's been a long week."

Alex ran a hand through his hair. "I'm sorry, too. You're right, it has been a long week. I promise, my lips are sealed. You might want to give Mal the heads-up though."

"I will," Lucas said.

Maggie stepped back. "It's a pity, though. If you were going public you could've brought Sara as your date to the ball."

Sara's stomach tensed all over again. Of all things, a goddamned ball. The only images the words *fundraiser* and *ball* brought to mind were beautiful people in the very expensive clothes and jewels that she'd seen in the papers. She couldn't afford even one-tenth of one of those gowns.

"It's okay," she said quickly. "I don't mind. Lucas can go. I have two left feet, anyway."

"No, you don't," Lucas said. He was frowning again. Damn.

"A ball means photographers and pictures in the papers, doesn't?" Sara said. "So, really not a good idea. It's okay, really. Plenty of time for balls later on."

Maggie's eyes narrowed. "There would only be pictures if you arrive or leave with Lucas. We're keeping the press out of the actual event."

"Who else would I be going to the ball with?" Sara said, confused.

Maggie smiled suddenly, and the expression was so full of satisfaction that Sara had a vision of her holding a wand and saying, *Bippity boppity boo*. Only in Maggie's case her fairy godmother wand was more likely to be a baseball bat.

"Well," Maggie said. "Last time I asked him, Mal hadn't lined up a date, either. You could use him as a smokescreen."

Beside her, Lucas made a noise deep in his throat.

"No, don't go all caveman on me," Maggie said with a flip of her hand. "Think about it. Mal can escort her through the press and out again at the end of the night. Once she gets inside, she's all yours. Cinderella can go to the ball!"

"Cinderella doesn't really want to go to the ball," Sara muttered, but she had a feeling that once Maggie Jameson got the bit between her teeth, getting her to back down from an idea was about as easy as landing a helo in a storm. "And Cinderella thinks that there will be a whole lot of people at the ball who know Lucas, so if he hangs out with me there, everyone will know anyway."

"Cinderella doesn't know what's good for her," Maggie retorted. "Admit it, you must want to see Lucas in a tux."

"I've seen him in a tux," Sara said. "I survived." Of course, it had also been the tux that had led her to the moment of madness that was her jumping his bones. Lesson learned. Avoiding Lucas in a tuxedo was the sensible thing to do.

"Oh really?" Maggie said. "When did you see him in a tux?" She tilted her head at Lucas. "The only tux-worthy event you've been to lately was that fund-raiser in the Hamptons."

"You don't know my every movement, Maggie," Lucas said. "I have events for the hospital as well."

Maggie pursed her lips. "Yeah but that was one that Sara flew you to, wasn't it?"

"Yes," Lucas said. "Now stop bullying Sara. If she doesn't want to come to the ball, she doesn't have to."

"Everyone wants to go to a ball," Maggie said. "Especially when I'm throwing the party." She shot a sideways glance at Sara. "I throw *excellent* parties. And besides, it would be nice not to be the only female dealing with the terrible trio." She shook her head at Alex who stuck his tongue out in response.

Sara bit back a laugh. "Are they really so bad?"

"Only when they're being difficult," Maggie said. "So basically all the time."

"Not letting you have your way about everything doesn't constitute being difficult," Alex said with a teasing tone in his voice. "Don't forget we employ you."

"Yeah, yeah, you'd be lost without me," Maggie said. Then she turned back to Sara. "See what I mean? I'm outnumbered. There's far too much testosterone around here."

"What about the players' wives and girlfriends?" Sara asked. "Can't they help you out?"

"They try. But they have to be nice to the terrible trio so they don't trade their boys to other teams."

"Oh yeah, they're so intimidated by us," Lucas said. "That's why I had Hana on the phone for half an hour yesterday demanding that I let her husband come home for the weekend. Hana's Brett Tuckerson's wife," he said to Sara as an aside. "Who is a former Olympic tae kwan do medalist and one of Maggie's pals. I'm not sure she's ever been intimidated by anyone in her life. She definitely didn't have any trouble telling me it was unreasonable for our starting pitcher to have to be in Florida for all of spring training."

Maggie laughed. "Well, that may be true but Hana's married to Brett, not one of you three. It's not the same thing. I need an ally." She made puppy-dog eyes at Sara. "You have to come help me out."

"Stop harassing the poor girl, Maggie," Alex said. "Let her think about it for a few days. After all, you haven't even asked Mal about this. Maybe he has a date by now."

"He would have told me," Maggie said. "Malachi is the sensible one."

"If you think that, then you really haven't figured Mal out yet," Lucas said. Sara's curiosity spiked a little. Mal was clearly the strong, silent type. There was a story there. But she wasn't going to try to pry it out of him.

If she stayed with Lucas then there'd be time to figure it all out. "I'll think about it," she said to Maggie. "It's a very nice invitation," she added. "But I need time to think."

Maggie opened her mouth to reply and Lucas held up a hand. "She said she'll think about it, Maggie."

He stood and planted a quick kiss on the brunette's cheek and then straightened and held out a hand to Sara. "We'll see you all later."

The silence when they got back to her apartment seemed to weigh a ton. Sara let Dougal off his leash, and he nosed around his food bowl hopefully. When no early dinner magically appeared, he flopped down in his dog bed and closed his eyes. He had the right idea. Ignore the whole situation.

Sara stowed her purse and keys and shed her jacket. Lucas hadn't made a move to take off his yet.

He'd been quiet during the drive back from Deacon. She wasn't sure she'd pinned his mood down, though. He didn't seem to be actively mad about anything, but he did seem . . . distracted. Distant. Almost how he used to be during those first few flights.

Was he upset because they'd run into Alex and Maggie? Upset about being outed? Upset that Maggie had invited her to the ball? Upset that she hadn't immediately accepted?

She took a deep breath. Too many options. Given that she wasn't a mind reader there was only one way to find out and that was to ask. But first it might be a good idea to restore some goodwill. She made her way over to Lucas and put her arms around him, tilting her head up to look at him.

His hands came to her waist—that was a good sign—and she stood on tiptoe and pressed her lips to his. Gently at first, but then the kiss turned hungry. She almost dragged him off to her bedroom but she didn't think that a postcoital glow was quite the time to have a relationship discussion. Better to do it with a cooler head and then use the sex part to smooth over any bumps the conversation might cause.

A cooler head and a full stomach, she thought as hers rumbled slightly, reminding her that it was past lunchtime and she hadn't eaten anything except a few cookies since breakfast.

"So, Dr. Gorgeous," she said, pulling back from Lucas a little. "How about you make me some lunch?"

Forty minutes or so later she was sitting at her kitchen table, biting into the pasta that Lucas had made and trying not to moan with pleasure. Apparently he not only cooked, he cooked well. Divinely.

Figured. He was the sort of man who made sure he excelled at something once he decided to do it at all.

Sara had stood at one end of the counter and watched as Lucas had sliced and diced tomatoes and eggplant and bell peppers and onions with knife skills that could only belong to a professional chef or a surgeon. It was like watching a dance in a way, every movement purposeful and elegant and controlled.

And it had been a complete and utter turn-on. She'd barely restrained herself from jumping him in the kitchen. Only the smell of the sauce he was concocting restrained her. She'd watched and found the herbs he'd asked for, and set the table and poured the wine he'd brought, but otherwise he'd insisted on doing it all himself.

"I could get used to this," she said, pausing before she scooped up another forkful of pasta.

Across the table, Lucas lifted his water glass and sipped before he said, "I could, too."

And there was the opening she'd been looking for.

She'd been avoiding having this talk with him, but meeting Maggie and Alex earlier had meant that avoiding wasn't going to work any longer.

"I know we said we'd just see how things go but this changes things, yes? If I go to the ball, it says something."

"It says you're going to the ball with me."

"It's taking things public. That will change things. Your world is . . . different." She didn't know if he understood just how different. She doubted he'd ever had to be aware of how much money he had to the exact dollar and do mental math to make it through another month. And if he had problems with an insurance company he could just set a whole squad of lawyers on them.

"I understand," Lucas said. "And I understand if you don't want to change the status quo. This isn't what you signed up for."

He wasn't what she'd signed up for. He'd tilted her world off its neat little flight path. She hadn't expected to like someone like him. Let alone let him start to get a foothold on her heart.

Foolish.

Not enough words to describe just how foolish.

But also too late to stop now. And the thing was, in her heart of hearts, she would love to go to a ball with Lucas. To stand at his side and let the world see that this gorgeous, ridiculous man was hers. Even if it was just for one night. Sanity was warring with desire and she had a horrible feeling that, just like it had every night she let him into her bed, sanity would lose.

"I need to think," she said. "I need to think about this. So do you."

She wished desperately that Viv were just across the hall like she had been in Manhattan. She would be an objective opinion. But she wasn't.

"I've thought about it," Lucas said. "And I want you to go. I want to show you off." He smiled at her. "But that doesn't mean I'll force you to go."

She pushed pasta around the plate with her fork. Such a seemingly simple choice, pasta. Red sauce, some vegetables, some chicken, some red wine. Simple. But dig deeper and there was a world of subtle complexity in the dish he'd made.

If only she could figure out her life as easily as she could decide if she liked the pasta.

"And if I say yes?" she said. "Do you think Mal will go along with Maggie's plan?"

"I think Mal likes Maggie and he's not dating anyone at the moment, so I can't see why not."

"I'm not sure that plan even makes sense."

"Probably not. Like you said, there will be plenty of people who know me there. No pictures will keep it out of the press and the wider world but not from them. But it's an option if you want to take it. I can understand not wanting your picture in the papers. I don't like it, either."

"Where is the ball, anyway?" she asked. It was a relatively minor detail at this point but maybe knowing the venue might let her figure out what level of craziness she was getting herself into.

"At the Paragon."

Huh. The Paragon. Right in the heart of the city.

Times Square. Better than it being somewhere ridiculously extravagant like the Met, but still, not exactly a hole-in-the-wall venue. About the only point in its favor was that it was in Manhattan, which meant the Staten papers wouldn't cover it. Or would they? After all, it was a Saints fund-raiser, and the Saints belonged to the island even if they were called the third New York team.

"And it's full-on black tie?" She didn't hold out much hope that it wouldn't be. She thought about her wardrobe for a moment. She had one simple long black gown that had seen her through a couple of wedding receptions and an army shindig or too. She hadn't pulled it out of her wardrobe in a while, though. God knew what shape it was in. Or even where it was. She thought of the boxes that she'd dumped temporarily in her parents' garage while she settled into this apartment. Hopefully it was somewhere in there. She couldn't even remember if she'd seen it in her city place since she'd gotten back from deployment.

She could afford a new dress; she could spend some of the money the Saints were paying her. But she couldn't spend the sort of money a designer ball gown cost.

"Yes," Lucas said. "Penguin suits and gowns all around."

She made a face. "They didn't want to buck the trend and do an all-jeans ball?"

"You have to look like money to ask for money," Lucas said.

It sounded like a quote. She wondered who from. Alex, perhaps?

"And," Lucas continued when she didn't say anything, "it's only fair. You already got to see me in a tux. I think it's only fair that I get to see you in a gorgeous dress." He stopped and tilted his head at her, humor gleaming in his eyes. "You do own a gorgeous dress, don't you?"

"Yes, I own a dress." She narrowed her eyes at him, but to be fair, he'd only ever seen her in her uniform, yoga pants, or jeans and casual things. It was warm in Florida but not yet dress weather. Not when she had to fly helos anyway.

"Just one?"

"More than one." She stuck her nose in the air. "And I look good enough in them to give you a heart attack, rich boy." Lies, damned lies, but he didn't have to know that. Though she did scrub up quite nicely.

He smiled then and waggled his eyebrows at her. "Oh good."

"What will you be wearing? That tux you wore to the Hamptons?" She assumed he probably had more than one, though it was hard to imagine he had one that made him look better than he had that night in the chopper.

He shrugged. "I guess. Why, did you like that tux? Is that why you jumped me?"

"I didn't jump you."

He snorted. "Yeah, you did." He poured more wine—the same red he'd used in the pasta—into his glass then topped hers up with water. She didn't drink if she was flying.

"It was a momentary lapse of reason," she said.

The glass tilted in her direction. "To momentary lapses of reason, long may they continue."

"I thought surgeons were all about logic and reason."

"Not when it comes to getting beautiful women into their beds, they're not. Then it's whatever works."

She rolled her eyes. "Like you ever had to work that hard."

"You might be surprised. And speaking of jumping me, if you need another incentive to come to the ball, then let me offer this. We're going to have to fly in and then fly out afterward. So if you want to drag me into a supply closet to have your wicked way with me, then the ball is going to be your only chance that weekend."

The vision of Lucas and a small dark room derailed her train of thought. "What?" she said, suddenly thinking of his hands sliding over her in the dark.

He laughed. "I said, it'll be your only chance to have your wicked way with me that weekend. If you're sticking to your no-sex-in-Florida rule."

"Yes, I am. I'd rather not deal with everybody I work with knowing about us just yet. So. You think I can't live without you for a whole weekend?"

His mouth quirked. "As much as I like our hotel phone sex, I prefer the live-action version. I think it's more like I can't live without you and I'm hoping I don't have to. So Cinderella, do you want to go to the ball?"

She forced her mind back to somewhere near the

vicinity of rational. As lovely as balls and supply closets sounded and as much as she definitely didn't want to go a whole weekend without getting some quality naked time with Lucas, she had to be sensible. Even though it was killing her. She took another swig of water, wishing that it were wine. "Cinderella wants to sleep on it."

Chapter Eighteen

Lucas tracked Sara down near the front of the bleachers halfway through Monday's game. She was munching popcorn and following the action with an expression of fierce concentration that was kind of adorable. A Saints cap shielded her skin from the sun. She looked pretty cute when she was so engrossed. He stood still and watched her for a minute or two.

When the batter connected solidly and the ball went flying across the park like a rocket, the crowd—small but not too bad for a Monday game playing the Pirates—erupted. Sara applauded, grinning and whooping along with the rest of the crowd.

Ha. The baseball bug was starting to bite. He made his way along the row and slid into the empty seat next to her. "You know, we have this nifty owners' suite back there."

She jerked her popcorn and bits of it shot everywhere. That earned him a sea-blue glare. "I think

you need to wear bells on your cufflinks or something."

"Sorry, but you looked kind of cute all intent on
the baseball. I didn't want to disturb you."

"Well, for once we seem to be winning. I thought
I should enjoy it while it lasts." She stuck out her
tongue. "Sam's doing pretty good, isn't he?"

"He's sitting on a 4.5 ERA—that's Earned Run
Average. Yep, that's not too shabby at all."

"Is he going to get a slot?"

"If he keeps pitching like that, then probably." He
grinned. He'd grown fond of Sam. He worked like
a dog and sucked up knowledge like a sponge. He
listened and he implemented. He kind of reminded
Lucas of himself many moons ago. Tico wasn't doing too badly, either. And there were still a few weeks
left until the season proper began.

"I'm glad, he's trying so hard." She held out the
popcorn. What was left of it.

He took a piece and looked at it before tossing it
into his mouth. "You know we have real food in the
owners' suite."

She wrinkled her nose and gestured widely at the
crowd with her free hand. "But isn't this what it's
about? Sitting with the crowd in the sunshine, eating junk, and enjoying the game?"

He smiled. A woman after his own heart. During
the real season he was going to have to be in the
owners' box because there would be sponsors and
VIPs and all that bullshit to deal with. He hadn't
really thought about it until now, but he wasn't going to get many chances to just sit in the stands and

kick back. Not unless he snuck out to non-Saints games. Damn.

Well, then. Today he was going to play hooky and sit here with Sara and try to be a fan for as long as he could. Alex and Maggie could hold the schmoozing fort.

He looked around, spotted a guy with a tray of hot dogs, and waved a bill at him. "If you put it like that . . ." He took the hot dog—loaded with mustard the way he liked it—and sat back down.

"Don't spill mustard on that suit," Sara warned.

"My dry cleaner laughs in the face of mustard stains," Lucas said and Sara laughed. "What?"

"Do you actually know who your dry cleaner is?" she said, voice amused. "Or do you have a housekeeper or someone who deals with all that stuff?"

"I know my dry cleaner." Well, he knew one dry cleaner, the one he sometimes dropped stuff off with at the hospital. He had no idea where his housekeeper took most of his suits. But he wasn't going to tell Sara that.

"That's a relief." She fished out more popcorn and grinned before she ate it, looking as though it was the best thing she'd ever eaten. That was baseball for you—it made even the junk food taste good.

He bit into his hot dog. It was gloriously terrible. Salty and beefy and tangy with mustard. He could almost feel his cholesterol spiking. But who gave a damn? He took another bite and chewed happily.

"Did you come to ask me something?" Sara said when he'd swallowed. "Do you need the helo?"

He frowned. It stung that she was surprised by him seeking her out. "Do I need a reason to come talk to you? Maybe I just wanted to see you."

Sara nudged his leg with her knee, and the quick flash of heat eased the sting. And replaced it with a surge of why-the-hell-was-he-stuck-in-Florida-where-he-couldn't-touch her?

"No reason required, Dr. Gorgeous. But I thought you'd be up with the bigwigs, doing your owner thing." She smiled, expression teasing.

"They'll live without me for a bit. But actually, I came to tell you that my office called. Your mom rang them earlier and your dad's going to have some X-rays and scans done Wednesday. Then I can see him Thursday before we come back here for Friday and Saturday night."

This time her smile was one of pure delight and relief. "Really?"

"Yup. It's all sorted. And it's on the house. I've got a friend who's looking at patella fractures and recovery times, so he can use your dad's data for his study and the hospital will cover it."

Her smile ramped up another few degrees until the happiness in her face just about blinded him. He really wanted to kiss her. Really. But other than Mal, Alex, and Maggie, no one else in the Saints knew about them. So he couldn't. That wouldn't be fair. He contented himself with grinning back at her while making a mental note to get her alone as soon as humanly possible.

"You're a good guy, Dr. Gorgeous," she said. "Want to take me to a ball?"

* * *

All dressed up with no date in sight. Aka where the hell was Lucas? He was meant to meet her at his apartment at seven and whisk her away to the ball. Once she'd said yes to him taking her, she'd decided she wasn't going to hide away and sneak in the back or turn up with Mal. In for a penny, in for a pound. Or something.

She was with Lucas. So let the world think what they would for however long that lasted.

Of course, making a grand statement like that would be easier if he would show the hell up.

It was nearly ten past seven and she was starting to feel like an idiot. She had a coat flung over her dress, but she was still getting some curious looks from the people going in and out of the building.

She checked her phone again. No message.

Damn it.

The revolving door in the lobby started to move and she looked up. Only to see Malachi walking toward her, looking apologetic.

"Mal," she said a little warily as he reached her. Mal bent and kissed her cheek. Since Lucas and she had come clean, she seemed to been moved into "approved friend" status with Alex and Mal and, other than in the office, they both had taken to kissing her hello and good-bye.

Which wasn't so hard to take.

Mal straightened, easing his tuxedo jacket back into place with a shrug. It was unbuttoned and the bow tie around his neck undone. He didn't wear the suit as naturally as Lucas did, but that didn't make him any less spectacular in it.

"Hey, Sara. Lucas sent me to pick you up. He's stuck in surgery but he'll be done in an hour or so. Doctor's hours, you know."

She nodded and pasted on a smile against the sharp snap of disappointment. Lucas was a surgeon. A great one. In demand. That meant a lot of emergency calls from athletes around the country. A heads-up might have been nice, but if he was in surgery and something had gone wrong then maybe there just hadn't been time.

She lifted her chin, determined to not let Lucas being late ruin her night. "Well, you're kind of cute in that tuxedo. So I guess you'll do."

"Always the bridesmaid," Mal said. He held out an arm.

Sara tucked her hand through it. "Somehow, I find that hard to believe. Pretty sure there would be potential dates lining up for you if you wanted them."

"Not much time for socializing right now. And Alex and Lucas keep beating me to the gorgeous women at the Saints." Mal navigated them through the revolving door and gestured toward the limo parked out front. "Our chariot."

It took a few minutes to wrangle dress and coat into the limo without ruining either of them or her hair, but she managed with Mal's help. He offered Bollinger but she took Perrier. She hadn't eaten since lunchtime, butterflies about the ball killing her appetite. Alcohol and low blood sugar didn't mix in her experience. Besides, she was flying later, so she'd rationed herself to one drink for the night. She was going to wait until she was with Lucas.

The fizzy water was cool, which was good because the limo was warm, even though she'd shrugged out of her coat once inside.

She watched Central Park, all dark green mystery and pools of light sliding by outside the windows. Limo travel would be easy to get used to. All the space was pretty sweet, and it smelled of clean leather and the deep smoky spice of whatever after-shave Mal had used rather than of sweaty cabdriver and fake air freshener.

All that was missing was Lucas himself. She tried not to think about what he might be doing to her if they were alone in a limo together but heat swept over her anyway. He'd kept teasing her about doing all sorts of things to her in a dark spot at the ball.

Part of her hoped he'd been joking but most of her, right at this moment, fervently hoped he hadn't.

She swallowed more Perrier, trying to cool herself down. Nothing was going to happen if Lucas didn't get out of his surgery.

Of course he would. She drank again.

"Nervous about tonight?" Mal asked.

"A little." Make that a lot. Lucas's parents were on the guest list, a little bombshell he'd dropped the night before. To be fair, he'd seemed surprised by the information himself, claiming that he hadn't expected them to accept the invitation. But she'd dropped him in the deep end with her own folks, so she'd just have to woman up and cope with his.

Mal topped up her glass. "It'll be fine. Just like any other party. Only bigger-scale."

"You mean kegs and grilled burgers and loud rock 'n' roll?"

Mal laughed. "I see you went to the same sort of parties in the army as I did. This is the same principle, just fancier booze and food. And then we ask them for money."

"I see." He wasn't really easing her nerves any. Army parties and pilot parties—which tended along the same lines—she could handle. This was a whole other level.

But if she wanted Lucas, this was apparently the life that came with it. Maybe she'd like it. She hadn't thought she'd like baseball but she was enjoying it now. She still didn't understand half of what was going on in the games and even less of what all the statistics meant, but she liked the crowd and the silly music and the seventh-inning stretches and the sense of fun. Plus watching guys built like Ollie Shields in tight pants and short-sleeved shirts wasn't too hard.

She didn't think tonight was going to have much silliness, though. But probably just as much stuff she didn't understand. Though Lucas would be there with her, and that was what mattered. Lucas who thought he could fix her dad's leg. Lucas who was *operating* on her dad next week. Lucas who had offered to get his lawyer onto the insurance company if they hadn't assessed the A-Star by the end of the month.

Lucas who made her brain melt every time he touched her.

For him she could do this.

Though, as they got closer to the hotel, the thought of braving photographers without Lucas holding her hand was making her palms sweat.

She'd seen pictures of paparazzi crowding around people, pushing and shoving and cameras flashing. She was pretty good with crowds and noises most of the time, but that seemed almost a guaranteed way to trigger herself into a panic attack. Not how she wanted to start the evening.

Which meant she needed to change the environment. Control things if she could. At least that's what her therapist would tell her.

"Mal, is there a back way into the hotel?" she asked. "I mean, if I'm not arriving with Lucas, do I need to go in the front?"

Mal tipped his head. "Something about photographers bother you?"

She swallowed. Mal had been in the army. He'd understand. "When I first got out, I wasn't good with people getting too close. And loud noises. And flashing things."

He nodded. "Combat stress. I know that one."

Relief made her smile at him. "I'm mostly better but I'm not sure I'm ready to deal with packs of photographers."

Mal nodded. "I don't like them, either. I'll call Gardner. He'll get us in another way."

"Don't you need your picture taken?"

"Alex can play poster boy for the night. The papers can live without my ugly mug."

She was doing the women of New York a

disservice. There would be plenty of them perfectly happy to drool over a picture of Mal in the paper. But they'd just have to drool over Alex instead. "Thank you," she said.

"Are you sure about this?" Mal said as the limo slid into the alley leading to the back of the hotel ten minutes later. "We can still go around the block and go in the front."

Sara shook her head. Having seen the throng of photographers and cameras outside the front of the hotel, complete with a red carpet, of all things, she knew she wasn't ready to walk that particular gauntlet. "Yes," she said sounding more certain than she felt. "Sneaking in the back suits me just fine."

"It takes a bit of getting used to," he said. "All the attention."

"So are you used to it yet?" she asked.

"Hell, no. If I could send all the paparazzi to a very deserted island somewhere in the Bering Sea, I would. Of course, that would still leave the actual legitimate press to deal with. And we need them." He didn't sound like he was happy with that situation.

That didn't ease Sara's stomach any. Malachi Coulter was taller than either Alex or Lucas and built on broader, more solid lines. He had shoulders that could probably cause a lunar eclipse. If he didn't like the media circus, what hope did she have of getting used to it?

"Well, I'm not going to have to deal with it tonight, at least. Thank you," she said.

Mal smiled, brown eyes warming. Which made him even nicer to look at. She could see why Maggie called them the terrible trio. Mal was easy enough to talk to and he'd been nothing but a perfect gentlemen since he'd climbed into the limo, but she had no trouble envisioning him kicking butt and taking no prisoners.

She wasn't sure exactly what he'd done in the army—it seemed rude to ask when he hadn't offered the intel—but she was guessing it had been something specialized and risky. And apparently he hadn't lost whatever don't-mess-with-me vibe it had instilled in him. Though, who knew, maybe he'd had that before he'd joined up.

"Gardener will be waiting at the door," Mal said. "He'll let us in and then we'll get you upstairs and deliver you to Lucas."

"Lucas isn't here yet and I'm not a package," she pointed out.

"No, but you're very prettily wrapped." Mal grinned. "Good dress choice."

She felt her face go hot. Maggie had talked her into the dress, and it had been in her price range— the shopping gods apparently smiling on her for once. Maggie's friend Shelly Finch, a player's fiancée, had shopping mojo that probably involved sacrificing goats to dark gods or something. Shelly had whizzed them to about ten little up-stairs-and-down-alley showrooms stuffed full of gorgeous clothes at the sort of price that Sara could afford before Sara could blink. She'd had no idea such places existed.

Affordable or not, she still wasn't sure she could

pull the dress off. But she'd adored it too much to resist, particularly with Maggie and Shelly egging her on. It had a soft blue bodice, made sparkly with a thousand or more tiny glittering silver beads curling around her body in waves. No straps held it in place, just boning and what Maggie had called *magic tape*. She just hoped that it wasn't going to do her any harm in sensitive areas when she had to take it off. Lucas might have been hoping for some action in a dark closet somewhere, but he was going to have to be very inventive to leave her looking respectable afterward. Not that she doubted his ingenuity in that department.

No, indeed. The man had skills. And very few inhibitions.

She wrenched her mind off that path and focused back on her dress. A far safer subject. The bodice, impenetrable or not, wasn't the best part. No, the best bit was the skirt, which was made from miles and miles of soft tulle, falling around her like a long tutu in layers of blue and gray and white in a hundred soft shades. It stopped just below her ankles, which let her show off the silver heels that she'd had to buy as well. Because they were perfect for the dress.

The dress swished and swayed and made her feel like some sort of sea fairy. She hadn't been able to resist it.

She'd curled her hair in loose waves and donned the pearl earrings her grandmother had left her and then decided to let the dress stand alone. She couldn't compete with the sorts of jewels that anyone else here tonight would be likely wearing, but she did have a killer dress. One that would, hopefully, make Lucas crazy.

"Earth to Sara," Mal said and she realized she was smoothing the skirt of the dress with one hand. "Worried about ruining your frock?"

"No," she said. "Not the frock." Just everything else in her life. Not that there was that much left to ruin. So maybe she should just suck it up and enjoy this one glittering night for what it was: a rare moment before the bell chimed at midnight and delivered her back to the pumpkin patch of real life. She put her hand on the door handle and summoned a smile. "Let's do this," she said to Mal and then climbed out to face the fairy tale.

True to Mal's word, Gardner was waiting for them at the end of the alley. He showed them through the door and then through a bewildering series of corridors and up two sets of stairs. The decor became progressively more luxurious as they moved from the service areas toward the public parts of the hotel.

They came out in the lobby, which was teeming with people, and then followed Gardner downstairs to the ballroom. The vast space was like a cross between a steampunk theater and a Golden Age ballroom. Sara had to remind herself not to gape when a guy dressed in black tuxedo pants, silver braces, and nothing else, his face hidden by a mask that was an explosion of white silver and blue feathers, waved a silver tray of drinks in her face as soon as they reached the bottom of the curving staircase.

She shook her head and stepped closer to Mal. He scanned the throng of people—there were advantages to being so tall—and then bent down and said, "I can see Maggie, we'll go that way."

Sounded like a good plan to her. He offered her his arm again and, between him and Gardner, they made their way fairly easily through the room. Maggie was standing near a table, speaking to a couple of women Sara didn't know.

Maggie wore white, long and slinky, with sky-high black stilettos. The collar of diamonds around her neck glittered blindingly. She'd bought the dress on their shopping trip as well and had been just as excited about finding a bargain as Sara was. But looking at the diamonds, Sara didn't think they were bargain-basement finds. Nope, they were the real thing. Maggie was at home in this world.

Sara wasn't. She really, really wanted Lucas to be here with her.

Maggie's face broke into a smile when she spotted them and she waved them over, introducing them to the women she was talking to, though the names flew out of Sara's head as soon as she heard them.

"This is amazing," Sara said, snagging a glass of sparkling water off the tray of the next feathery boy who passed by.

"I told you I throw excellent parties," Maggie said with a grin.

"Yes, you do," Mal said. "And now I have to mingle." He smiled at Sara then made an apologetic face and broke away from their group, melting into the crowd.

He was one of the hosts, and he had to work to do, so she couldn't ask him to stay just because she was nervous.

Relax. She focused on the conversation and tried to act like a normal person. It was hard to hear over the music and the sound of the crowd, but she followed well enough to be able to nod and smile at the right moments.

She was starting to feel a little more comfortable when Alex appeared by Maggie's side. "Sorry, ladies," he said, "I need to steal Maggie for a few minutes." He smiled at Sara. "Hey, Sara. You look gorgeous."

She smiled back and watched as Maggie abandoned her to follow Alex. Though Maggie did stop and whisper, "Shelly's somewhere over by the main bar. Go find her," before abandoning her.

Shelly being one of the few other people she was likely to know here, Sara decided that was good advice. She would have felt better if the players had been here. She was getting to know a few of them in Orlando—Brett Tuckerson the pitcher had talked to her a few times, and Ollie had introduced her to some of the other guys. And then there were Sam and Tico, of course, who like to come and hang out with her and ask her about helicopters and try to teach her baseball stats.

But they were all in Florida. She stood on tiptoe to try and figure out which direction the main bar was, then excused herself to the two women she'd been talking to and headed in that direction.

She was about halfway across the room when she nearly bumped into an older woman whose dark hair was pulled back into an immaculate chignon, framing olive skin and dark eyes. She wore dark-red silk, and rubies the size of malt balls glittered in her ears and around her neck.

"I'm sorry," Sara said.

"That's all right, dear," the woman said. "I wasn't looking where I was going." She looked Sara up and down. "Did I see you come in with Malachi earlier?"

"You know Mal?" Sara perked up.

"Yes, he's a friend of the family," the woman said. Then she held out a hand weighed down by even more diamonds and rubies and tipped with blood-red nails to match. "I'm Flavia Angelo."

Chapter Nineteen

Oh crap, Lucas's mom.

Sara managed to keep the smile on her face from freezing in place and took Flavia's hand. "Sara Charles." Flavia's skin was cool and Sara kept the handshake brief, withdrawing her hand as soon as possible.

"How lovely to meet you, Sara. So are you here with Malachi?" Flavia asked, lifting the champagne glass in her left hand to tilt it in the direction that Mal had disappeared earlier. "I hadn't heard that he was seeing anybody."

Sara didn't think that Lucas had the kind of relationship with his mom that meant he was calling her with updates on his friends' love lives. But she'd done some research on his family, and the Angelos were firmly cemented in the Manhattan social scene. Flavia probably had a network worthy of a spymaster. Sara only hoped that it hadn't revealed anything about Lucas and her.

"We're just friends. Colleagues really."

"Oh? You work for the baseball team?"

The tone in which she said *baseball team* should have dropped the temperature in the ballroom a good few degrees. The look in her eyes dropped it farther still. Brown eyes should be warm. But Flavia's were a shade you might get if you froze bitter chocolate. Lucas must have gotten his eyes from his dad. And he apparently hadn't been kidding about his family's views on baseball. She might be here at the fund-raiser, but Flavia was definitely not a Saints fan.

Where the hell was Lucas? Though maybe it was just as well he wasn't here. She didn't want Flavia's chill directed at her personally. "Yes, I work for the Saints," she said.

"That must be interesting."

There was that tone again. Sara set her teeth. "Yes, it is."

"What is it you do there?"

"I fly their helicopter," Sara said.

Surprise flared in the dark eyes, and Flavia's forehead wrinkled infinitesimally. It seemed Lucas's mom liked her Botox. For some reason, that made Sara feel slightly better.

"I wasn't aware they had a helicopter."

"It's a trial thing," Sara said. "While spring training is on." She wasn't going to offer any more of an explanation. Over Flavia's shoulder she thought she caught a glimpse of Shelly's pale-blond head. She wasn't going to stand here and chat to Lucas's mom without him any longer than she had to. And she definitely wasn't going to offer the news that she was dating Lucas when Flavia had shown no reaction to her name. Which meant Lucas hadn't told his parents about her.

Why the hell hadn't he told them about her? He hadn't mentioned that he hadn't when he'd said they were coming.

She managed to smile at Flavia. "It was lovely to meet you but I see someone I have to speak with. Enjoy the ball." She made her escape, heading toward Shelly, but she was fairly sure she could feel Flavia watching her as she left.

Shelly was standing by the bar, talking to the bartender.

"Sara, hey," she said. "That dress looks fab."

"Thanks to you," Sara said.

"Nope, the dress is nothing without the woman inside it." Shelly smiled. Her dress was a short shift—kind of flapper style—silver embroidery glimmering over black net. "Now, I was just asking Tom here if he can make me a very dirty martini. Do you want anything to drink?"

She had never wanted alcohol more in her life, but she was flying later. "No, I'm fine."

"Are you having fun? Where's Lucas?"

Maggie had, out of necessity, told Shelly about Sara and Lucas during their shopping adventure. But Shelly had promised to keep her mouth shut until the news became public. "Held up in surgery," Sara said, trying not to sound annoyed. With Flavia prowling the ballroom, she really wished Lucas were here.

Shelly grimaced in sympathy. "That's the problem with surgeons. Always on call. Well, the ones who do anything interesting, at least."

"Given that I tend to be on call, too, I guess I can't complain about that," Sara said. She wondered whether to mention that she'd just met Lucas's mom but decided to wait for the man himself to arrive to discuss that particular experience.

She stood and chatted with Shelly for a bit, telling her about spring training and letting Shelly— who worked as an entertainment columnist—give her the lowdown on half the people in the room. Just as she was starting to think that Lucas was never going to arrive, the crowd parted and he was suddenly in front of her.

"Oh thank God," she muttered as he bent to kiss her hello.

"Sorry," he murmured against her lips. "Surgery."

"So Mal told me," she said.

"Good." Lucas pulled back from her, still holding her hands. Then he scanned up and down and up again. His eyes went hot and dark and the breath caught in her lungs as an answering heat stroked her skin.

"You look beautiful." His fingers tightened a little on hers, stroking gently as he looked at her. "More than *beautiful*."

Her breath caught, the room suddenly shrinking to just the two of them. He really did think she was beautiful. And he wanted her. Both those things shone clearly in his eyes. The certainty suddenly arrowed through her, making her knees go weak. What

Lucas saw when he looked at her wasn't what she saw in the mirror. No, it was better. And maybe, just maybe, it was the real her. Not the mess of a woman who couldn't keep a business afloat, but the woman who filled Lucas's eyes with wonder and happiness.

She didn't know what to say. Didn't quite know if she could make lips and tongue cooperate to find any words.

Instead she stepped in and stood on tiptoe to kiss him again. Let her body say what she wasn't ready to say. A kiss of heat and tenderness in equal parts that didn't do much to still the spinning in her head.

Lucas *saw* her. And gloried in what he saw.

There was a word for that, but she wasn't ready to even think it. She pulled the shreds of her self-control back around her and stepped back from him.

"Thanks, you look pretty good yourself," she managed with just the right tone of casual delight.

"Turn around," Lucas said. "I want to see the rest of that dress."

She spun obediently, feeling the layers of skirt waft against her skin with a delicious rustle. Only she didn't want silk and tulle touching her. She wanted Lucas. "Do you like it? Shelly and Maggie helped me find it."

"They did good work," he said fervently. "But I really need you to tell me how to get you out of it."

She laughed. "Patience is a virtue, Dr. Gorgeous. You just got here."

His eyes were still that hot midnight shade. "That's long enough. I can get a room in the hotel in about ten seconds flat."

She desperately wanted to say yes. But he was here to work. His partners were here. His parents were here. She couldn't let him drag her off and do wonderful things to her, no matter how much she wanted to.

"Down, boy," she said softly. "You haven't even said hello to your mother."

That seemed to do the trick. His eyes lifted from hers, narrowed, started scanning the room. "You met my mother?"

She nodded.

He winced. "You did. Christ. Sorry. I told Maggie to keep an eye on her. I wanted to introduce you myself. Was she nice to you?"

"Well, she didn't seem overly impressed that I worked for the Saints. But I didn't tell her we were seeing each other."

"No, you didn't, did you?" Flavia's voice came from Sara's left and her stomach nose-dived.

Holy buckets of crap. That was definitely not how she wanted Lucas's mom to find out the news.

She turned, Lucas moving as she did, and tried to smile at Flavia. "Mrs. Angelo—"

"Mother," Lucas said, and he bent to kiss his mother's cheek. "Be polite."

Flavia's eyes were hot as they looked up at him. "I'm not the one forgetting my manners. Or did I miss the part where you told me about your new . . . friend?"

The ice was back in her voice. Only this time it was cold enough to seed a glacier.

"I was waiting to introduce you tonight," Lucas said. "There hasn't been time."

"I see," Flavia said. Her eyes flicked to Sara. "I guess this explains why your little venture suddenly has a new helicopter pilot."

The words *helicopter pilot* had never sounded so much like *gold-digging floozy*. Sara bristled, every muscle in her body tightening in denial.

"Sara is an excellent pilot and she was hired for that reason, not any other."

Lucas's voice was almost as icy as his mother's. There wasn't a single drop of heat left in his eyes. No, they'd gone cool and distant.

Crap. She'd known this was going to happen. There were reasons why she didn't date guys like Lucas. Jamie had snuck around with Callie and she'd strung him along, promising that he'd meet her family "soon." Jamie had told Sara that one night, not long before the accident. He hadn't told her whom he was seeing, just that they were serious and he was going to meet her parents.

Who knew, maybe it was true. But Sara didn't think so. Jamie had been Callie's little slumming-it fling. And Flavia Angelo was looking at her as though that was exactly what Sara was to Lucas.

"Whatever you say, Lucas," Flavia said. "We can discuss this another time."

Lucas reached down and took Sara's hand. "There's nothing to discuss. Sara and I are involved. The end."

His words lifted Sara's mood a bit but the fury

in Flavia's eyes—clear despite the carefully pasted-on social smile—made it plain that this wasn't the end of the discussion. Not by a long shot.

Sara's mouth was bone-dry and the room was suddenly far too hot. "I think I need a drink," she said and turned away from both of them, pushing away through the crowd.

Lucas caught up to her halfway across the room, his hand closing around her arm. She pulled it free with a jerk.

"I'm sorry about that," he said. "I didn't—"

"Didn't what?" Sara said. "Didn't think your mother was going to have an issue with you dating a lowly helicopter pilot?" She shook her head, trying to ignore the sting in her eyes. She'd been looking forward to tonight, to dancing with Lucas in her beautiful dress.

Music and moonlight and romance.

The perfect fairy tale.

Only now reality was rearing its ugly head, and she felt like a child caught playing dress-up. One who'd been told the wrong theme to the party, at that, and turned up dressed as a clown when everyone else was wearing space suits.

The outsider.

"I need some air," she said and turned away from him.

But he didn't just let her go. Instead he took her hand and led her up the staircase, out of the claustrophobic crowd, and then into the nearest elevator.

It surged upward silently. Neither of them spoke. The elevator stopped and the doors opened.

"Where are we?"

"Roof garden," Lucas said. "We hired it for the afterparty. There shouldn't be anybody up here."

Sara stepped out, shivering as the breeze hit her. Lucas slid his tux jacket off and slipped it over her shoulders. Then took her hand and led her across to the far side of the garden. The space was lit with a million tiny white lights winking through the lush foliage of the trees and bushes dotted throughout the space.

The quiet was nearly deafening after the noise of the ballroom, the sounds of the city traffic faint beneath them. Sara stared down at the lights of Manhattan, the sparkling arc of it, the patch of sparser darkness that marked the swath of Central Park. It looked different than it did from her helo, but familiar just the same.

"Better?" Lucas asked.

She nodded, not looking at him.

"Sara?"

She looked up. "Yes?"

"You know I don't care about what my mother thinks, don't you?"

He kept telling her that. But this was now. The future still had a hell of a lot of *then* to play out. And in the long term, in her experience, family tended to win out. "Maybe you should. Family is important."

"Not everyone has a family like yours. Mine isn't close. And I disappointed them a long time ago. That's what my mother's attitude is about, not you."

"Oh, I'm pretty sure she's no fan of mine," Sara said.

"That makes no difference whatsoever," Lucas said. "My mother isn't part of this relationship."

"She is, though. Family always is." Sara shivered. "Family is important. Who you are and where you come from is important. And you come from this world." She made a sweeping gesture at the garden and the rooftop. "I don't. We don't fit."

"The hell we don't," Lucas said. He reached for her but she moved back.

"Sex doesn't last. And it's not enough. It doesn't work to hold people together. Been there, tried that."

"What does that mean?"

"It means heat doesn't last. And when it goes, we're too far apart."

"So you dated some jerk who dumped you when the chemistry wore off and that means you and I can't make it work?" he said incredulously.

"Close enough. It wouldn't even matter if your family loved me. There are always going to be people who look at me like your mother did just now. Like I'm the money-grubbing trailer trash after the rich guy. And I can't do that."

"I won't let them," Lucas said fiercely.

"How are you going to stop them? That's the way the world works."

"Not for everyone," Lucas said. "Not for people who are decent." His eyes were dark, the blue glinting in the reflection of the fairy lights. He took a deep breath. "It doesn't have to be like that. It doesn't have to end badly. You're not your brother."

The words hit her like a slap. "What do you mean?"

"Your dad told me about Jamie," Lucas said. "About what happened. That was shitty. Tragic and shitty. But I'm not a scared nineteen-year-old girl. I'm not going to hurt you." His voice softened. "Can't you trust me? What have I done that you can't trust me?"

He sounded so right. Solid and true. She wanted to believe it. But she didn't know if she could. "I want to trust you . . . it's just . . ."

"Then how about this, how about we just take this a day at a time for now? I want this to work, Sara. I want to be with you."

She reached up and touched his cheek. "I want you, too."

"Then let's just hang on to that, okay? We can make this work, I promise." He leaned down and kissed her. Softly. Hands cradling her face. His touch was enough to make the doubts fade away. For now.

And because she wasn't ready to let the doubts win—not just yet—she kissed him back. And tried to ignore the fact that deep in the back of her mind she could hear a clock starting to chime midnight.

The week that followed was fractured and difficult. The Saints lost their game on Saturday and followed it up with another loss—to the Mets, which only made it worse—on Tuesday.

Lucas was doing his best to pretend that nothing was wrong, but Sara couldn't shake the feeling of doom. He might not care about his family, but she didn't know if she could brush off that icy fury in his mother's eyes so easily. After all, what would happen if she and Lucas kept going? If they got married? Flavia didn't seem to be the type who would thaw easily. Did she want to spend time with people who thought she wasn't worthy of their son?

It didn't sound appealing. A lifetime of cold-war family gatherings and events. Of what she assumed, having met Flavia, would be not-so-subtle insults and dismissal.

But the alternative meant no Lucas.

And that wasn't a future something she was ready to choose.

The only highlight was Lucas deciding that he could fix her dad's leg, or at least improve the current situation. Even better, Sean had agreed to another surgery. Which Sara thought was testament to just how painful his leg had gotten, given how much he'd hated being laid up the first time around.

Other than that, she was on edge and stressed.

She tried to tell herself she was just getting tired from the endless travel. But that wasn't going to change if she stayed with Lucas and the Saints, either. Baseball teams traveled, and so did their owners. If she wanted Lucas, that was part of the package.

By the time they made it back to Manhattan on Wednesday, she was exhausted and chased Lucas off to his apartment to sleep alone. Alex and Mal were going to Florida the next day, when the Saints were playing the Yankees back in Florida. But one of Lucas's patients had gotten an infection that had to be treated before the surgery could go ahead and he'd slotted her dad's operation into the resulting gap in his schedule.

She wanted him to sleep the night before he operated on her dad, not spend the night with her. Their nights were full of frantic, hungry, sex, both of them trying to chase their demons away, maybe, with the feel of the other. Hardly restful. She needed a good night's sleep, too.

But despite the comforting weight of Dougal beside her, filling the space where she was used to Lucas being, it took her a long time to fall asleep.

The next morning Sara was gritty-eyed and nervous. She drove to her parents' house to pick them up, and their trip from Staten into the city was largely silent. Her mom made a few attempts at chattiness before she gave up and subsided into quiet. Sean stared out the window, and Sara tried to concentrate on the early-morning traffic and getting them there in one piece.

Once Sean was settled in his room, Sara left in search of coffee.

Caffeine would only make her more jittery, but given a choice between jittery and facedown on the floor through lack of sleep, she was going to take jittery.

When she got back to the room, Lucas was with her dad. He looked grim and her dad was looking irritated.

"What's up?" she asked, hurrying.

"Wonder boy here has to reschedule," Sean said grumpily.

Her hand tightened abruptly around the takeout cup. "What? Why? Lucas?"

"I'm sorry," Lucas said. "But something else has come up."

"But Dad needs his surgery," Sara said.

"Sara, it's okay," Liza said. "We can wait a few more days."

"No," Sara said, temper snapping. "Dad's leg is important."

"Sara—" Lucas started.

"I want you to fix his leg," she said, feeling tears pricking in her eyes. Damn it. Her dad was important, not some lesser being to be shunted around just because some rich athlete had stubbed a big toe or something.

"I will fix his leg," Lucas said. "Just not today."

"Why not today?"

"Sara." Lucas came across to her. "Why don't we go talk about this outside?" He turned back to her dad. "One of the residents will be in to see you and work out the rescheduling. I'm sorry about this, Mr. Charles."

Sean grunted and Lucas took Sara's hand and led her out of the room. She shook him off, but he took it again and opened the door to an office a little way down the hallway, shutting it behind them.

"What's going on? Dad needs that surgery."

"There was an accident in Vero Beach," Lucas said. His voice had gone flat. "Some of the guys were fooling around—they were goofing off. Tico climbed up on the roof above the announcer's box. Sam climbed up after him, to get him to come down. But somehow Sam fell off. He's fractured his shoulder. His *right* shoulder."

Sam was right-handed. Fuck. But still Lucas was here, not there. And her dad was here, too.

"They have surgeons in Florida, don't they?"

"I'm the team surgeon now," Lucas said. "He's being airlifted here."

"So do my dad's surgery now and then Sam's when he gets here."

"I can't. I wouldn't be finished in time. And I have to look at the scans the ER sent across, work out my plan of attack."

"So Sam's shoulder is more important than my dad's leg?" Sara asked.

"His shoulder is his livelihood," Lucas snapped. "He's just starting out."

"My dad's leg is his livelihood," she retorted. "He needs two good legs to fly. And he's been waiting for nearly a year."

"Which means he can wait a little longer."

"No. What it means is potentially rich baseball star trumps boring old average helicopter pilot," Sara snarled.

"Don't be ridiculous," Lucas said.

"I'm not being ridiculous. I'm right."

"It wouldn't matter who it was if their case was more urgent," Lucas said. "I'm a surgeon, I have to prioritize."

"And I'm not high on that list," Sara said, realizing with a crack of her heart that it was true. For Lucas baseball and his medical practice trumped her. Trumped what they had.

He shook his head. "You're being unreasonable."

"Am I? Well, that's too bad. I don't think it's unreasonable for the man who's in my bed every night to want to put me first."

"Sam's injury is new," Lucas snapped. "Every minute makes a difference at this stage. Your dad is stable. A few days won't make a difference."

"They make a difference to me," Sara said.

"I'm sorry, then," Lucas said. "But there's nothing I can do about it. I promise I'll operate on Sean as soon as I can."

"I'll find another doctor," she said.

"Another doctor will cost you about a hundred thousand dollars," Lucas said. "I didn't think you had that sort of cash."

She stared up at him. "So I need you because of the money?"

"No." His mouth twisted. "That's not what I meant."

"It's what is sounded like. Poor little Sara needs the big rich doctor to save her family. Well, guess what, Lucas. I can save myself. And you can find yourself a new pilot. And a new girl to rescue. I quit."

His mouth was flat. "Actually I think you quit back in that ballroom. You let my mother scare you off. Funny, I always thought you were brave. That you wouldn't let other people hold you back."

"I don't," she said. "I just let them make me forget about reality sometimes. But now I remember." She reached for the door handle. "I have to go. And so do you. Your priorities are waiting."

Chapter Twenty

"Sara, if you don't at least pretend to eat I'm going to have to do something drastic," Liza said three days later.

Sara looked up from the meat loaf she was pushing around her plate. "Sorry, Mom. It's great. I'm just not that hungry." But she made herself eat a forkful, which tasted pretty much like nothing, and forced it past the seemingly permanent lump in her throat, washing it down with water.

Across the table, her dad was frowning at her. "Have you heard from—"

"Sean, don't," Liza said sharply. "Sara said she didn't want to talk about Lucas."

"Sara's being pigheaded," Sean muttered, but he subsided without saying anything further. He'd been very quiet since they'd come back from the hospital without him having surgery. He didn't seem angry, just quiet. Though apparently not quiet enough to keep his opinion about Lucas to himself.

Sara ate another bite then pushed her plate away. "I have to go, Mom. I need an early night."

Yeah, that was a plan. Go to bed early so she could lie awake staring at the ceiling and replaying the fight with Lucas over and over again for even longer. But it was Monday tomorrow and she would have to go into Charles Air and start working on getting the A-Star fixed. There might be enough money from what she'd earned at the Saints in the last month or so to make a good chunk of down payment on the repairs, even if the insurance company wouldn't come to the party.

If there it wasn't enough, then she'd just find another job and save until there was.

And then there was the fun task of finding a new surgeon for her dad. So far every orthopedic surgeon in Manhattan and the whole damned state seemed to be booked up for months. No one could even see her dad for a consult.

So she would start trying out of state if she had to.

She drove home with Dougal and gave him his last walk of the day. He looked almost as dejected as she felt. Every time there were footsteps in the hallway, he went to the door and stood there wagging his tail hopefully, obviously waiting for Lucas.

Watching him was torturous. Three days. Three days and Lucas hadn't called her. No one from the Saints had called her. She'd thought maybe Maggie might, to try to talk her out of quitting, but apparently not.

She'd called the hospital to see if she could find

out how Sam was, but they'd refused to give her the information over the phone. There was no way in hell she was going in person. Not when she might run into Lucas at the hospital.

Lucas whom she missed like she might miss a limb if she lost one.

But despite the fact that she'd smashed her heart to pieces, she didn't think she'd been wrong. She didn't want to be low down on the list with someone who was supposed to love her, and she couldn't ask Lucas to give up being a doctor or to give up baseball. So he was always going to have competing priorities. Nothing was going to change about that.

Damned fairy tales. She should have remembered they were written to teach people lessons.

She almost caved to temptation and called Lucas on Monday morning. She'd lain awake most of the night again, and the emptiness where he should have been lying next to her had pushed at her and made the pain even worse for too many hours before she'd fallen into an uneasy sleep.

Just one last conversation. Closure. Isn't that what they called it? End things on a better note. Tell him it just wasn't meant to be. Maybe then it would be easier.

But before she gave in, her phone rang and she found herself, much to her shock, speaking to the assessor from the insurance company. Who wanted a final look at the A-Star. That afternoon.

She resisted the urge to whoop in triumph down
the phone and instead limited herself to a silent
Snoopy dance of victory around the kitchen as she
agreed to meet him at the airfield at two.

A record-fast shower and breakfast—hope apparently returning some of her appetite—and she was
on her way, determined to have every single piece of
paperwork the assessor could possibly want organized before he got there. She was going to call her
parents and tell them the good news but decided to
wait until she actually had some details. That might
cheer her dad up at least.

The assessor even turned up at the appointed time
and clambered up and around the A-Star with rapid
efficiency. He took another statement about what
had happened, collected copies of the paperwork—
which the insurance company already had, but she
wasn't going to argue—and told her he'd call her in
the morning with his final verdict.

Sara could have kissed him but she just nodded.
Finally, finally, something was going right. Maybe
losing Lucas had been the last kick in the teeth
karma had in store for her. She went home, intend-
ing to call her parents, but decided on a nap first.

She woke when her phone rang. Sunlight streamed
through the window, highlighting the clock on her
nightstand. Which said it was twelve p.m. Which
couldn't be right—it had been nearly seven p.m.
when she'd gotten home. Holy crap. She couldn't
have slept for eighteen hours or so, could she?

But apparently she could, because the screen on her phone agreed with the clock. And told her it was Liza calling. She hit the button to take the call, still not quite believing she'd slept for so long. "Hey, Mom," she said.

"Honey, were you sleeping?"

"I took a nap. What's up?"

"Now, don't be mad, but I'm at the hospital with your dad. He's just out of surgery."

"Surgery?" Sara said. Maybe she was still sleeping. Dreaming the conversation. She thumped her thigh, which did nothing but hurt. So she must be awake. "What surgery?" She rubbed her thigh, trying to make her brain work.

"Lucas found another opening," Liza said. "He called us yesterday."

"And you didn't tell me?"

"We weren't sure how you'd take it," Liza said diplomatically. "Your dad wanted to go ahead, so we decided to tell you afterward."

Sara fell back on her bed, brain whirling. Lucas had operated on her dad? "Did the surgery go okay?"

"Lucas says so," Liza said. "But he also said it was early days. He said something about a trapped nerve. He had to reset the kneecap, so it's going to take a while."

"I—" She stopped, not knowing what to say. "Where's Dad now?"

"Still in recovery. They said he'll be down in a few hours but might be a bit groggy. Visiting hours start at four. Why don't you come then? Lucas said he'd check in tomorrow morning."

Which meant that Sara wasn't going to run into him if she went this afternoon. "Okay, Mom. I can't believe you didn't tell me but okay. I'll see you later." Then she paused. "Is Dougal still at your place?" She'd left him there Sunday night, hoping he'd cheer her dad up.

"Yes. We fed him this morning and Nancy next door is going to walk him at lunchtime. So he's fine."

Her dad was kind of spaced out but he was sitting up in bed, the covers tented over his leg with a metal frame, when Sara arrived just after four. He managed a slightly stoned-looking smile as she came through the door. "Hey, honey."

She leaned down to kiss his cheek. "How are you feeling?"

Sean nodded. "So far so good. He gives out the good stuff, your man."

Sara shot a look at her mom, who mouthed *morphine* at her with a smile.

"Dr. Angelo isn't my man," she reminded Sean.

"Then you're missing out," Sean said. His eyes drifted closed a little. "He's a good one, that one. Did he tell you, he said he fixed my leg?"

Sara felt her heart tighten, tears prickling. "So I hear. Why don't you sleep for a bit, Dad?"

"Might just rest my eyes at that," Sean agreed, eyes drifting shut. He promptly started snoring.

Liza shook her head at him fondly. "He never did do very well with drugs. He'll sleep awhile now. Why don't you go get me a coffee or something? I don't want to leave him just yet."

"Okay." Sara walked around the bed and gave her mom a quick kiss as well. "One coffee for the sneaky woman coming right up. Are you hungry?"

"I wouldn't say no to a muffin," Liza said. "It's been a long day and the sandwich I had for lunch in the cafeteria was forgettable."

"I think there's a coffee cart outside the hospital," Sara said. "I'll see what they have. Call me if he wakes up or anything."

"He's pumped full of enough stuff to kill a horse," her mom said. "So I wouldn't hold my breath."

Sara left the room, closing the door quietly behind her. She looked up and down the corridor, trying to get her bearings. The ortho ward was quiet, just a series of private patient rooms leading off the corridor. The nurses' station was about halfway down the row. On impulse, Sara headed toward it.

"Excuse me, is there a Sam Basara on the ward?" she asked when the nurse staffing the station looked up.

"Room Two Oh One. Go down the end of the hall and turn left."

"Thanks."

She would check in on Sam, she decided. Her fight was with Lucas, not with him.

But as she rounded the turn in the hall as directed, she saw Maggie coming in the other direction. Both

of them stopped. Then Maggie smiled and moved
forward.

"Sara, what are you doing here?"

"My dad's down the hall," she said. "So I thought
I'd see if Sam was still here."

"He is," Maggie said. "But they've just taken him
off for some scan or other. I've been trying to keep
his parents company. They flew in from Missouri
and they don't know anyone in New York."

"They must be worried. How's his shoulder?"

"Lucas—" Maggie broke off. "Sorry."

"You can say his name," Sara said. "I'll survive."

Maggie pursed her lips. "Let's go get some coffee
and I'll tell you all about it."

Maggie didn't take no for an answer. Sara found
herself across the street in a Starbucks with a Frap-
puccino in one hand and a blueberry scone in the
other before she had time even to try to argue.

"You were going to tell me about Sam's shoulder?" Sara said when they were seated at a table.

"I will," Maggie said. "If you tell me what's going on with you and Lucas. He's been miserable for
the last five days. What happened?"

"We broke up."

"That much I gathered. Can I ask why?"

Sara started crumbling her scone. "It wasn't going to work out."

"Because he pushed your dad's surgery?" Maggie
sounded disbelieving.

"No, that's not it. I mean, I was mad about that on the day but I understand why he did it."

"Then what's the problem?"

"The problem is that it's always going to be like that. Lucas is a surgeon. He owns a baseball team. He's always going to have something. It's too complicated. He needs someone who's used to his kind of world."

"His kind of world?"

"Your kind of world," Sara said. "I'm not rich, Maggie. I don't know how to do fund-raisers and press and disapproving mothers."

"Ah. Flavia. Quite frankly, Flavia Angelo's a bitch," Maggie said, shaking her dark hair back from her face. "Luckily, Lucas seems to be well aware of that fact, and he doesn't let her get away with pulling her shit with him. But I take it she pulled some of it with you?"

"I met her at the ball," Sara admitted. "We didn't hit it off."

"Sweetie, the number of people that do hit it off with Flavia Angelo can probably be counted on one hand. I don't know how on earth she snagged Sandro. He's much nicer. If you get him away from his wife."

"I didn't meet him," Sara admitted. "Flavia was enough. She made it perfectly clear I'm not good enough for Lucas."

"And you agree with her? Don't be an idiot."

"I don't want a cold war with his family."

"It's doable," Maggie said. "My dad's partner,

Veronica, doesn't care much for me, but we coexist.
It's not like we have to live together. And you wouldn't
have to live with Lucas's family. He doesn't see them
much. I see Veronica quite a bit but she knows I'm
not going anywhere and she knows that if push came
to shove, if she ever really tried to get between me
and my dad, then she'd lose."

"Yeah but he's your dad, not your boyfriend. You
know he'll choose family."

"And Lucas would choose what he wants, not
what his family thinks he should want. He's proved
that many times already," Maggie said. "Flavia
knows that. Every time she's fought Lucas on something, Lucas has won. He does what's right for him,
not what's right for Flavia. She didn't want him to
play baseball but he did. She didn't want him to be
a doctor but he is. She definitely doesn't want him
owning the Saints. Do you see him caring about
that? He's a grown-up. So maybe you could give him
the benefit of the doubt? Especially when a case like
Sam kind of pushes his buttons?"

"Buttons? What buttons?"

"Lucas hurt his shoulder when he was playing
college ball," Maggie said. "I won't tell you how—
you can ask him that—but it wrecked his chance at
a career. So if you want my two dollars' worth of
Lucas Angelo psychoanalysis, I think he sees quite
a bit of himself in Sam. And wants to give him the
second chance that he didn't get."

"I can see that," Sara said slowly. "But that doesn't
make his life any less complicated."

Maggie shrugged. "No, it doesn't. But if he was

happy with simple, he wouldn't be the guy you've fallen for. Trust me, I know it's complicated. Guys who do the kind of stuff that Alex and Lucas and Mal do, they're complicated. But the complicated is worth it. It's not as though you're so simple, Sara. You're a helicopter pilot. You were in the army. You're up in the air, technically risking your life every day. Lucas hasn't asked you to give that up, has he? He's willing to take the hard with the good. Besides, things won't always be this crazy with the Saints. It will calm down once they find their feet a bit more and the season starts. This first year will be the worst. I remember Dad telling me once that he wasn't sure how he made it through his first year of ownership without going crazy."

"That's not exactly encouraging," Sara said.

"At least Lucas wants to take you with him in the crazy," Maggie said. "The man is spending hours every week in helicopters—and he really does hate flying—just so he gets more time with you. He's smitten. And I think you're kind of smitten, too. And being smitten with one of the terrible trio doesn't seem to shake off all that easily. So why don't you try again? You never know, it might just work out."

It might just work out. Sara stared up at Lucas's apartment building three hours later, Maggie's words still ringing in her ears. She'd gone back to sit with her mom until her dad woke up and then made sure her mom ate before driving back to Staten Island, having waved off Sara's offer of paying for a hotel room for a few nights.

And then Sara had found herself in a cab, giving directions for Lucas's apartment. She'd never even been inside yet thanks to Lucas being late the night of the ball. She had no idea if he was even home, though Maggie had told her he was in New York, not heading back to Florida until later in the week.

But she asked the concierge manning the front desk. He lifted a telephone and someone at least answered because shortly she was shown into a lift and directed to the top floor. The top floor. The damned penthouse. Figured.

The lift dinged discreetly when it came to a halt. Sara walked out into a small foyer with a smooth black lacquered door facing her.

"Here goes nothing." She reached out and knocked.

Then held her breath for ten very long seconds, counting Mississippis in her head until the door swung open and Lucas stood in front of her.

He wore a black T-shirt and very dark jeans and his hair was rumpled, as though he'd been sleeping. His feet were bare. A scruff of five o'clock shadow darkened his jaw.

She'd never seen anything as delectable in her life.

"Sara," he said, voice reserved. "Is there something I can do for you?"

"Can I come in?"

"Of course." He stepped back politely. She walked past him, feeling her knees wobble a little when she got a waft of the damned delicious smell of him.

For a second she just wanted to throw herself at him and drag him off to bed, but she fought off the temptation. If this didn't work out, if reality was going to win over the fairy tale, then one more taste of him would just make walking away even more difficult.

"Come into the living room, I was watching a game."

She should have guessed that part.

She followed him, looking around curiously. The whole place was floor-to-ceiling glass on one side, looking out over the darkened park. The floor was a dark polished wood and the walls a deep blue-gray.

He showed her into a room with three huge overstuffed sofas upholstered in navy. They flanked a huge TV. The walls were bare except for one massive abstract painting that echoed the grays and blues above the flat screen. Lucas bent down and killed the TV with the remote. Then he turned to look at her, face still impassive.

"I came to say thank you," she said simply. "For my dad's leg. For still operating."

He nodded, expression not changing, eyes wary. "I said I would."

"No one would have blamed you if you hadn't. Not after the way I behaved."

"You were worried about your dad. I get that."

"Still, thank you. It means more to me than you know."

"His prognosis is good," Lucas said, with a half hitch of his shoulder that only drew attention to the way the T-shirt hugged his body. "And you know, even if he doesn't get full use of his leg back, he can probably still fly. I asked Alex about it—Ice has an aeronautics division—and he said there are modifications for disabled pilots. He said he'd be happy to get someone to talk to you about it, once we know what's going on with your dad's leg."

Disability aids? Why hadn't she thought of that? Maybe because she'd barely had time to breathe. But Lucas had. Lucas was fixing things for her. Even though she'd run out on him. She bit her lip.

"Sara?"

"How did you hurt your shoulder?" she asked suddenly. "Maggie said you used to play baseball in college but you hurt your shoulder."

Lucas nodded. "I did."

"How?"

He sighed. "It was a long time ago."

"How?"

"There was an explosion at a game. A group of those survivalist-type wackos tried to blow up the stadium."

"You got hurt in the explosion?"

"No, I got hurt helping people afterward. Pulling them out of the wreckage." He rolled his shoulder suddenly. "I don't actually remember what I did. Alex says we lifted a concrete beam off someone and that's what did it. But I don't remember. Don't remember much after running back into the bleachers. Not until I woke up in the damned helicopter being medevaced out of there."

The man ran into burning stadiums to save people. Sara sat down suddenly. Grateful for the sofa behind her so she didn't just sink to the floor. God. She was an idiot.

"Sara?"

"I'm sorry," she said. "I'm an idiot."

"You're not an idiot." He came closer then. Not quite close enough.

"I am. But I can't help it. You scare me, Lucas. This"—she flipped her hand at the room—"scares me. I'm just an ordinary girl from Staten. I never imagined anything like this would be part of my life."

"And that's a bad thing?"

"Yes. No. I don't know." She laughed then, and wasn't sure it wasn't half a sob. "I'm an idiot."

"It's just money, Sara," Lucas said. "It's not me. It's nothing to be scared of. Money is just a tool. It lets you do good things. It makes life easier in some ways, yes, but it doesn't have to change who you are. Like I told you, you're not your brother. History doesn't have to repeat itself. I won't let it. We won't let it. So what if you never expected me? Sometimes the unexpected turn is the best thing. I never expected to be a doctor. I never expected to own a baseball team. I never expected to fall in love with someone who flies goddamned helicopters."

"I never— Wait, what did you just say?"

"I never expected to fall in love with a chopper pilot."

"It's helo pilot."

"I don't care," Lucas said.

"You'd care if I called baseball softball."

"Well, yeah, maybe. Okay. Helo pilot. That's not

the important part. The important part is that you scare me, too. All my life I've had people running after me because of my name. Because of my money. But you. You don't care about that. In fact, you want to run away from it. And apparently that makes me want to run after you. I want to be the guy who makes you happy, Sara Charles. Because I've fallen hard for you and these last few days nearly killed me. Losing you nearly killed me, and that's pretty scary."

She wasn't sure she'd heard him right. Maybe because of the blood suddenly roaring in her ears. The world narrowed to one very specific spot. The one where Lucas was standing. "You've fallen for me?"

He nodded. "Yes. And don't say you don't believe me, or I'll have to agree with you that you're an idiot."

"I believe you," she said. She did. Because he was the guy who meant what he said. Who came through. Who ran into burning buildings. Who saved people.

Who wanted her. Who would keep running after her.

"So then, the question is, do you feel the same way about me?" he said, eyes very blue. "Scary or not, have you fallen for me, Sara Charles?"

She was never going to get tired of that blue. Or the way he said her name. Or the fact that the only possible answer to his question that she could come up with was yes. She stood up and he moved closer. So close. "Yes," she said and heard her voice quiver.

"Then I have one more question," he said. "To confirm the diagnosis."

"Which is?"

"Do you want to be scared together? See if we can help each other through all the crazy?"

"Hell, yes," she said and pulled him down to the sofa to prove how much.

Epilogue

She was going to be very happy when spring training was done. Sara wriggled on her sofa, found a more comfortable spot on the cushion propped under her head, and closed her eyes again, trying to let the sunbeam coming through the window lull her to sleep.

They were flying back to Vero Beach in a few hours. Just a few more games to go. Just over a week. And then she'd be home for months.

Well, apart from the part where the team traveled to play games. Which probably meant Lucas and Alex and Mal would want to travel with them sometimes.

They'd asked her to stay on for that. So they were sorting out the details for Charles Air to become the official charter helicopter firm of the New York Saints. Her A-Star was fixed, so she could hire another pilot to do any charters that clashed with team commitments until her dad was back on his feet.

She smiled sleepily.

Too much work.

Nice problem to have really.

If only she had time for just a bit more sleep. Though really, it was Lucas who was leaving her sleep-deprived, not the Saints' schedule.

She rolled over again, trying to make herself give in to the sleepy. From a distance she heard the sound of footsteps in the hallway and then a familiar bark.

Lucas and Dougal. Back from checking on her dad. They'd been gone longer than she'd expected, but maybe Sean had coaxed Lucas into watching some of a game with him.

No point getting in the way of male bonding.

The front door opened. She should probably force herself up.

"Take it to Sara," she heard Lucas say and smiled again. He'd been teaching Dougal new tricks. Taking things to specific people was one of them. And the damned dog looked so proud of himself every time he delivered something, it was hard to resist.

Dougal's nails clicked across the kitchen tile; then she heard him gather speed across the living room.

But wait, wasn't Lucas supposed to have left Dougal with her parents? After all, they were flying out later.

She opened her eyes just in time to see Dougal arrive beside her, a little green-blue bag dangling from his jaws from a white handle.

She knew that blue.

Her heart began to pound. "What's this?" she said as Dougal dropped the bag on her chest and licked

her face before racing back to Lucas, who stood in
the doorway, half leaning against the frame. The
blue T-shirt he wore matched his eyes.

"Open it," he suggested.

She eased open the bag. Inside was a matching
blue box tied with white ribbon. A small box.

"Lucas?" she said uncertainly, lifting it out of the
bag.

He smiled crookedly. "Dougal and I had a talk,"
he said. "He told me he wanted me to stick around.
I told him it was up to you." He patted Dougal's ears
then walked across the room and lifted the box out
of her hands. His clever surgeon's fingers made short
work of the ribbon, leaving him with an even smaller
black velvet box in his palm.

The room tilted around her for a moment.
"That's a—"

"Yes," Lucas agreed. "I think if I'm going to stick
around, then it should be forever. So, the question
is, Sara Charles, what do you think?"

He flipped the box open. The ring nestled inside
had a brilliant blue stone set in diamonds and a
silver band. "It's a blue diamond. The color made
me think of your eyes," Lucas said. Was she hearing things or had his voice wobbled a bit on that
last part?

He held out the ring. "I know this is fast," he said.
"But I know what I want. And what I want is you.
You said you'd do crazy with me. So I figured, why
not go all the way? Sara, will you marry me?"

Across the room, Dougal barked once.

"Hush, dog," Lucas said. "I'm asking Sara."

She looked from the blue ring to the blue eyes. And knew there was only one answer.

"Yes," she said.

Lawless in Leather

Chapter One

Damn. It smelled like a ball park. Mal Coulter breathed deeper, closed his eyes, and let the grin spread across his face as he took in the mix of sweat and grass and old beer and well-worn wood and leather that spelled baseball.

It made his palms itch for a bat.

It made his gut twist as, once again, he contemplated the possible monumental insanity that had led him to buy a baseball team with his two best friends. He still suspected Alex had put something in that very good bourbon they'd been drinking when he'd gotten Mal to say yes to his crazy proposal. Or maybe Lucas. Lucas was the doctor. He had plenty of access to drugs.

Still, here he was. New York. Though, right at

this moment, Staten Island. Part owner of the worst team in the major leagues. The New York Saints. And currently in charge of bringing the security in their stadium up to scratch.

That wiped the grin from his face. Deacon Field was a rabbit warren. A beat-up, crazy rabbit warren. Figuring out how to keep it, the players, and the people who would fill the seats safe—because if one thing was for damn sure, it was that no one was getting hurt in his ballpark—had been keeping him awake at night for months now.

Rabbit warren or not, Deacon would be safe.

There would be no repeat of the attack that had changed his life and the lives of his two best friends, now his partners, on the rabbit warren and the team that played in it. No explosions and fire and death caused by deluded evil.

Not on his watch.

He'd had practically half a squadron of contractors in here doing what they could, but there were limits to what could be achieved without some major remodeling.

Which wasn't feasible with their budget or the time they had before the season started. In fact, he was starting to think the only way it would be feasible to do the work that really needed to be done was if the Saints relocated to a different field for a season. A choice that wasn't going to be popular with their fans. If it could be done at all.

Yet another thing to worry about.

And now there was only one week left until the

first game and he had a to-do list that was so long, he didn't want to think about it.

Lack of sleep wouldn't kill him though, and he found himself arriving for work at the crack of dawn each day, heading for Deacon Field first instead of his own offices and climbing to a different part of the stadium to sit and smell the air. Today, finally, he'd let himself into the owner's box, sliding back the windows to let the early morning air seep in and carry the smell up to him.

It was the closest to peaceful things got these days, these first few minutes. The rest was sheer chaos.

Good thing he liked chaos.

OOH, BABY, SHAKE IT!

Music smashed through the morning silence. His eyes flew open. What the fuck?

SHAKE, BABY, SHAKE IT!

Mal stalked to the front of the box and stared down at the field. Took in the twenty or so women wearing skimpy little gym bras and leggings and shorts and groaned. He'd forgotten the damned cheerleaders.

SHAKE IT LIKE YOU MEAN IT!

He gritted his teeth. Cheerleaders. Hell. Baseball teams didn't have cheerleaders. Adam could call 'em a dance troupe and spout off about getting butts on seats all he wanted, but they were cheerleaders and they didn't belong in baseball. No matter how good they might look prancing around down there, all long legs and long hair and big boobs.

He allowed himself a moment to appreciate the view and found his eyes drawn to the woman at the front of the squad. The one in charge, judging by the way the others were following her moves as she bent and stretched in ways that were arresting despite the goddamn annoying music.

Half a foot shorter than the shortest of the others, her hair a short vivid slick of scarlet—unlike the long falls of blond and brunette surrounding her—she was also built sleeker. She lacked the curves that were testing the limits of the Lycra worn by the others but, as the music changed to some sort of sinuous beat and she started to demonstrate a kind of twisting hip shimmy thing, he felt his mouth go bone-dry as he watched her.

Da-a-amn.

It was surprising the turf beneath her feet wasn't scorching with each sinuous step she took.

Sex on legs.

He blinked and tried to bring his mind back to the job at hand.

Hot or not, he didn't remember clearing a cheerleading practice for this morning so that meant he had to go down there and find out what the hell she was doing on his field.

"And five, six, seven, eight." Raina Easton bounced to her left, expecting the squad of dancers in front of her to mirror the move. Instead, to a woman, they stayed right where they were standing, looking past her shoulder, with varying expressions of surprise, approval and assessment on their faces. *Uh-oh.* She spun on her heel and took in the very tall man striding across the ballpark toward them, wearing jeans, a dark gray tee-shirt, a perfectly beaten-up black leather jacket, and a thunderous expression.

She knew who he was. The other one. She'd met Alex Winters—he of the shirt/blazer/jeans/GQ good looks—when he'd interviewed her for this position. She'd met Lucas Angelo—six foot plus of immaculate suit, gorgeous Italian model face, and divine blue eyes—when she'd been talking to the team doctor about the training plans for her dance squad. But she hadn't yet met the last of the three men who'd bought the Saints.

Malachi Coulter. She'd wondered about him. A girl would have to be made of stone not to wonder what the last third of the trio might be like when the first two were so delectable. And she'd never claimed to be made of stone. Not in the slightest.

Though the man walking toward her might be. His expression was pretty stony. It didn't make his face, which was angles and jaw and deep dark eyes, any less appealing. He looked, as her grandma might have said, like a big ol' parcel of man trouble. Her favorite kind. Or rather, her *former* favorite kind.

Bad boy written all over him.

Pity he was sort of her boss. No. Not a pity. A very good thing. It would help her remember that bad boy was her former preference. Still, regardless of her stance on bosses or bad boys, there was nothing to say she couldn't enjoy the view. Or the irony of his approach being backed by a song about men who drove you crazy.

She summoned her best knock-'em-dead-in-the-back-stalls smile as he reached her and extended her hand. "Hi. I'm Raina Easton, your dance director."

He didn't take her hand. She raised an eyebrow. He didn't change his expression. She sighed and dropped her hand back to her side. "What can I do for you, Mr. Coulter?"

"I didn't clear anyone for the field this morning."

Damn. His voice fit the rest of him. It rumbled pleasingly. It made her girl parts want to shake pom poms and she wasn't a cheerleader. Imagine what it might do if he didn't sound so pissed.

She squelched the thought. She wasn't going to imagine any such thing.

"The dance practice schedule was agreed a week ago," she said, wishing she wasn't in practice clothes and very flat dance sneakers. With a few inches boost from her favorite heels, he wouldn't loom over her quite so much.

"You're supposed to get a security clearance from me before entering the stadium."

Oh dear. He was going to be one of those. Tall, dark, and grim. Pity. She didn't do humorless. Life was too short for men who couldn't make you laugh. And, right now, she didn't do men at all.

"I'm sorry, nobody told me." She tried a smile. "I swear we're not some other team's troupe sneaking in for illicit practice." She was tempted to add a line about it being pretty hard to conceal a weapon in a crop top but figured that would be pushing her luck. Besides, if he announced he was going to search anyone, she'd likely be trampled by the dancers behind her stampeding to be first in line.

Mal's gaze lifted, scanned the women behind her, then returned to her, looking no more pleased than previously. "Other baseball teams don't have cheerleaders."

He sounded like he thought that was a very good thing. She wasn't going to let on that she agreed with him. Alex Winters was paying her a boat-load of money to whip his dancers into a lean, mean cheering machine and she was keeping her opinions about cheerleaders and baseball being sacrilege firmly to herself. She had plans for that boat-load of money. Which meant she also had to make nice to Malachi Coulter. "Dance troupe, not cheerleaders," she said, tilting her head back to meet his eyes. "Now, we've only got another hour of practice. Can we stay or do you need us to leave?" She hit him with another smile.

"You can stay," he said after a pause where the only noise was the pounding of drums and squealing guitars as the song on the sound system built to a crescendo. "But come and see me when you're done."

"Sure," she said after a little pause of her own. "I look forward to it." Then she turned back to the dancers so she wouldn't watch him walk away.

Two hours later, Raina finished slicking lip gloss on and decided that she needed to stop procrastinating.

She'd spent longer than she should showering and changing after the practice session and talking to the women in the squad. She'd only met most of them a week ago at the auditions, and she was still trying to get a feel for their personalities and strengths. They could all dance, she'd put her foot down about that—nixing a couple of the more blond and busty candidates who had looked freaking spectacular but had been less than blessed in the coordination and moving to music with some understanding of the basics of a beat and rhythm department—but just being able to dance wouldn't necessarily turn them into a team fast enough for her liking.

It took time for personalities to gel and right now it wasn't helping her cause that the best dancer of them all—the truly stunning green-eyed, dark-haired Ana—was shaping up to be a diva of the pit viper temperament variety.

Still, this was a rush job and she didn't have time to hire any more dancers, let alone give up one as good as Ana, so she was just going to have to do her best. Think of the very nice chunk of change she would be earning and give up on the idea of spare time for a couple of months.

But none of that changed the fact that she still had to beard the boss man in his den, so to speak. The tall, dark, grumpy, and disturbingly handsome boss man.

No chickening out just because he'd sent her hormones ratcheting into high alert.

Damn it.

He had that bad boy vibe practically radiating

for miles around him. There was the slightly too-long hair. The jeans and t-shirt "I don't care" outfit. Alex Winters had worn jeans and a dark gray blazer when she'd met him, but his jeans had been one hundred percent designer. Whereas she was pretty certain that Malachi Coulter's were well-worn Levis that had come by their faded patches and mysterious stains honestly.

There was also the tattoo snaking down his arm. She hadn't let herself focus on the design, only noticing the bold color and geometric black edges before she'd looked away.

And if she had to put money on it, she would have bet a fair portion of her next Saints paycheck that the big black motorcycle she'd spotted in the parking lot earlier belonged to him, too. He was, after all, wearing a well-worn pair of biker boots.

So, the bad boy. Even if he was bad-boy-made-good—after all, he was part owner of a baseball team—he was still a bad boy.

And she'd sworn off bad boys.

Pity.

But necessary for her sanity.

She grabbed her things, stuffed them into her bag, and headed out of the locker room—which she had her suspicions, based on the aroma of fresh paint, hadn't been a female locker room until shortly before Alex had hired her and held his auditions.

The next week in particular was going to be hell. By taking this job at the last minute, she'd managed to give herself the mother of all scheduling head-aches. Her next big-themed review at the club was starting the same weekend as baseball season. Which meant days here on Staten Island making the Fallen Angels—she hadn't been able to change Alex Winter's mind about the ridiculousness of that name—baseball's next big thing in dance troupes and then nights and any other spare seconds rehearsing at Madame R before they opened for the night.

Which left her, as far as she could figure it, maybe six hours a day for sleeping, eating, and basic hygiene.

She was going to need a lot of caffeine. And possibly a clone army.

She reached the reception desk after riding the creaky lift up to the office tower where the Saints' management and administration operated and smiled. The blond she'd met earlier in the week wasn't there; instead a woman with shoulder-length, light brown hair and blue eyes was sitting behind the desk. "Hi. Where might I find Malachi Coulter's office?"

The woman looked up from her computer screen. "Does Mal know what this is about?"

"He asked me to come by," Raina said. "The name's Raina Easton."

Blue eyes lit. "You're the dance coach? Is that the right word?"

"It's as good as any," Raina said. "And yes, guilty as charged."

"I've been hearing all about you," the woman said. "I'm Sara. Sara Charles. I fly the team's helicopter."

"And man reception?"

Sara shrugged. "Just helping out while Letty has

her break. Anyway, I'll let Mal know you're here."
She picked up the headset on the desk—which gave
Raina a lovely view of the sizeable diamond grac-
ing the ring finger of her left hand, a diamond that
was an amazing shimmering blue that matched
Sara's eyes—put it on, and touched something on
the computer screen in front of her.

"Mal," Sara said after a moment. "Raina Easton
is here to see you. Okay, I'll send her around."

She touched the screen again and pulled the
headset off with ease. Once again the ring sparked
in the light.

"He said to come round. You take this corridor,
then the second turn right, and his office is the end
of the row."

"Thanks," Raina said. "I'd better go or the boss
man will be cranky."

"His bark is worse than his bite," Sara said.

"Oh I figured that part out," Raina said. "But
he's still signing the paycheck."

She smiled a good-bye and headed off in the direction Sara had given. In the minute or two it took
to find her way, the nerves returned, a fleet of butterflies apparently trying out their step ball change
skills in her stomach.

Malachi Coulter's bark might be worse than his
bite, but she had the feeling she didn't want to really see him growling.

She wasn't sure that she wanted to see him in a
good mood either. Add a smile to the chiseled lines
of that face and a girl might be in serious trouble,
anti–bad boy resolutions or not.

The door to the office at the end of the hall was open. She took a breath and stepped into the doorway.

Malachi was sitting at a desk, but his chair was turned to face a bank of monitors showing what she assumed was security footage of the ballpark.

"I thought security offices were down in the basement," she said. "They always are in the movies."

The chair swung back around to her. "Ms. Easton. Done with your practice?"

"For now." She walked into the office, not waiting for his invitation, and put her bag down near the desk. She jerked her chin at the bank of screens, feeling a little bit of tech envy. She had as good security as she could afford at her club, but that was still limited to cameras on the main floor, and a few others covering strategic points in the building and the entrances and exits. The twelve monitors behind Malachi's desk each showed views from four cameras, and she suspected they rotated through even more than that. "Nice setup."

His eyebrows rose. "Just the key feeds," he said. "Our main monitoring room is on one of the lower levels. Close enough to a basement, I guess."

"I can't imagine having to run crowd control for a place this size," Raina said. "Must take a hell of a lot of people."

"Yes, it does," Malachi said. He tilted his head at her. "Security isn't a subject I'd expect a dancer to know a lot about."

She shrugged. "Maybe I ran away with a rock

band when I was a teenager and spent my formative years hanging out with roadies and security teams."

He shook his head. "According to your background check, you spent your teenage years in a number of different schools around the country until you landed in New York for Juilliard. Where you lasted a year before you started working on Broadway."

They'd done a background check on her? Well, she shouldn't be surprised. Alex Winters wasn't the kind of guy to not obtain all the information he needed. And Malachi didn't strike her as any more easygoing. "Busted. No rock bands for me. Well, not the kind with arena tours. But dancers spend their lives in theaters and other venues. And these days, those come with security. I pay attention."

"I guess burlesque clubs come with security, too," he said.

"Yes, they do," she said. So he knew about the club. And what she did these days. She waited to see what he said next. A lot of people assumed burlesque meant stripper. Mal said nothing. "But not like this."

"That might be a good thing," Mal said. Then he waved a hand at the chair. "Please, sit."

She waited for him to say something else, but he didn't. "So, you asked to see me?" she said as she sank into the chair. The leather was old and soft, and she ran her hand over the arm, appreciating the feel of it. "Is there a problem?"

"Just thought we should get things straight about the security protocol around here."

"O-kay." She leaned back in the chair. "I'm sorry, no one told me that I had to do anything about security. I sent my practice schedule to Alex two days ago."

"It's probably still sitting in his in-box," Mal said. "He's been flying back and forth to Florida every other day with the end of spring training."

"So, I should send it to you as well?"

He nodded. "Then you'll be on the books and we can leave passes for you all at the gate for next time."

She rummaged in her bag for her phone and then found her contacts. Held it out to him. "Fine. Give me your e-mail and we'll be all set."

He took the phone, and as his head bent as he typed, his hair fell forward over his face and she had another flash of "Oh Lord, he's attractive." In a perfect world he'd be giving her his details for a whole 'nother reason, but this wasn't a perfect world and she'd learned over the years that men like Mal were among the least perfect things in it.

Damn it.

"There." He passed the phone back to her and his fingers brushed hers. Brushed and lingered. Just for a second or two. Then she pulled her hand back, resisting the urge to shake her fingers to get rid of the tingle in her skin.

"Thanks," she said. "I'll send you that schedule."